THE TREASURE OF PARAGON BOOK 2

WINDY CITY DRAGON

USA TODAY BESTSELLING AUTHOR
GENEVIEVE JACK

Windy City Dragon: The Treasure of Paragon, Book 2
Copyright © Genevieve Jack 2019
Published by Carpe Luna, Ltd, PO Box 5932, Bloomington, IL 61702

First Edition: April 2019
eISBN: 978-1-940675-49-7
Paperback: 978-1-940675-50-3

v 3.0

Winter in Chicago cut deep. It raged with wind that snapped and cold that gnawed, a four-month attack by Mother Nature that ravaged the city like a relentless, icy beast. For Dr. Tobias Winthrop, whose core temperature was normally a blistering 113 degrees, the cold was both shocking and harmless to his constitution. Dragons couldn't freeze to death or catch human ailments. He hadn't suffered so much as a cough in over three hundred years.

Nor had he pondered his dragon nature in decades.

All that had changed when his brother had phoned him out of the blue weeks ago. Gabriel had needed his help combating a life-threatening voodoo curse. Although Tobias had done all he could for his brother and his mate, Raven, he hadn't heard from the pair since.

He was afraid to look too closely into his brother's fate. If his queen mother's warning to stay apart from his siblings wasn't enough to keep him away, Gabriel's forbidden relationship with the witch Raven was. Tobias had sacrificed his principles to try to save his brother's life. Besides tacitly accepting their forbidden relationship, he'd broken his mother's rule to stay away from his sibling. But the turbocharge on his slip and slide into hell had been helping them go back to Paragon. All these years, he'd worked tirelessly to put his dragon past behind him and become the healer he was meant to be. Helping Gabriel had ripped a scab off a wound he'd thought had healed. He vowed again to do his best to blend in and live as a normal human would.

Except this one time.

Tobias toyed with the amulet in his pocket. Helping his brother hadn't entirely been a selfless act. He'd asked for one thing in return, a healing amulet that once belonged to the indigenous guide who had led him and his siblings through the wilds of early America. With any luck, the amulet would save a child's life.

Despite decades practicing medicine with superhuman precision, one case had been his nemesis. He hesitated outside room 5830, looked both ways to confirm the hall was empty, then slipped inside his patient's room.

The child, Katelyn, slept curled on her side, the tubes and machines she was wired to lording over her tiny body like the appendages of a mechanical monster. Her pale blond hair curled against the pillow, her eyelashes softly feathering her alabaster cheeks. He frowned at the dusky-blue rim of her bottom lip.

Katelyn suffered from a complicated condition. A nasty, yet-unidentified virus had infected her heart and was slowly, torturously bleeding her life away. A heart transplant was her best chance of survival, but it was risky. No one understood this virus; therefore no one could say if it would attack the new heart as well. Active systemic infection was a contraindication of a heart transplant. As long as the virus was in her blood, she would not get the heart she needed.

Without his help, Katelyn would die.

Sick children died every day. Tobias should have faced the inevitability of human death and dealt with it as all doctors did, with grace and acceptance. Instead, he'd sold his soul for a miracle. Silently, he removed the one-of-a-kind, ancient healing amulet from his pocket and positioned it around her neck.

By the Mountain, he was pitiful.

Her eyes blinked open, and she drew a heavy breath through her nose. The oxygen tube there cut a line across her cheeks, and the air bubbled in the humidifying chamber with her effort.

"Hi, Dr. Toby," she said in her sweet child's voice. Her giant blue eyes locked onto him. Total trust. Total innocence. She did not question what he was doing even though he and the nurses had poked her limbs with needles and performed every manner of painful procedure on her over the past several months. She showed no fear. The brave girl only thought to say hello. No tears. No complaints.

"Shh," he said. "I didn't mean to wake you. I need you to wear this special necklace for a few hours. I'll be back to get it later."

"Why?" She looked down at the pearlescent white disk against her skin.

"It's a secret."

"Where did you get it?"

"Where do you think?"

"It looks like a seashell. I think you got it from a mermaid," she said between breaths.

Who was he to deny a sick little girl a fantasy?

"Our secret," he responded, placing a finger over his lips. "I'll be back later to retrieve it. The mermaid king loaned it to me for one night only."

"Whoa." Eyes wide, she strained to smile. "Really?"

"Close your eyes, Katelyn," he said. He was relieved when she obeyed. "Good girl. Now, dream of a mermaid kingdom. I'll check on you later." He tucked the blankets around her.

A few hours with the amulet should heal her, although he couldn't recall it ever being used on an illness like this. If memory served, Maiara, the native healer who had created the amulet, had used it mostly on injuries, not illnesses. It didn't matter. Indeed, he had no other choice but to try. His own magic wasn't right for this situation. Dragons could heal but only by binding, and binding one so young would be unforgivable. No. This was his last hope. He was sure it broke all sorts of ethical boundaries.

It was not like Tobias to break the rules. He wasn't proud of his newfound flirtation with rebellion. Not one bit.

He left the room, completely distracted by his conflicting emotions on the issue, and slammed right into a blur of red and surgical green careening down the hall. Coffee splashed. A box flew and skimmed across the floor. He squatted down to retrieve it.

"Sorry," he said. "I didn't see you." When he handed the box back to the nurse he'd collided with, he did a double take. Sabrina Bishop. He didn't work with her as often as he'd like, but when he did, the experience was memorable.

Sabrina reminded him of cherry pie—fresh, sweet, warm. She was the type who always asked about a patient's feelings, who held a parent's hand during a procedure, who spent way too much time talking to the hospital chaplain. Her hair, which was the bright red of maple leaves, and her milky complexion didn't hurt the comparison either. He frowned at the coffee stain on her scrubs. "Let me get you something for that."

"Never mind. I've got it." She rounded the corner of the nurses station and took a seat behind the desk. Grabbing a fistful of tissues, she set the red box he'd retrieved down on the counter and dabbed at the spill.

"Animal crackers?" Tobias eyed the snack box, the corner of his mouth twitching upward. "Are those for you or a patient?"

She flashed him a smile. "For me. Why?"

"It's just I haven't seen anyone over the age of five eat animal crackers in a while... like ever."

Leaning back in the chair, she raised her chin and stared down her nose at him. "I'll have you know I do it as a mental health exercise."

He snorted. "How is eating animal crackers a mental health exercise?"

"Have you heard the saying 'How do you eat an elephant? One bite at a time'?"

"Sure."

"Well, how do you eat animal crackers? One elephant at a time." She tore open the box and popped a cracker into her mouth. "It makes me feel like I've accomplished something."

He narrowed his eyes and shook his head. "That makes no logical sense."

"Logic is highly overrated, Doctor. You should ditch logic in favor of magic."

Their eyes caught and held. Her use of the word *magic* unsettled him. It hit too close to his open wound. Could she see through his facade to who he actually was, not human but dragon? Did she suspect he'd just slipped a healing amulet around the neck of a dying girl?

He pushed off the counter. "I should continue my rounds."

"Sad case, huh?" She gestured toward Katelyn's room with her head.

"We work in a pediatric hospital, Sabrina." He cracked his neck and sank his hands into the pockets of his lab coat. "All cases are sad. Children do not belong in hospitals."

She popped another cracker in her mouth and stared at him with a piercing green gaze that seemed to cut straight to his soul. Was she assessing him? The look on her face was strange, unreadable. He didn't need this right now. If a woman like her pulled the right string, he might unravel like an old, worn sweater.

"Well, I should, er—" He moved away from her.

"Doctor, can I talk to you for a moment in private?" Sabrina gestured over her shoulder with her thumb.

He gave her a confused look. "We *are* alone."

"It's important. I need to show you something." Sabrina pointed toward the corner stairwell. She led the way, holding the door open for him. Reluctantly, he followed her, trying to avoid noticing the way her scrubs hugged her backside. The tips of his fingers itched to stroke the silken red length of her hair. This was probably not a good idea.

He hurried after her.

Only when they were both in the stairwell and the door was closed behind them did she address him. "You don't have to pretend with me." She stalked toward him.

He retreated, keeping space between them until his back hit the wall and he could go no farther. "What are we talking about?"

"You don't have to act like you don't care about these kids. You're not some kind of medical machine."

"Miss Bishop—"

"I watch you, Tobias. I see how much you love these kids, how much it kills you each and every time you can't fix

6

a patient's heart. You say it's all part of the job, but I can see that it's an act. The more you deny it, the more it's going to eat away at you." She stepped in closer. By the Mountain, she smelled good, like honey and moonlight.

Tobias's body responded. It had been decades since he'd been with a woman. Decades since he'd trusted anyone enough to be intimate. Trust was difficult when you were an immortal living among humans. Relationships brought with them complications, the risk of exposure, the reality that he could never truly share who or what he was with anyone. How could you have intimacy when the other person wasn't just a different gender but a different species?

"Thank you," he said curtly. "If I ever need a shoulder to cry on, yours will be the one." He shifted to the side to walk around her but she blocked him with a hand to his chest. Her eyes searched his. A circle of heat bloomed where she touched him.

"Nothing rattles you, does it?" she said softly. "Nothing raises your blood pressure. Sometimes I wonder if you *are* a robot. Do you have a beating heart, Tobias, or are you made of chips and wires?"

"I am not a robot," Tobias said firmly. His pulse quickened. Could she feel that? He had no control over it or his growing erection. He needed to get out of this stairwell. "Sabrina, this is—"

Without warning, her lips slammed into his. The kiss was hard, searching. He didn't have the strength to stop her even if he'd wanted to. Something primal and urgent caused his hand to tangle in her hair and his tongue to sweep into her mouth. By the Mountain, she tasted good. He forgot where he was, forgot *who* he was.

All too soon, she planted both hands on his chest and

pushed him away. "Not a robot." She panted, breathless. She wiped under her bottom lip.

He opened his mouth to say something, anything, but his mind had gone completely blank. Should he tell her the kiss was inappropriate? How could he when he desperately wanted to kiss her again? She placed a finger over his lips before he could say a word.

"Look me in the eye," she commanded. He did and was surprised when her green eyes glowed a bright, silvery blue. "You will not remember this. If anyone asks what we did in here today, you will say we talked about Katelyn. We never kissed. You will wait here for five minutes and then go about your business." Her eyes stopped glowing, and she smiled sweetly up at him, her cheeks rosy. Was it his imagination, or did her skin look more vibrant than a moment before? "Thank you, Dr. Winthrop. I find our talks incredibly refreshing. You have a good heart."

She turned on her heel and strode from the staircase with a new pep in her step. Tobias blinked once, twice, three times. He pressed two fingers into his lips and chuckled under his breath. Was she a witch? No. He would have smelled her if she was. But she was something. Something that didn't realize her mind control had no effect on him.

He wiped a thumb over his lips and grinned, striding for the door. "Miss Bishop?" he called as he opened it. She was gone, but there was someone else at the end of the hall, someone he hadn't been sure he'd ever see again, and the sight of him was a bucket of ice water on his libido. He made no attempt to disguise his scowl.

"Hello, brother," Gabriel said. "Aren't you going to welcome me to the Windy City?"

CHAPTER TWO

With the taste of Tobias still on her lips, Sabrina raced toward the women's restroom. Thank the goddess the other nurses were busy with patients tonight. If someone had seen her, her superhuman speed might have raised eyebrows. Calling attention to herself was the last thing she wanted to do.

She burst through the door and lunged for the sink, splashing cold water on her face. When she raised her head and looked at herself in the mirror, she got a horror-movie-worthy view of her fangs slipping back into her gums.

Fuck! What the hell was wrong with her? She hadn't sprung fang involuntarily in years. As a vampire-human hybrid, she didn't need to feed on blood like other vampires. Energy was enough. And holy hell did Tobias have energy. She could feel it coursing hot and fast through her veins, warming her cheeks and rushing through her torso like she'd done the world's biggest shot of espresso. She used a paper towel to dry her face and took a shaky step back from the sink.

To say she was surprised was an understatement. Oh,

she'd suspected that there was more to Tobias than his reserved and reticent exterior. He'd always conjured a clever quip on the rare occasions they'd had time between patients to converse. She'd found him interesting for years. Only, until tonight, she'd assumed his pool of emotional energy was relatively shallow.

Humans with sharp tempers, a quick laugh, or easy tears usually provided the best meals, and Tobias was the exact opposite. He was conspicuously cool, calm, and collected, even in the most stressful situations. She'd never seen so much as a flicker of emotional volatility until tonight. When he'd emerged from that patient's room, he'd been almost glowing with joy. That's why she'd targeted him. His unguarded aura was irresistible. And so, it seemed, was the taste of him.

She touched her lips. Tobias had turned out to be a wellspring of deep and intense emotion like she'd never felt before. It was like drinking from a fire hose.

Her fingers found her temple, and she wobbled on her feet. Oh hell, espresso had nothing on Tobias's energy. Sabrina felt almost... high. Her nervous system was sending up fireworks, and all the twinkling lights were going off in her head. She steadied herself on the bathroom stall.

A long, loud burp escaped her lips. She giggled. *Damn*.

Her butt tingled. Stopped. Tingled again. Oh, her phone! She pulled it from her pocket and cursed. Texts. Lots of them. From Tristan. She was late, and oh hell the vampire was not reading a magazine or playing *Words with Friends* to pass the time. If the texts were any indication, he was livid. She shoved the phone back into her pocket and rushed toward their rendezvous point.

The blood bank was on a different floor of the hospital, and units of blood were strictly monitored. But being a vampire had its advantages. A human mind was no match for vampire persuasion.

"Hey, Julie. I have a requisition." Sabrina smiled at the older woman and handed her a blank sheet of paper. The tech often worked nights and was easily susceptible to vampire persuasion.

"This is blank," Julie said in confusion.

"Look at me." Sabrina grabbed Julie's arm and she obeyed. "I have an order for twelve units of blood. You're going to let me back there to get it. Once I'm done, you will forget I was ever here."

The older woman stared vacantly at her, pupils dilating. "Of course. Everything is in order. Take what you need." She absently placed the blank sheet of paper on her pile of requisitions and unlocked the door to the blood bank for her.

Sabrina wasn't even to the first cooler when a breeze on the back of her neck and the scent of cigar smoke told her Tristan was right behind her.

"You're late," he said.

She glared at him over her shoulder. Tristan was the quintessential Chicago vamp, short and stocky with a thick head of slicked-back hair as dark as his soul. His eyes were brown and always ringed with silver. The effect was a rheumy and dull appearance she was glad she didn't share with her brethren.

"I was working. I had a patient emergency. Do you want this blood or not?" Sabrina popped out a hip. Her emotional grid was buzzing with the negative vibes Tristan was putting off. Jealousy sliced through her psyche like arrows, and anger and malice pummeled her emotional radar. As always, she hid any reaction. Full-blooded vampires couldn't read emotions like she could. It was a private talent. Nothing good would come of flaunting it.

"Oh, I want the blood," Tristan said. "I also want to know why you look like you're overfed. Your cheeks are red and you're unsteady on your feet like a... like a mortal."

She scoffed. "I am not like a mortal. But I did have an errand to run for Father in daylight today, so I might need rest. You wouldn't know anything about that though, right?"

He recoiled, his lip curling. Unlike Tristan and the rest of the Chicago coven, Sabrina was born, not made. Half human and half vampire. That meant she was the only one in her coven who could daywalk. Although her skin burned easily in the sun, it wasn't in an obviously inhuman way. She could believably blame her Irish complexion for any quick redness. It would take prolonged exposure to kill her, unlike Tristan, who would burst into flames the moment a UV ray touched him.

Along with her ability to subsist on human food and energy instead of blood, her hybrid nature was a boon for the coven, allowing her to hold the human job that kept their emergency blood stores full. It also meant she was her father's favorite. Her daddy, the only vampire to ever sire a hybrid, was coven master. He'd never hidden the fact he planned for Sabrina to take his place one day. She'd been training to do so from birth.

It was times like this she didn't mind using her place to put Tristan in his. The guy was genuinely a dick. She snatched his messenger bag from his hands. It was specially lined to keep the blood cool until he could make it back to coven headquarters. She started loading the bag with an assortment of blood types.

"You know, Sabrina, you think you're so important, so *untouchable*." Tristan sneered. He swaggered toward her and lowered his voice. "The coven doesn't even know for sure that you're immortal. Although I'd be happy to test you for immortality if you'd like. Drowning would be the easiest way. If you come back, you're one of us. If not, you're one of them."

She thrust the full satchel into his hands and ushered him toward the door. "I'll make you a deal, Tristan. I'll let you drown me the day you can do it outside, at noon, in full sun. Until then, you'll just have to assume I'm immortal like you."

"You are nothing like me." He looked at her then like a dog about to bite. "It's only a matter of time until your father and the coven sees you for what you are. You're not master material. You'd rather be here caring for these walking bloodbags"—he gestured toward Julie—"than leading our coven."

"You need to leave."

"Why don't you just admit it and save us both a lot of trouble? I'm older than you. I'm stronger. I have more experience. If it wasn't for your father—"

"You'd be out on the street, fending for yourself. Be thankful he keeps you around. Although if we ever have a conversation like this again, I swear to you I will relay every word of it to him."

"He'll never believe you. Your Dad and I go way back, sweetheart. He knows I have a significant following in the coven. He's not going to cut me loose because you say I hurt your feelings."

"No? Care to test that theory?"

Tristan buckled the messenger bag and turned to leave. "Fucking bitch," he muttered under his breath.

A hot wave of rage crashed through Sabrina and her vampire side engaged as if he'd thrown a switch in her torso.

In an instant she was on him, fangs fully extended. Before she could even process what she was doing, she'd fisted his greasy black hair and forced his head back on his neck until he had to arch on his tiptoes to keep his head attached to his shoulders. She rested the blade of a pair of open scissors at the base of his throat. When had she picked up the scissors? She couldn't remember. She must have swept them into her hand instinctively, just as what came out of her mouth next was the product of pure, unadulterated instinct.

"Say that to my face," she hissed into his ear. "Or would you rather apologize?"

"Sorry," he said, groaning. He held up the blood between them. "Let me go. I've got to get this back to the coven." The scissors couldn't kill him—they'd have to be made of wood or silver to do that—but she could hurt him. She was strong enough to carve that smug grin off his face and seriously ruin his day.

Cursing, she pushed him away from her. He was gone in the blink of an eye. Damn, where had that come from? She normally didn't lose her cool over the likes of Tristan. Not that Tristan didn't have it coming. Vampires were naturally aggressive. She'd been dealing with his shit for years. He just wasn't worth the effort. Father always said violence was only the answer when you didn't want anyone to ever ask a certain question again.

With a sigh, she pulled the blank sheet of paper off Julie's pile, and slipped out the door.

"Thanks, Julie. Have a good night."

"You're welcome, sweetheart," the woman replied without looking up. "Anytime."

Sabrina chuckled softly. She fully intended to take her up on that offer.

"WHAT ARE YOU DOING HERE?" TOBIAS STOPPED SHORT, his eyes darting to the hall behind Gabriel, hoping to catch another glimpse of the intriguing Sabrina. The hall was empty. He inhaled deeply but couldn't catch her honey-and-moonlight scent under the smoky odor of his sibling.

"Is that any way to greet your flesh and blood?" Gabriel arched a brow. "Last you saw me, I was at death's door."

Tobias's eyes widened, and he checked for eavesdroppers over both shoulders. He gripped Gabriel by the upper arm and shoved him down the hall. To be sure, his brother had always been the more powerful of the two, and had he not wanted to move, Tobias couldn't have made him. Thankfully, he was conveniently compliant.

"This way." Tobias guided his brother into a consultation room and closed the door behind them. "Are you insane, Gabriel? This is my place of work! What are you doing here?"

Gabriel paced to the window on the far wall, glancing out over the city of Chicago. Giant white flakes swirled on the other side of the glass. Snow again. To Tobias, it felt like being locked inside a medical snow globe. He braced himself for a firm shake.

As his brother's hand came to rest on one of the consult room's beige chairs, Tobias noticed that Gabriel's emerald ring glowed brightly again. Solid emerald green. "I see you broke the curse on your ring."

"I should have called. My apologies." Gabriel turned to face him. "My survival did not come easily."

Tobias shook his head. "I'm relieved you're alive. I am."

"That's good to know. I'd find it disconcerting if you'd gone from indifference to wanting me dead."

15

"I was never indifferent, Gabriel. Don't be dramatic."

"Then why does this welcome feel as cold as your city?"

"Dr. Tobias Winthrop doesn't have a brother, you understand. I have an identity here, a life, a career. People know me. They'll ask questions."

Gabriel closed his eyes and frowned. When he opened them again, he placed a hand over his heart. "And I called you *brother* in public. My sincere apologies, Tobias. Truly, I was careless. From now on, you are Dr. Winthrop and we are simply old friends."

Tobias focused on his brother's emerald ring again. "How did you break the curse?"

"Raven."

"The witch."

"My mate, yes. Raven killed the voodoo queen who cursed me. It is a long, complicated story, but suffice it to say, she saved my life."

"I am relieved for you, brother, although you know how I feel about your relationship with Raven. The law is clear. I hope you've come to your senses about pursuing it further."

Gabriel sighed, the city lights like stars behind his head. There was an intensity in his eyes Tobias hadn't seen before. The mating bond, he supposed. He could still smell her on him. What would it be like to be crazy from love? The concept seemed so foreign to him.

"I've asked Raven to marry me."

"By the Mountain." Tobias cursed. "Gabriel, you cannot continue a relationship with this witch. It's forbidden!"

"Forbidden by whom, Tobias? Mother and Uncle are ruling Paragon beyond the rule of law, and that's not even considering the immorality of their incestuous relationship. I hardly think that some edict Brynhoff handed down a few centuries ago holds any weight given the circumstances."

Tobias slashed a hand through the air. "Two wrongs don't make a right. I knew what she was and I helped you. I don't regret that. I'd do it again. And I'm happy for you. I understand, I do. You've shed the old ways. We all have to some extent, living here. I've buried the past so deep sometimes I forget I was ever a dragon. But you might say old habits die hard. I think mating with a witch is dangerous, brother, and now that you're safe, I can't condone it. I can't be a part of it." He stared at his brother for a long moment. "Why did you come here?"

Gabriel rubbed his jaw. "She's here, Tobias."

Tobias swore. "Where?"

"Downstairs. In the coffee shop."

"Why?"

"Raven wanted to get to know you. We're getting married in the human tradition. We wanted to thank you for what you did for us and invite you to the wedding. Our family has stayed apart too long. It's time we got to know each other again."

Tobias shook his head. "Mother warned us to stay apart for our protection."

"Everything Mother told us was a lie," Gabriel said.

Tobias cringed, his stomach locking down, his hands fisting.

Gabriel didn't let up. "Raven and I saw her on the throne. She's ruling at Brynhoff's side."

Tobias shook his head. "I don't believe it."

"Have you ever known me to be a liar?"

All of Tobias's instincts said no. Gabriel had never been dishonest before. He'd been trained as a warrior in Paragon, a position that valued honesty and valor.

"Why would I lie to you?" Gabriel asked.

Tobias was quick to answer. "If the rule of law in Paragon is corrupt, then there is no reason you can't take Raven as your bride, is there? I think you have a strong motivation to lie, brother, as out of character as the behavior might be for you."

"That is not what is happening here!" Gabriel growled and rushed Tobias, stopping mere inches from his face.

Tobias flashed back to Paragon, to being slammed onto the practice mat by his older brother like a royal practice dummy. He held his ground, but his stomach clenched. He did not miss those days. Not at all. "Are you going to pummel me for old times' sake?"

"I'm telling you the truth." Gabriel rubbed the back of his neck as if he desperately needed to keep his hands busy. Perhaps pummeling Tobias was more of a temptation than he'd assumed. "We came here to properly thank you for your help and to show you that you're family. I also came to warn you about Mother and Brynhoff. She didn't see me, but she did see Raven. If she suspects—"

"You're welcome," Tobias interrupted. "I've heard your story; now I think you should go. When it comes to Mother and Paragon, I..."

"You don't believe me." Gabriel's jaw tightened. "You don't believe that Mother was part of the coup and lied to us all those years ago."

"I don't know what I believe. Paragon may be a different place now. Maybe you saw something, but I'm not sure it means what you think it means. What I am sure about is we are not in any danger. If either Brynhoff or our mother, assuming she is in fact still alive, wanted to pursue us in this realm, they would have done so long ago."

Gabriel narrowed his eyes. "Hmm. Don't you want to find out? Don't you want to know for sure?"

"Not really." Tobias watched his brother gape in disapproval. "I live as a human now, Gabriel. Aside from helping you, it's been years since I've thought about Paragon. Longer still since I gave up on ever going back. Let me make it clear, in case I didn't before—I don't care what's happening in Paragon."

"You don't mean that."

"It has nothing to do with me or my work."

"Then my being with Raven shouldn't bother you. My being near you shouldn't concern you. If you aren't concerned with Paragon, why would you be concerned with the old law?"

"I think you should go." Tobias took a deep breath through his nose. His brother's logic was sound, but it made Tobias nervous having him around. Gabriel wore his otherworldliness like a cologne. Not something that stood out in the New Orleans French Quarter where the supernatural was practically a cottage industry, but here in Chicago, he and Raven were a risk to Tobias's tenuous human life. He'd worked hard to bury the part of him that was once dragon. He didn't need Raven to snap her fingers and ruin it all.

Gabriel nodded slowly. "As you wish, brother, but can I ask you for one small favor before I do?"

"What kind of favor?"

"It's the middle of the night. Raven is exhausted and we have no place to go. Please, Tobias, allow us to stay with you, at least until I am able to arrange transportation back to New Orleans." The direct eye contact Gabriel doled out made it clear that there was only one answer acceptable to their kind.

Tobias rolled his head on his neck and stared at the

ceiling tiles. They were in Chicago. The city had about fifty thousand hotel rooms. He could call the local Four Seasons and pay to put them up. But as Gabriel was aware, proper Paragonian etiquette required a royal to host another royal when asked. It would be hypocritical for Tobias to harp on Paragonian law but not keep to the social expectations of his people.

Besides, he genuinely missed his brother. And although he didn't welcome the disruption to his well-ordered life, he could not deny they had a bond or that this was a rare chance to foster it. He'd once loved his siblings, all of them. He was their practice partner, their confidant, the one who wasn't strong enough to be a threat in the training room so could be a true friend outside of it. There was a reason Gabriel had called *him* when he needed help. Having Gabriel here provoked a deep tug in his sternum, a feeling between reminiscence and nostalgia. What could one night hurt?

"One night. Tell Raven no witchcraft in my house."

"Thank you, Tobias." Gabriel bowed his head slightly.

"You'll have to wait until I finish my shift. We'll go back to my place together."

"Fair enough."

Tobias nodded. "One night and then we go back to the way things were, understood?"

"Understood."

With a curt nod, Tobias readied himself to make a hasty exit only to be pulled into a firm hug by his brother. His spine stiffened. Hesitantly, he patted Gabriel's back before pulling away again. Without another word, he turned and briskly escaped into the predictable sterility of his work.

CHAPTER THREE

At times Raven believed that the day she had woken in her hospice room to find Gabriel standing at the end of her bed was the first day of her real life. Everything before that moment, when he'd fed her his tooth, cured her cancer, and ignited what would become her blazing passion for him, seemed like another lifetime—nothing but practice for the real thing. This... this was *real* life, cruising down the road in a new city, eating new foods, feeling like the person next to her was the piece of her soul she'd been missing all along.

"Wow, the architecture here is different from home. These houses look like castles." Raven watched the brownstones go by as Gabriel turned from West Fullerton onto Lincoln Park West, guided by the GPS that came with their rental vehicle. They'd started out following Tobias's Toyota Land Cruiser but had been cut off by a yellow cab. The roads were icy, and Gabriel chose to slow down rather than risk an accident. A few texts later and he had Tobias's address. It appeared they were close.

"I've been meaning to ask you, why isn't Tobias's last

name Blakemore? You're brothers." She stared absently out the window.

Gabriel laughed. "We've had many last names over the decades, all invented. In Paragon, we are addressed by our first name and our title. No surnames. Winthrop is simply the name he's chosen for this identity."

"And you just reinvent yourself over and over as the humans around you age?"

"Something like that. Dragons can change their appearance at will. We can age ourselves when we need to, alter certain features. It's not as difficult as you might imagine."

"Sounds lonely."

He cast her a small smile. "Not anymore."

She pecked him on the cheek.

"Here it is." Gabriel turned between two snowdrifts and proceeded down a narrow drive that bisected the row houses. At the back of the residence, he parked next to Tobias's SUV in a small parking lot. But, although his hand rested on the keys in the ignition, he did not turn the engine off.

"What's wrong?" Raven asked. "Why aren't we getting out?"

"There's something I need to talk to you about before we go inside. I didn't tell you everything about my conversation with Tobias."

Raven leaned back in her seat. "You hardly told me anything. We talked more about the deep-dish pizza than your brother. What's going on?"

Gabriel's eyes met hers. "He doesn't approve of your being a witch."

Tracing the cupholder with her finger, she thought back to her short interaction with Tobias in New Orleans. "Oh, he has no problem with my being a witch. He's known witches before, remember? He told us so... the friend he knew in college. He has nothing against witches per se. What he has a problem with is his brother being mated to a witch. That's the forbidden part, isn't it? Which means he still puts faith in your mother and Brynhoff."

Gabriel glanced toward the door to the house. "He wasn't with us when we saw them together in the Obsidian Palace. He doesn't believe us."

Raven groaned. She should have expected this. Tobias's reaction when Gabriel told him she was a witch wasn't positive, and although he'd always treated her kindly and had been charming in his own way, he had left abruptly after they'd returned from Paragon. Her heart sank. She'd wanted this to be a friendly family reunion, a celebration of their engagement. Now she felt like she was coming between Gabriel and his brother.

"Maybe he believes you," she said as the thought occurred to her, "but he doesn't believe you saw what you think you saw."

"He mentioned something about that. It is possible he assumes there is another explanation for Eleanor's behavior."

"There's only one thing we can do." Raven turned toward him in her seat. "We have to win him over. If we can gain his trust, we can convince him that what happened in Paragon is real."

Gabriel nodded. "I agree, little witch. That's why it might be better for you to not mention witchcraft while we're here. We don't want to scare him away. If you don't use your power in his presence, he might come around faster. And..."

"What?" Raven placed a hand on his arm, imploring him with her eyes to explain this turn of events.

"He said we couldn't stay here unless you promised you wouldn't use witchcraft."

"Right." She inhaled deeply. A wave of disappointment crashed into her. As a new witch, practicing her craft was both fulfilling and necessary. Raven absorbed magic. What she practiced stayed with her. What she didn't was lost. But the fear of losing her power wasn't nearly as disturbing as the nagging feeling that Tobias disapproved of *her*, not only what she was but *who* she was. She placed a hand on Gabriel's. This was hard for him too. There wasn't room for her to wallow in her own emotions. "I was your everyday powerless human for twenty-three years. I'm sure I can pretend to be one for the length of our visit. How long are we staying?"

Gabriel raised an eyebrow. "I persuaded him to let us stay the night."

"Oh. Not a long time to pretend then." Raven froze. Over Gabriel's right shoulder, she saw something move in the arborvitae behind the small parking area. "Gabriel, I think someone is watching us. Not Tobias."

Gabriel glanced over his shoulder, a low growl percolating deep inside his chest. "I see him too."

"Who do you think it could be?"

"I'm not sure, but I don't like it. Let's get inside where it's safe. Stay close to me." He turned off the engine and opened his door.

A surge of icy wind stung Raven's cheeks, and she pulled her new heavy wool coat closer around her neck. She climbed from her side of the car and walked around the hood to Gabriel. From where they parked, they'd have to pass the shadowy figure to get to Tobias's back door. She pressed close to Gabriel's side.

"Stop," a man's voice said as he sprang from the evergreens. A dark hood concealed his face, and there was something in his gloved hand, partially hidden by the sleeve of his puffy blue-and-orange coat. A gun?

"*Pagoma!*" Raven's hand arced through the air, her emerald ring glowing like a star—she'd recently enchanted it to magnify her magic—and the man froze. His body tilted forward precariously. She'd stopped him midstride.

"I thought we agreed no magic," Tobias stage-whispered from his door. He jogged down the steps toward them.

"He had a gun," Raven said, although, now that the man wasn't moving, the thing in his hand didn't look as threatening as it had before.

Tobias groaned and closed his eyes for a beat. "It's his phone, Raven. This is Mr. Gilbert from next door. He monitors the parking lot. I forgot to tell you they require parking decals here." He held up a rectangular card with a number on it and pointed toward the dashboard.

"Oh. Oh no." Raven's chest felt heavy. Right after promising Gabriel she wouldn't, she'd used magic right in front of his brother. She eyed Mr. Gilbert contritely, chewing her lip. There was only one way to fix this. In for a penny, in for a pound. A memory wipe should do the trick. She strode to the man and took his frozen hand in hers.

"Wait. Don—"

"*Freskaro,*" she said.

Mr. Gilbert blinked his eyes and shook his head before looking down at their coupled hands.

"It's so nice to meet you," Raven said. "I really appreciate your taking the time to introduce yourself."

The man cleared his throat, looking utterly confused. "Dis is private parkin'."

"We have the placard now, see?" She pointed to the

parking pass on their dashboard. "Tobias brought it out for us."

Mr. Gilbert showed a few yellow teeth. "Right. I says to Tobias, you can't have your people comin' in here without a pass. Glad ta see he did da right thing. You guys enjoy your stay now."

Raven tried not to laugh at the man's thick accent. He made "here" sound like two syllables and made "without" sound like "wit out." It was charming. She released the man's hand and gave him a warm smile.

"Thank you, Mr. Gilbert," Tobias called, ushering Gabriel and Raven inside. As soon as the door was closed behind them, Gabriel started to apologize. "It was a simple misunderstanding—"

"Save it, Gabriel." Tobias's hand waved dismissively between them. His face had gone red and his lips were a thin, tight line. "You promised she wouldn't use magic in my house. You broke that promise. I think you should stay in a hotel tonight."

"Please, Tobias, I never used magic *in* your house." Raven met his eyes and placed a hand gently on his forearm. "I wouldn't have used it at all if I hadn't felt we were threatened. Please don't blame Gabriel. It was my slip and it won't happen again. You have my word."

When Tobias's gaze dropped to the place she touched him, she sensed a warm tingle of power that moved through her skin at the point of contact. She was absorbing his energy without even trying. Raven needed to get that under control; it was a dead giveaway that she was a witch. She removed her hand, hoping he hadn't noticed.

If he had noticed, he didn't mention it. Instead, he swallowed and said, "Okay. As long as we have an understanding."

Gabriel smiled. "I'll get the bags out of the car." He pulled his coat tighter around him and slipped out the door again.

"You have a beautiful home," Raven said. They were in a mudroom with pale gray walls and white cabinetry. There was a washer and dryer against one wall and a large folding table. It looked like something out of a magazine, tidy and clean, not a stray detergent cup or speck of dryer lint anywhere.

"You've only seen my mudroom, but thank you." The corner of Tobias's mouth twitched.

His build and coloring was so different from Gabriel's; it was hard to believe they were brothers. Although both males were exceptionally tall, where Gabriel was dark and stocky, Tobias was long and lean. Pale and blond, he reminded Raven of a 1950s poster child—straight white teeth, not a hair out of place.

Raven gave him her warmest smile. "If I've learned anything about you in the short time I've known you, it is that you are meticulous. You want things done right. I respect that about you. I know, without seeing it, that your home reflects your perfectionism." She shrugged out of her coat, and he hung it up on one of the hooks near the door.

"Laying it on a little thick, aren't you? Gabriel must have told you I'm not comfortable with your mating." Tobias scoffed, his smile fading.

"Yes. But every word I said is true. I do respect you and I want a chance to earn your trust."

Tobias's shoulders sagged as if her admission was a weight on his back. Was it that difficult to hear that your future sister-in-law desperately wanted your approval? Raven was rehearsing things to say to him in her mind when a blur of orange flew at her face. She raised her hands and caught the thing before it collided with her nose.

"Sorry. Let me—" Tobias reached for the wriggling ball of fur in her hands.

"Oh, what a sweet kitten!"

Tobias growled. "No. That is the spawn of the devil. I've been trying to catch her to take her into the humane society for days."

"Humane society? Why?"

"That cat is evil. Frankly, I'm surprised she's not scratching your eyes out. The thing doesn't like anyone, especially not me."

Raven tucked the cat against her chest and scratched it behind the ears. It wasn't orange at all but calico with a black spot over one eye that looked like an eye patch. The other eye was surrounded by bright orange fur that set off a white chin and belly. Raven buried her face in the cat's soft coat. "I don't know what you're talking about. This is a sweet cat."

Tobias reached out to stroke the cat's head and the feline hissed. It swiped at him with outstretched claws. "Yeah, right."

Raven laughed. "I've always had a way with animals."

"That explains your relationship with my brother." Tobias's face was impassive, but the longer he stared at her, the harder she laughed. She was rewarded with a small smile.

The door opened and Gabriel ducked inside with their bags. "I think it's starting to snow again."

"It's the end of February. I hope you guys brought warm clothes because Chicago is brutal this time of year."

"You have a new friend," Gabriel said, looking at the cat as they followed Tobias into the main part of the house. He reached out to stroke the cat's head and was met with a growl, hiss, and a swipe.

"Maybe she hates men. Or dragons."

Raven scratched the cat's neck. "Tobias, what did you say her name was?"

"Devil's Spawn. I sometimes call her DS for short. I found her in my dryer vent around Christmas and took her in. Clearly I'm not a cat person, but I couldn't let her freeze to death."

"Devil's Spawn can't be her name," Raven protested. "She needs a real name."

"What do you suggest?"

Raven looked at the patchwork kitten. "She's not a devil. She's a survivor... a warrior... like a goddess. Can I call her Artemis?"

"You can call her anything you want if you can keep her from pissing on my kitchen mats."

Raven rubbed her nose against the cat's. "Artemis. Do you like that?" The cat purred in her arms.

Gabriel looked at the animal sternly with what Raven swore was jealousy. She rolled her eyes. She'd make him purr soon enough.

"Come on in. I'll show you to your room." Tobias led them into the main part of the house, through the kitchen, dining room, and what he called the living room.

The house was narrow but deep and as meticulously kept as she had expected it to be. It was hardwood and steel with clean, modern lines and the occasional perfectly framed work of art. Tobias turned under a modern crystal chandelier and started up an ebony staircase. This was the main foyer of the home, she realized. They'd come in the back entrance. She appreciated the vintage white molding that framed blue-gray walls.

Gabriel's expression soured as he took in the place. He eyed the minimalist decor as if it were repulsive to him.

Raven elbowed him in the side. "What's wrong with you?"

"Where is your treasure room?" Gabriel asked. Raven didn't miss the note of disapproval in his voice.

Tobias stopped short and turned around slowly, casting a heated expression toward his brother. "You will find no treasure room in this house. No treasure at all, actually, aside from the art on the walls. I don't need it."

Raven watched Gabriel's face crumple. "Where do you shift? Spread your wings?"

Tobias snorted. "I don't. I haven't shifted, even partially, in almost a century."

Gabriel cursed, and Raven brought her fingers to her lips. That couldn't be right, could it?

"I told you, I live as a human." Tobias opened the door to a room halfway down the hall and gestured for them to enter. "Here you are."

Raven followed him into a posh space with a fluffy white bed and dark wood furniture.

"Now, if you'll excuse me. It's late and I have surgery tomorrow. Good night."

Raven was still gaping at the beautiful room when the door closed and she realized Tobias was gone. With the cat still in her arms, she turned toward Gabriel, who set the bags down on the floor and started peeling off his parka. He looked concerned.

Cheerfully, she offered, "I don't know about you, but I think that went well."

The look he gave her told her he did not agree.

CHAPTER FOUR

Although Tobias's surgery wasn't until late morning, he hastened to leave the house the moment his eyes popped open. His work served as an effective escape from all the awkward and uncomfortable goings-on at home. If he played his cards right, Gabriel and Raven would be gone by the time he returned home. It was for the best. If Raven had proven one thing last night with the spell she'd cast on poor Mr. Gilbert, it was that she couldn't fully control her magic. Tobias wanted no part of it or their ridiculous story about Paragon. It had been three hundred years. It was ludicrous to believe Brynhoff or his mother, if she was truly still alive, would come after them now.

If he were being honest, there was another reason his steps hastened toward the hospital. Sabrina. He hadn't seen her since their encounter in the stairwell, but oh, had he thought about her. Her honey-and-moonlight scent, the taste of her like fresh cherries on his tongue, the firm and close feel of her against his body. And the best part, she wasn't human after all. The mystery of what Sabrina was teased him like the ribbon of a glittering bow on an unexpected gift. He'd enjoy a chance at peeling back her outer wrappings.

But as was always the case with Tobias, his work came first. He swept his thoughts of Gabriel and Sabrina into a compartment at the back of his mind. With total focus, he performed his scheduled surgery, blocking out everything but the open chest in front of him, the tiny heart he was patching, and the steady thrum of the bypass machine. With utmost care, he corrected the ventricular septal defect that had plagued the five-week-old baby boy, his fingers working with precision far greater than any human's. Once the last stitch was in place, the boy was wheeled back to recovery. Tobias stripped off his rubber gloves and deposited them in the red receptacle near the doors before exiting the operating suite. Everything had gone textbook. The operation was a success. Why then was he not elated?

As he pulled off his mask and cap, all the thoughts he'd put on hold while he operated came back with a vengeance. He washed his hands, scrubbing under the sapphire ring he kept invisible while he worked. The ring made him think about his brother and the crazy story he insisted was true. Normally he wouldn't call his brother a liar, but there was no way his mother had been part of the coup that banished them from Paragon. She was their savior. She'd kept them safe.

Tobias had been elated to hear Eleanor was still alive. That part he wished were true. All these years, he'd assumed she'd been murdered. It was too much to accept that she was both alive and an active and consenting partici-pant in Marius's death. He would never believe such a thing. Not unless he had incontrovertible proof.

He closed the locker he was using and made his way to the floor's break room. A cup of coffee and a moment alone would clear his head. He fed the machine a dollar and hit the latte button.

"Are you waiting for the machine to hand it to you?" Sabrina stood beside him. When had she come in?

Oh! His coffee was done, steaming at the base of the machine. He grabbed it too quickly and it splashed over the back of his hand. *Fuck*. If he'd been human, that heat would have blistered him. Instead, he set his cup down on the counter and dabbed at his wet hand with a paper towel.

"Sabrina," he said. "I was looking for you last night after we... talked. You disappeared."

"Busy with patients." Her tone was nonchalant, but her eyes shifted as if the topic made her nervous. "Dr. Allen asked me to find you though. There's been a major development in one of your patients."

Dr. Allen was Tobias's partner and shared a medical office across the street with him where they provided consultations and ongoing care for their patients. There was only one major development she could be referring to. *Katelyn*. Dr. Allen must have examined her that morning.

"Thank you, Sabrina."

"No problem." She turned to leave.

"Can we talk sometime? Maybe grab a better cup of coffee than this?" He held up his cup. Tobias surprised himself with the brusque solicitation. *Smooth*, he thought. *Play it cool, dragon*. She intrigued him. He had to know who she was and, more importantly, *what* she was.

She whirled, her face unreadable. "Sorry—I don't date people I work with."

"No?" he drawled, swaggering toward her. He sent her a slow grin, his gaze settling on her full lips. "You draw the line at kissing your coworkers in the stairwell? Tongue wrestling's perfectly okay, but coffee's completely out of the question?"

The nurse went absolutely still, all the color draining from her cheeks. Her green eyes darted toward the break room door before landing back on him. As they had the night before, her irises glowed silver under the fluorescent lights.

"We never kissed," she said. "We're friends, nothing more."

The silver faded and Tobias observed her curiously. He narrowed his eyes and gave her a knowing smile. "Whatever you're trying to do didn't work last night, and it sure as hell isn't going to work now."

She staggered back, scanning him from head to toe. Her hand pressed into her stomach. "What do you want?"

"Nothing."

"What are you?"

"I'm the man you kissed." He moved in closer to her. "I'd like that to happen again, which is why I asked you out for coffee."

"And if I don't?" Her face tightened. "What will you do to me?"

Tobias stopped. Now that really pissed him off. Here he was being forthcoming with her, practically admitting to her that he wasn't human. And what did she do? Assume he was threatening her.

"Nothing." He cast a disappointed look down his nose at her. "I thought we shared something last night, and I thought you might want to drink a caffeinated beverage with me and discuss it. I thought it might be refreshing for you to talk to someone who was... like you. Well, at least more like you than the other employees of this hospital. But your secret is safe with me. I'm not into extorting things from my coworkers."

She stared at him for a long moment.

"Now if you'll excuse me, I have hearts to mend." Tobias moved around her and slipped out the door, walking quickly toward the elevator.

"Wait," she called, following him into the corridor. Sabrina's shoulders sagged with her exhale. "Coffee would be great. But not here at the hospital. Someplace we can talk candidly."

Interesting, Tobias thought. Luckily, he was an expert at flying under the radar and knew just the place.

"Maverick's Café," he said. "It might seem crowded, but the patrons are really good at not seeing or hearing a thing."

"I'm just starting my shift," she said. "Tomorrow morning?"

Tobias smiled. "See you then."

THERE WERE FEW THINGS SABRINA HATED ABOUT BEING half vampire, but the constant need to protect her secret was definitely one of them. The coven had rules with serious consequences. Telling a human was out of the question under penalty of death for the human. The law was more lenient with regard to other supernaturals. If Tobias wasn't human, she could reveal what she was so long as he did not present a threat to their kind. Which begged the question, what exactly was she dealing with when it came to Tobias?

Before yesterday night, she would have sworn he was human. After all, not many supernatural creatures made a habit of being as restrained as the good doctor. Tobias was passionate about his work at the hospital without an ounce of ego to muddy the waters. It was rare to find a supernatural being who cared so much or strove for perfection the way he did.

Still, he couldn't be human. She'd never tasted human energy like his. When she'd fed on him, she'd felt high and weirdly energetic for hours afterward. Coupled with her inability to influence his mind, the evidence leaned toward Tobias being supernatural. Only, what type was anyone's guess. He was too smart to be a werewolf, and she would have smelled a witch.

She pulled open the door to Maverick's Café and spotted him waiting for her near the back. He gestured for her to join him at the tiny café table. Two to-go cups rested in front of him, and she caught herself hoping one of them was for her. Something was going down at the counter that had nothing to do with coffee. Three men had gathered near the cash register and were having a heated conversation in another language while another large man with a triangular symbol tattooed on his neck watched from the shadows. She'd rather not interrupt the conversation to order a latte.

"Is one of those for me?" She slung her messenger bag across the back of the chair and took off her hat and parka.

"I got you a cappuccino. Believe it or not, they're good here." He gestured toward the counter and the men Sabrina had noticed earlier. "I would have waited for you to order, but you do not want to interrupt that."

"Looks intense."

"Trust me, it is. I got ours in just before things got heated."

She sank into the chair across from him and grabbed the cappuccino. Warm, foamy heaven slid down her throat. It was exactly the drink she would have ordered for herself. Delicious.

"It's good. Thank you."

Tobias's expression turned clinical. He was studying her, like a cell under a microscope. "There goes one theory."

She leaned her elbows on the table, the cup nestled in her hands between them. "You have a theory about me?"

"I thought you might be a succubus, but if my research is correct, in that case you would not eat or drink human food."

"I'm not a succubus."

"A witch then?"

"No."

He took a long drink. Damn, his eyes were something out of a dream, a very good dream. Sapphire blue, they twinkled beneath his dark blond hair, perfectly matching the brightness of his ring. Holy hell, that was some sapphire ring. The blue gem on his right hand looked lit from within and was as big as her thumbnail. It enthralled her. That thing must be worth a mint.

"I never noticed your ring before," she said. "Is that a wedding band? Are you married?"

Tobias looked like he might blow his coffee out his nose. "No. I am not... married. The ring is a family heirloom. It's against hospital policy for me to wear it at work."

That was a strange way of putting it, she thought. "It's beautiful." *And so are you,* she finished in her head. Tobias was square jawed and full lipped. She wasn't used to seeing him without his lab coat on. The muscles of his shoulders stretched his black sweater. She'd always thought of him as academic, reticent, sometimes phlegmatic, but now his curiosity was evident. She was a puzzle he needed to solve. Good. She intended to remain puzzling.

"What are you?" he asked.

"Shouldn't I ask you the same thing?"

"What makes you think I'm not human?"

She lowered her voice. "I know. You didn't taste human. Not at all." Her fingers brushed her bottom lip.

"You fed off my energy." His eyes narrowed.

She nodded. There was no point in denying it. "Are you a werewolf?"

"Please," he scoffed like he was offended. "No, I am not."

Good, she thought. *What a relief.* Werewolves were her coven's mortal enemies and not allowed within their territory. She wouldn't want to deal with the repercussions if he'd admitted to being one. "Warlock?"

"No."

"Fairy?"

He shook his head. "You?"

"No."

Sabrina swirled her coffee. "Game is up, Doctor. Tell me."

"The road goes both ways, Ms. Bishop."

She thought about it. It was clear he wasn't human, so she wasn't breaking any rules telling him the truth. She nodded. "At the same time then."

"On the count of three: one, two, th—"

"Vampire."

"Dragon."

Sabrina stared at him. Had she heard him correctly? Did he say *dragon*?

"Did you say vampire? But you didn't drink my blood and you walked in here in broad daylight."

"I'm half human. I can feed on energy instead of blood,

and the only thing that will happen if you leave me in the sun is a bad sunburn."

"By the Mountain..."

"What does that mean?"

Tobias cleared his throat and shifted in his seat. "It's an expression. Dragons are born from a mountain. In your vernacular, you might say 'oh my God.'"

"Goddess," she corrected.

"It means you're extraordinary."

She lifted a shoulder. "The only one of my kind in existence."

Unless she was totally misreading his body language, the look he gave her bordered on awe.

"So, uh, you're a dragon? Like you can shift into one? I thought dragon shifters were a myth."

He chuckled softly at that. "Not a myth, although our numbers are few. I look like a man on the outside, but I am a dragon on the inside."

"And you change shape... like a shifter?"

Tobias shrugged. "Yes."

Sabrina sipped her coffee to hide her frown. This was bad. He might not be a werewolf, but if her father knew there were dragon shifters in Chicago, he'd want them out. He'd see them as a threat.

"Are there more like you?" she asked him.

"Here, living in Chicago? No. We are mostly solitary creatures."

She let out a held breath. One dragon was hardly a problem for her coven. In fact, she didn't see the need to even mention his existence to her father.

"What about you?" he asked. "You said you can feed on either energy or blood. Can you exist solely on one or the other?"

"I have. On either or both. I can go months on human food alone, but it would be like a human going without iron. Eventually I run out of my stores and can hardly move. I know. I tried when I was a teenager. I wanted to be a normal human. It didn't work."

"I can relate to that. I've lived as a human for a very long time." He leaned his chin against his fist.

"You're good at it. We've worked with each other for years and I never suspected you were anything but."

He leaned forward, his gaze lingering on her mouth.

"You want to see them, don't you?" she said, suddenly feeling like a kid at show-and-tell.

"Yes." The word came out in a heady drawl. His face was close, so close. His breath brushed her cheek, a gentle caress that warmed more than her face.

She smiled slowly. Should she indulge his curiosity? What was it about his boyish smile that made her want to? Maybe it was because he was focused on her like she was the only woman on the planet. Hell, the only *thing* on the planet. No one—human, vampire, or anything else—had ever looked at her in quite the same way. It made her feel significant.

"Okay," she said softly, allowing her fangs to drop behind her hand. But she didn't get a chance to show him anything. At that moment, a shot rang out. In superspeed, she turned her head. Spotted the tattooed man with a gun, the bullet moving toward Tobias.

He'd moved. His body was in front of her, shielding her.

Eyes widening, she reached out and grabbed his elbow just as the bullet pierced his flesh.

CHAPTER FIVE

Tobias hadn't exactly decided to do it. Something happened when the gun went off. His inner dragon reacted from a deep instinctual place. Sabrina must be saved. Before he fully realized what was happening, he'd placed his body between the bullet and her.

She'd grabbed his arm and everything had turned to mist, black swirls of energy, the smell of honey and night air, the disorienting weightlessness of falling. When they formed again, they were in the alley behind Maverick's. Tobias had never traveled in such a way before, and he pitched forward and heaved. A sharp pain tore through his shoulder. Blood dripped down his side.

"Crap, you've been hit!" Sabrina said.

"It's nothing. I'll heal."

"Only if you get the goddamned bullet out." Sabrina tore the sleeve of his sweater and the button-down underneath and pressed her hand into the bloody wound. "If you heal with that thing inside you, you are going to be in a world of hurt. Vampires in my coven have delayed their healing by years because their bones grew around the bullet and fused together."

Tobias's forehead furrowed. "Do members of your coven get shot often?"

"If you must know, yes. We are the supernatural presence in this city. It has consequences." She moved behind him to inspect the wound at the back of his shoulder. "Come on. My apartment is nearby. I'll extract the bullet while the wound is still open."

Her voice sounded funny. When he turned to see why, her fangs were extended, razor sharp, long and curved over her bottom lip. Beautiful. Fierce. His heart quickened.

"Sorry," she said, raising her hand in front of her lips as if she had a case of bad breath. "It's a reflex. I won't eat you, I promise."

He wasn't sure he wanted her to keep that promise. He wrapped a hand around her wrist and pulled her hand away. "Beautiful," he said, and he meant it.

She blinked rapidly and looked away. A police siren closed in. "We should get out of here."

"Lead the way."

"Oh, you can't walk through Chicago like that." She looked pointedly at his bloody side.

"No—" he began when she reached for his arm again.

She ignored him, took his bicep in a formidable grip, and dematerialized.

Tobias came apart at the tug of her power and hurtled through space only to come back together in a homey apartment overlooking the city. It hadn't taken long, but when they re-formed, Sabrina was panting and the smell of ozone permeated the air.

"Where are we?" he asked.

"My condominium. Marina Towers."

Tobias was familiar with the corncob-shaped twin towers called Marina City that overlooked the river. The buildings had been completed in 1962 under the concept that a person could live, work, and play within the same complex. He remembered the year it opened, how modern it had seemed at the time. Aside from the wedge-shaped units with beautiful views of the city, the place included the House of Blues, a bowling alley, and a grocery. But it was the history of murders and suicides in the towers that came to mind now, knowing what she was.

"Are you the only vampire who lives here?" he asked, suddenly very aware that he was bleeding on the floor.

She gave a breathy laugh. "Just me. Too much sun for the others. But if you're thinking about the suicides, I can't say that vampire business has never taken place here or that it's never become violent. I just... I try to stay out of coven politics, you know?"

He did know. In fact, he knew exactly what it was like to be born into a family whose business was not his own. A drop of blood fell from his shoulder onto the wood floor.

She cursed. In a rush of speed fast enough for him to lose her in the blur, she raced to the kitchen. He watched her pull a towel from one of the drawers and return to press it against his wound. So, a vampire's relative swiftness wasn't folklore. She'd moved faster than any dragon.

"Hold this here. I need to get the medical kit."

He did as she asked, although his shoulder rewarded him with a stab of pain. He grabbed a napkin from the table and bent down to clean up his spilled blood from the hardwood.

"By the way, you weigh a ton," she called from the bathroom. "Do you have bricks in a hollow leg or something?"

He laughed, which made him wince in pain. Tossing

the bloody napkin in the garbage, he was careful to keep pressure on the wound with his opposite hand. "No bricks. But I do carry a dragon's worth of bones, scales, and organs inside me. Even with magic, I'm about a hundred pounds heavier than a human of my size."

She returned with the medical kit, eyes wide. "Right, you're a dragon. Also, I'm weaker during the day, which makes everything seem heavier." She dug a fist into the small of her back. "I think I pulled something."

"I'm sorry. I would have called an Uber if you'd given me a chance."

"I'm sure that would have gone over well. Two people covered in blood, staggering toward an innocent human with a side gig in a Toyota Corolla. We'd have been lucky not to get shot at again."

"True. It's unfortunate we were shot at at all. I knew those humans looked like trouble but I've never had a problem at Maverick's before."

"Just the wrong place at the wrong time. The guy completely missed the human he was aiming at. I hope the Chicago PD nailed him." She opened the kit and picked up a pair of rubber gloves. "Can you catch human infections?"

"No."

"Good. Then I won't bother with aseptic technique. Sit down." She pointed at a chair at the kitchen table. "Sit sideways so I can reach the wound. Oh, and I'm going to need you to take your shirt off."

He removed the towel and stripped the bloody sweater and button-down from his body, folding it neatly so that the bloody part was inside the dry part. He placed it on the table.

"Still Tobias," she murmured, positioning herself behind him. He felt her press the towel against his wound again and watched her choose a pair of forceps from the kit she'd retrieved.

"What do you mean by that? 'Still Tobias'?"

"You are the most meticulous man I've ever known. I've never met anyone more thorough or precise."

"Thank you." His shoulder throbbed and he suppressed a growl.

"This is going to hurt a little. The bullet is against the bone. Try to think of something else. Tell me what it means to be a dragon. Aside from shifting, what else can you do?"

Lightning bolts of pain shot through his shoulder and chest as she dug deeper. He winced. "Invisibility, speed, strength. We can fly, both in this form and our beastly one." His jaw tightened as she jabbed the forceps in and twisted.

"Where do you come from? I've never met a dragon before."

"Dragons come from a place called Paragon. We're not native to this world. I was... left here after a problem in my native land."

"You can't go home?"

"No."

Awkward silence stretched between them.

"What about you? You said you're the only half vampire. Does that mean the only one in your coven?"

"I'm the only half vampire in the world."

"The only one... anywhere?" Totally unique. Dragon catnip. He inhaled her moonlight-and-honey scent and quelled a rush of desire.

"As far as I know. My mother was a human who practiced necromancy. After my parents met and were mated in the 1940s, she cast a spell to temporarily reverse my father's vampire nature... um, raise him from the dead. Basically she made him human for a short time, and he fathered me." She paused. "I was five when she was murdered by a werewolf while my father was sleeping."

"I'm sorry." Tobias watched her over his shoulder. There was so much pain in her expression. All those years working with her, and he'd never known.

Sabrina sighed. "It was a long time ago."

He took a deep breath and let it out slowly. "As someone who lost their mother over three hundred years ago, I can say unequivocally that the pain never goes away no matter how much time has passed."

"Three hundred years?"

"That's when we came here, to this realm. Unfortunately, my mother didn't make it." Only half of Sabrina's face was visible behind him, but her wince was unmistakable.

"You don't look a day over two hundred and ninety."

"I was an adult when we lost her. I can't imagine what you must have been through as a child."

Sabrina paused what she was doing. "My father became both parents to me, and he's never failed me. Not once. But I remember her sometimes. Her face comes back to me at the strangest of times, and I feel the hole. Do you know the hole? That mother-shaped wound that never quite heals. Something is missing inside, and you just hope it doesn't make you defective."

He nodded. "I can relate."

"It's a sad thing to have in common."

"You're not defective, Sabrina."

She grinned. "You haven't tried my cooking."

Another slice of pain traveled through his shoulder and he winced. "How many vampires live in Chicago?"

"Thousands," she said softly. "My coven runs the city. Nothing happens here that we don't have a hand in."

"What, like the mob?" He laughed lightly as he said it, but when she looked at him, her expression was serious. "How have I lived here for so long without knowing this?"

"We operate under the surface. Other vampires sleep during the day, but there are a few humans that work for us. We can accomplish everything we need to through a few strategic relationships. We try not to disrupt the lives of workaday humans."

Tobias turned that bit over in his head. It almost sounded like her coven was influencing the humans in power to do their will. Chicago was no stranger to mob activity, and it really wasn't a surprise that vampires were part of that. But he was thankful she was different. She was a nurse. Her coven's activities didn't reflect on her personally.

"Got it!" Pressure and a tug precipitated a gush of blood that splattered grotesquely on the floor. She dropped the forceps—still locked around the bullet—on the table and pressed a towel to the geyser sputtering from the back of his shoulder.

"I heal faster than a human, but it will take some time in this form. I apologize for the mess."

"You definitely don't heal as fast as a vampire." She pressed harder. "I know this sounds strange, but vampire saliva has healing properties. It's how we close up the wounds we make when we feed on human hosts. Would you mind if I...?"

"Lick the wound?"

"It's gross to you, isn't it? Ugh, this is awkward. Never mind."

He looked at her over his shoulder, her red hair falling in a wave across her right eye. By the Mountain, she was beautiful. She could lick any part of him she pleased.

"If you're willing, I would be grateful for your help."

Her green eyes widened and silver flashed along the edge of her irises. "Okay." Long, cool fingers traveled up his back and hooked over his shoulder, kneading the base of his neck. He felt the pressure on his wound ease. The bloody towel landed on the table. He swallowed, a tingle rising in his torso at the thought of her bubblegum-pink tongue touching his skin. Out of the corner of his eye, he watched her lower her head.

His imagination hadn't done the deed justice. Warm, wet heat lapped over the back of his shoulder. If she caused him any pain, he didn't notice. He was too distracted by the way his body reacted to the feeling, an instant erection punching into his fly. She licked again, the feeling like hot honey oozing over his flesh. Her lips grazed his skin. Her breath came cool and soft against the wet path she left behind. He reached between his legs and adjusted himself.

She moved lower on his arm, stroking a long trail from his elbow to his shoulder, then another along his ribs. Her nails scraped up the back of his neck and into his hair. She moaned, and didn't that just light his inner fire?

Tobias had an inkling that his wound was healed; there was no more blood dripping to the floor. But he couldn't bring himself to stop her. All his awareness narrowed on the feel of her warm mouth on the back of his arm and the resulting tingle in the head of his cock. In his quiet ecstasy, he didn't notice the rise of his inner dragon until it was too late. The rumble of his mating trill rose in his chest, a deep vibration that seemed to rattle the walls.

"What was that?" she asked.

"What was what?" He knew exactly what it was. It was his inner dragon's way of calling *mine,* possessive and feral. Something he could not explain to her and was wholly inappropriate in the age of the #MeToo movement. He might as well tell her he wanted to club her over the head and drag her back to his cave by the hair.

Instead, he turned to her, rising from the chair. "Thank you." He placed his hands on the outside of her shoulders, met her gaze, and moved in closer.

She didn't pull away. In fact, her expression was hungry, her gaze lingering on his mouth. Damn, her lips were close, flushed with blood, parted for him. What he'd like to do to that mouth. He stroked up her arms to cradle her face. He was going to show her exactly how she'd made him feel.

"I'm going to kiss you."

"Yes," she whispered, rising up on her toes and brushing her lips softly against his. He teased her lower lip, then repositioned to take the kiss deeper. Her head rolled and she leaned into him.

"Sabrina?" Her weight sagged in his arms.

"Your blood is good," she slurred. "Really good."

"Are you okay?"

In answer, Sabrina swayed violently on her feet. He caught her before she hit the floor.

◆

SABRINA WOKE ON HER COUCH, WRAPPED IN AN afghan she'd bought from Pottery Barn. Tobias was gone. As she sat up, a headache jackhammered in her skull and she cursed. If she'd thought his energy was intoxicating, his blood made it look like a virgin cocktail. For the life of her, she couldn't remember anything as erotic as the taste of Tobias's blood, except maybe the act of licking it from his tightly corded shoulder.

Dammit, she had the hots for the doctor. Pressing a fist into her forehead, she chided herself. One come-hither look and she'd spilled secrets like a busted piñata. She didn't even know this guy. Well, she'd *known* him for years, but not the real him. She'd known a human version of him. Worse, she had no idea what her coven's rules about dragons actually were. Before today she would have questioned their existence. At least he'd said he was alone here. That increased the chances he wouldn't be viewed as a threat.

Stretching her arms over her head, she stared out her floor-to-ceiling windows. Almost sunset. She'd slept all day. Time to get cleaned up and join her father for the monthly coven assembly. Heading for the bathroom, she stopped short when she noticed a note on the sparkling-clean table. In fact, the entire dining area, floor included, had been scrubbed to a shine. It looked like Tobias had even washed out the towels she'd used on his shoulder and hung them on the rack to dry. No trace of blood anywhere. And the coat she'd left in the coffee shop was hanging off one of her chairs. He'd retrieved it for her.

She lifted the paper from the table. It was from the pad she kept on her fridge: purple-lined and trimmed with a picture of a cat with its claws out. The caption read REASONS I SHOULDN'T KILL YOU IN YOUR SLEEP. Cheeks warming, she squeezed her eyes closed. Great, if he hadn't thought she was a psycho before, he did now. She opened her lids again and read what he'd written.

Had to go. Dinner tomorrow?
—Tobias.

She smiled and picked up her phone to text his number.
Have to work tomorrow night. Lunch date?
Saturday? There's something I'd like to show you.

She grinned. *I can't wait.*

She returned the phone to her pocket and hurried into the bathroom. If she didn't get to the tunnels quickly, her father would be angry, and if there was one thing Sabrina didn't want to do, it was make Calvin Bishop angry. When Calvin got angry, people died... or worse. She showered and donned the ruby-red Armani gown she'd purchased for the event. Once her hair was curled, her makeup applied, and her ruby and diamond jewelry in place, she dematerialized to her father's luxurious living quarters in the tunnels.

Few humans were aware of the network of freight tunnels forty feet under the city of Chicago that had become the home to the Lamia Coven. In the early 1900s, they were constructed to be utility tunnels, used to run telephone and cable wires to the city's inhabitants, but soon they were expanded to haul freight and mail. The network was hijacked in the 1920s by the mob, who smuggled alcohol for their speakeasies in through the narrow passageways. That's when vampires got involved. The vampires of Chicago had a long history of working with organized crime. Vampires provided Capone with muscle and manpower; he provided them with blood—lots of it. There seemed to be no limit to the number of bodies the man wanted to disappear, and her kind was more than willing to do the honors.

Once the twenty-first amendment ended Prohibition, the mob forgot about the tunnels and the Lamia Coven took over for Capone. Aside from those who were on the payroll or who were dinner, no human had come down there since 1959.

"Good evening, Ms. Bishop. You look beautiful tonight." Paul, a member of her father's human security detail and one of Chicago's finest, smiled up at her from his seat outside her father's chambers. He was in full dress today, his badge shining from the chest of his blue uniform. Two conspicuous puncture wounds shone from his left carotid artery. Good to know her father was eating.

"Hello, Paul. I take it he's up?"

"Yes. He's expecting you. Go right in." He stood and pulled the vault door that served as the entrance to her father's apartment open. Sabrina hurried inside.

"Sabrina! Right on time." Her father spread his arms wide and she embraced him, giving him a peck on the cheek. He looked dashing tonight with his sleek dark hair and oversized gray eyes. His skin might have never seen the sun, but it glowed with the kind of vitality that only came from recently taking a vein.

"Good to see you, Father."

"You smell absolutely delicious. Is that a new perfume?"

Sabrina realized what he was smelling. Although she'd brushed her teeth and washed her face, the scent of Tobias's blood leached through her pores, and it was absolutely captivating. It made her mouth water for him. But she couldn't tell her father that. This was not the time or the place to bring up dragon blood.

"Perfume. I don't know what it's called. Some girl spritzed me at Macy's."

He grinned. "I hope you bought a bottle. If not, you should go back. That's worth whatever they're charging."

Although her father's home was underground, it was far bigger than her own and as posh as any penthouse. It was also a study in the passage of time, an eclectic mix of the finest in decor from the past five hundred years. The art on his walls included an original van Gogh. He'd been friends with the artist and even supported him occasionally in exchange for his work. This one was called *The Beauty of*

Blood, and no human had ever seen it except Paul and the few others who'd entered his chamber. It resembled *The Starry Night*, only there was an embracing couple at its center, surrounded by swirling shades of red instead of blue. Sabrina found it both haunting and romantic, a representation of loving someone so much you'd give the life force from your veins for them. Her father had loved her mother like that once.

"The main hall is already full. We have record participation tonight." He straightened his bow tie.

Sabrina brushed her hand across the back of his tux, removing a bit of cave dust. "Of course they came. They want to hear what's going on with the werewolves."

His expression became somber as he looked at her in the mirror. What a funny thing it was that humans believed vampires didn't have a reflection, as if a stretch of silver only reflected life and not magic.

"The day that Frenwald killed your mother while I was sleeping, I swore I'd avenge her. I had his head in my hands before the night was through, but it wasn't enough. I needed to end the Racine pack and make this city safe for our coven once again." His fangs extended as he spoke, and Sabrina saw a bead of blood form in the corner of his eye. Vampire tears. "Today I get to announce to the world that we've accomplished our goal."

Sabrina grinned. "Truly? Racine has fallen?"

He turned to face her. "Yes."

"Wonderful news! The war is finally over." She wrapped her arms around his neck and gave him a peck on the cheek. Although he was a vampire and his skin was cold, he had never been anything but warm to Sabrina.

He embraced her fully. "You remind me of your mother," he said, pulling away. "She had red hair just like yours

53

and the same fire in her soul. Veronica was a force of nature."

"I wish I could have known her."

"She would have been proud of you. When you take your place as master of this coven, we can include a tribute to her in your coronation ceremony."

Sabrina laughed. "I'd love that, but I think you're going to be around for a long time." She'd always known she was in line for his throne. She was his favorite. Calvin had sired other vampires, but she was the only one born the human way, out of love. A love that had driven her father for decades. He was immortal though. He'd be running this place forever unless he was killed by their enemies, and given the crazy amount of security that surrounded him twenty-four seven, she doubted that would be happening anytime soon.

Thank the goddess. She wasn't sure she'd ever be ready to do what he did every day. As much as she loved her father, she recognized he was a different person than she was. Fierce. Strong. Sometimes brutal. The coven needed him.

He gave her a knowing smile. "It's time."

She allowed him to lead her from his suite, through the tunnels to the great hall where she climbed the short flight of stairs to the dais at the front of the ballroom they called Lamia's Star. The cavernous hall was the central destination of every tunnel from all over the city. There had to be over a thousand vampires there now, their pale faces staring up at her and her father, standing shoulder to shoulder and overflowing into the tunnels that branched off the sides.

Sabrina took her usual place in front of the smaller of two blood-red thrones set up at the center of the dais. It wasn't her father's way to sit. With as much poise as she could muster, she stood supportively by his side, a smile plastered on her face as she scanned the crowd.

She pretended not to notice Tristan, who scowled at her from the front row. He whispered something to the vamp beside him whose name she couldn't remember. What was he up to? The little worm had been gunning for her for years.

The echoing rumble of conversation went silent as her father stepped to the microphone. "Welcome, my coven. I thank you all for joining me on this merry occasion."

She tried to ignore Tristan's seething glances as her father spoke about the advances the coven was experiencing. Their numbers were increasing. All of their kind were amply fed and the coven's reserves were plentiful. Their territory was secure.

Sabrina had heard all these things before. She was part of making them happen, and she folded her hands in front of her hips, her spine straight, an unfaltering smile showing she supported every word.

"And now I have a surprise for all of you," her father said.

Sabrina smiled wider. The coven would be so happy to hear the war was over.

"I am pleased to announce that the Racine werewolf pack territory has officially fallen."

Cheers rose up from the crowd. Sabrina expected her father to go on, to tell the coven that they didn't need to fight anymore. The war was won. Instead, he looked directly at Tristan and motioned with two fingers. The slimeball disappeared for a moment. When he returned, the crowd parted to allow him passage. Tristan had two men and a woman in tow. Bound and gagged, the three had fresh red blood and dark purple bruises marring their exposed skin. Sabrina's eyes flicked down to their bound hands. The ropes were enchanted. They'd be powerless with them on.

Her father beamed at the crowd of vampires. "I give you the alpha male and female of the Racine pack and their shaman!" Her father made a grand sweep of his hand, and the coven cheered in delight. "I want you to know I was compassionate. I gave them a choice: to surrender or die. They chose death. So here we are."

An icy fist formed deep within Sabrina's chest. She rubbed the base of her neck against the discomfort and locked her smile into place. This was her father's big moment. Why did she suddenly feel ill? She chided herself for drinking Tobias's blood. This internal shiver that plagued her must be a side effect.

But when her eyes met the female werewolf's in front of her, the truth barreled into her like a cold wind. She was feeling their fear. The human side of her, the side that could absorb energy and sense emotions, was picking up on the sheer terror of the three captives in front of her. She'd never felt this before, not like this. Most vampire emotions were wispy to her, hardly detectable, and human emotions normally caused her barely more than prickle at the back of her neck. What these three shifters were feeling was strong enough to rattle through her as if the emotions were her own.

And then another horror dawned on her. Was her father truly going to execute these three people in front of her? If he did, would she feel it? And what about the rest of the coven? There were new vamps here with no control. It could start a frenzy.

She swallowed hard and swayed on her feet. Her father stopped what he'd been saying and reached behind him to slide his hand into hers, offering her a reassuring smile. He had this under control. He would never put her in any danger. She squeezed his fingers.

All at once, a sharp pain hit her between the eyes. She winced, her attention drawn almost magnetically to the shaman. He couldn't be using magic, could he? His bindings were enchanted against it. Unless, of course, the witch they'd hired to cast the spell had only taken into account their shifting abilities and not anything magical. The wolf's gunmetal-gray eyes cut into her and the pain throbbed anew. He was causing the pain, she was sure it. Well, she wouldn't give him the satisfaction of reacting to his little trick. He'd be dead soon enough, and the fear and ache he was pumping into her head would be gone with him.

An image appeared in her mind, four wolves running through the snow. They were free, wild. Four friends in perfect connection with nature. These three friends... and one more.

"Would you care to do the honors?" Her father whispered in her ear, breaking her out of the vision.

Sabrina blinked rapidly, clearing her head. She motioned at her dress. "It's Armani."

"You truly are a princess." He laughed and turned away from her. "Tristan, if you please."

Tristan drew a dagger from his black leather boot and gave Sabrina a knowing smile. Without breaking eye contact with her, he brought the blade to the alpha's throat. Sabrina tensed. The wolf image came back full force, flooding her mind until she could feel the snow on her skin. Now she saw herself running with the wolves, the cold in her nose, the soft powder under her feet. Her forehead throbbed and she rubbed her temple. She wanted to scream.

She composed herself, refusing an urge to look at the

shaman again. No way. She squared her shoulders and ignored the wolf.

Tristan sliced the alpha's throat, throwing him to the ground by his hair. The female beside him screamed, her shrieks stopping when they turned to sobs. Sabrina felt it all, the grief barreling into her heart and tearing it in two. She would not cry. She would not—

She was in the woods again with the wolves but she was covered in blood, the alpha's blood. She blinked and the white female flopped on her side, her neck gushing. At least that ended the ache in her chest. She no longer felt like her own mate had died. But she was still locked in the vision, unable to see or hear her own coven at all. The snow felt cold. The wind blew through her hair. The air smelled of pine and ice. Everything white was splattered in red.

Another blink and it was just her, the shaman, and a single black wolf standing in the snow.

He opened his mouth, snow catching on his eyelashes and bottom lip. "You will never be the same as them. If you try, you will lose your soul."

A wound opened in his neck, a crimson tide staining the white at her feet. The wave of nausea that crashed into her almost made her double over. Almost. The image faded from her mind fast enough for her to remain standing. The last thing she saw before it faded completely was the black wolf running into the woods. She came back into reality to find all three wolves bleeding out on the stone, the last twitches of life rippling through their dying bodies. Thank goodness. The pain in her head was gone.

Beside her, her father leaned toward the microphone. "It is said that werewolf blood is intoxicating to vampires. This is my gift to you. Feed, my children. Don't waste a single drop."

As if the coven were a tightly coiled spring that had been released, the vampires surged forward, swarming the three werewolves until Sabrina couldn't see them at all. She could smell them though. The scent of their blood filled the space, and the sound of their tearing flesh echoed above her clawing brethren.

After saying a few closing words that were largely ignored by the frenzy of vampires, her father led her back to his suite. Her well-practiced smile was still in place, but whatever the shaman had done had left her exhausted. She planned to say good night to her father as soon as possible and go to bed early.

"I know what's bothering you," her father said.

"Nothing's bothering me. I'm so proud of you. You've avenged my mother."

He shook his head. "You think you missed out on the wolf blood. Don't fret, Sabrina. I had them put some aside for us before the wolves were ever brought forward." He poured two shot glasses of blood from a decanter on the small credenza in his living room and handed her one. The vessel was enchanted to keep the blood fresh and the glass felt warm in her hand. Raucous growls of vampires feeding in the main hall echoed in the tunnels outside his front door as he raised his glass to her. "Here's to you, future coven master. It won't be long now. I hope you've been taking notes."

"Oh, I think I have time." She shook her head. "You're more powerful than ever. You're not going anywhere."

"But that's where you are wrong, daughter. Now that the werewolves are conquered, someone needs to take over the Racine territory. That someone is me."

"I don't understand."

"Only I have the experience to start a new coven there.

59

And that means"—he grinned like he was handing her the world on a spoon—"you, Sabrina, will become the new Lamia coven master."

She didn't say anything. She couldn't.

He laughed and nodded his head. "It's okay. This is overwhelming. Give it time to sink in."

"It's... so unexpected," she said breathlessly.

He clinked her glass. "Congratulations, darling, you deserve it." He tossed back his drink while Sabrina tried her best to steady her shaking knees. She wasn't ready for this. Not by a long shot.

CHAPTER SIX

Tobias pulled his coat tighter around his bare chest as he walked from his Land Cruiser to the back door of his house., His shirt hadn't been salvageable. After he'd left Sabrina's, he'd tossed it in the dumpster before returning to Maverick's to pick up their coats. At times like this, he was thankful dragons could make themselves invisible.

It had started to snow again, big fluffy flakes that turned the world white and covered the cars in the parking lot with a thick blanket of the cold stuff. Gabriel's car was gone, but he hadn't left long ago based on the thin film of white where it used to be. So they'd returned to New Orleans as planned. Good. That was for the best. He rushed inside, kicked off his snow-covered shoes, and placed them in the utility sink before wiping the excess snow from the floor with a towel. He removed his coat and hung it on the hook. Shirtless, he veered from the mudroom into the kitchen.

"Oh!" Raven raised her hands to shield her eyes. She was sitting at the counter, Artemis curled in her lap. "What happened to your shirt?"

"What are you doing here?"

He jogged past her and to his room, grabbed a T-shirt from his drawer, and pulled it over his head. When he returned, Raven looked confused.

"I'm sorry I caught you off guard." Her cheeks reddened. "Gabriel went to the store for some hot-chocolate mix. This weather makes me crave it, and you didn't have any. I still haven't adjusted to the cold, so he offered to go to the store without me." She trailed her fingers over Artemis's back and bit her lip.

Tobias shot her a pitying look. "No one ever adjusts to Chicago cold. What I meant to ask was, why are you still in Chicago at all? Gabriel told me you were going home today."

She frowned. "Why would he say that? We haven't even had a chance to talk to you."

"About what exactly?"

Raven stared at him for a long, assessing moment. "About what happened in Paragon. I think it would be better if Gabriel were here for this conversation." She stroked the cat again. "I'm uncomfortable saying anything more without him present."

"How diplomatic of you," he said stiffly. "I think my brother has failed to mention that we've already discussed this, and as I told him, I'm not interested in getting involved."

He crossed to the refrigerator and looked inside. No wonder he felt like a bent twig about to snap. Not only had he missed dinner, but he was still a little drained from his ordeal at Maverick's. He opened the meat drawer and grabbed the salmon fillets inside.

"You don't like me very much, do you?" Raven asked from behind him.

He took a deep breath and let it out slowly. "Don't take

it personally. Dragons and witches are not meant to be... related. I realize you are not familiar with our customs, but your mating to Gabriel breaks one of our most sacred laws. I can't condone it."

He preheated the oven and then tossed the fish into a pan with some lemon slices and fresh dill from his windowsill herb garden.

He glanced back at Raven to find her staring at him. Even though he was hungry enough to eat every ounce of fish he was preparing, he wasn't a monster. "Have you eaten yet? There's enough here for two."

"Thank you, but I'm set. Gabriel and I ordered burgers earlier."

He nodded and slid the fish into the oven.

"You're very comfortable around the kitchen. You don't have oreads to help you?"

Tobias chuckled. "No. Unlike my brother, I prefer to cook and clean for myself. It makes me feel human."

"You said that before, that you live as a human. No treasure room. Why do you want to be human?" Raven cleared her throat. "What I mean is, why aren't you happy being what you are?"

He looked at her over his shoulder. "When in Rome. The best way to disguise oneself as a human convincingly is to become convincingly human."

"Oh."

He poured himself a glass of white wine and pointed a finger toward an empty glass. When Raven nodded, he poured her one too. "I've accepted that I will be living on this Earth for a very long time. Maybe forever. I'd just as soon live like the natives do."

She nodded, but he hated the hint of pity he saw in her eyes.

"It doesn't surprise me that Gabriel keeps oreads. Even in Paragon, my brother wouldn't walk somewhere he could fly," he sniped.

Raven accepted the wine and took a small sip. "Did Gabriel ever tell you that he saved my life with his tooth?"

"He told me he healed you but not what he healed you from."

"Brain cancer. Glioblastoma."

He leaned against the counter. "No shit?"

"No shit."

"That's a harsh diagnosis."

"It was a harsh condition. I was sure it was the end until your brother came along. He saved me and I agreed to work for him, to help him break Crimson's curse. That bond, though, was not why I fell in love with him."

"Why did you?"

She stared straight ahead for a minute, focusing on nothing in particular before answering. "I kept hearing about this bond, about how Gabriel could force me to do things. I'd agreed to it when I was ill. I didn't know I was a witch at the time. If he had threatened me, I would have done what he'd asked. But he never did. In fact, he freed me, time and time again, at his own peril. Gabriel won me like a flower wins a bee; he held very still and offered me love and kindness like nectar. I came willingly, starving for my soul's nourishment. I couldn't resist. I kept coming back again and again until I never wanted to leave."

Tobias snorted. "I bet my brother loves being compared to a nectar-filled flower."

"Cancer is a prison. He broke me out. There isn't a thing I wouldn't do for him, Tobias. You have a rule in Paragon that dragons and witches cannot mate because they'd be too powerful. I get that. But I'm not the same kind of witch that rule was made for. I'm not from Paragon. I'm a human girl who was dying in a hospital bed less than a year ago. I don't want power or to rule Paragon. I just want a simple life."

"You may want a simple life, but it is said your offspring will be monsters with uncontrollable power."

"I can't have children. The chemo took that from me. I'm barren."

Tobias frowned. He was aware of the type of chemo she must've been on. What she said rang true. "I'm sorry," he said genuinely.

"Well, with my condition it wasn't like they were worried about preserving my fertility. I wasn't going to be around long enough to bear children."

He stopped himself from saying he was sorry again and instead blew out a deep breath.

She continued, "So you see, what you call a witch and what I am are two different things, and Paragon is an entirely different world. I love your brother, Tobias, with my whole heart and my whole soul. I just want us to be a family."

At last she stopped talking. He wasn't sure he could listen to any more. She was breaking his heart. The truth was he liked Raven. He had liked her since the first day he'd met her. But Tobias was a male who believed in the law. There was a right and there was a wrong. Rules existed for a reason.

He reached into the fridge and retrieved some leftover tabbouleh salad while he was thinking what to say to her. "Look. You seem like a nice person, Raven. It's nothing personal. I know you guys thought you saw something in Paragon that made you believe our mother was partly responsible for the coup. But I wasn't there. And I know our mother. She told us to stay apart in order to keep us safe. She saved us. Whatever you saw, it couldn't be what you thought it was. I plan to keep doing what she told us to do, and that means staying away from Gabriel. I'm sorry."

"Okay." She played with the cat's ears.

Tobias retrieved a plate from the cupboard and stared at the oven hungrily. Ten more minutes.

"I'm not buying it, you know."

He looked at her over his shoulder. "Buying what?"

"The 'I never break the rules' crap. You wanted Gabriel's healing amulet for a reason. I bet you've already used it."

He stared at the empty plate in his hand, his teeth clenching. True or not, the severity of his infraction was minuscule compared to an interspecies mating like hers. *Interspecies mating.* The memory of Sabrina's tongue coasting over the back of his shoulder filled his mind. He stiffened.

"Can you honestly tell me that in all your five hundred years you've never been with someone who wasn't a dragon?" Raven asked pointedly.

"Sexual relationships with humans are acceptable for dragons. Humans are considered a harmless distraction."

"And you've never been with any other species? Never even been tempted?" Raven crossed her arms, the wineglass cupped in her right hand. "I find that hard to believe."

Tobias's mind lingered on Sabrina. No, they hadn't slept together yet, but he wanted to. Oh hell, if he could woo her into bed, he'd have the feisty redhead right now.

"Your silence speaks volumes," Raven said.

"I'm not mated to anyone." He took a long drink of wine.

"Yet." Her intense gaze cut right through him, and one

corner of her mouth curled. "I see you with someone, and she isn't a dragon."

"What does that mean? Are you reading my mind or something?" Tobias scowled.

Raven shook her head. "I can't read minds. Just a hunch. You walked in here tonight shirtless and smelling of blood and perfume."

He thumbed the stem of his glass. Perhaps he was a bit of a hypocrite. Could he blame Gabriel for Raven if he planned to pursue Sabrina? Vampires weren't forbidden like witches, but the relationship would never have been sanctioned in Paragon. Dragons and vampires didn't commingle much in that realm. He gave his head a shake. Who was he kidding? There was no relationship to speak of, not yet anyway. At this point all he could claim was a permanent erection with Sabrina's name on it.

"Don't take this the wrong way, Raven, but as soon as I finish eating this, I'm going to bed. Today has been, in a word, draining, and this conversation isn't helping."

Raven gave him a warm smile. "Okay. I just want you to know I'm not the enemy. I'm here because I love your brother. Nothing more. You have nothing to fear when it comes to me."

"Understood. But what *you* have to understand—" The timer cut him off, and he spun around to retrieve his dinner from the oven. When he turned back to finish his sentence, she'd left the room and taken the cat with her.

CHAPTER SEVEN

New Orleans

A crack and a flash of light, not unlike thunder and lightning, heralded Scoria's arrival. He landed in a crouch in a grassy area that smelled of animal dung, the marble-sized orb Aborella had given him gripped tightly in his gloved fist. As the captain of the Obsidian Guard, he was among the strongest and fastest of his kind, capable of wielding all manner of Paragonian weapons, but that didn't stop his knees from shaking. Traveling between dimensions under any circumstances could be a dicey affair. Following the echo of a weak tracking spell rather than opening a portal was like feeding your body through a sieve.

But the empress wanted the girl.

Once, centuries ago, Scoria had prided himself on his devout adherence to the law of the Mountain, handed down by the goddess at the birth of Paragon. He'd learned the stories on his grandfather's knee and had believed every word of them. Now there was only one law. Her law. Eleanor was the most powerful dragon who'd ever lived, and she was now Paragon's high ruler. If she wanted the girl, it was Scoria's duty to retrieve her. He'd sworn his life to the crown, and he had every intention of following through.

He opened his fist. Cradled in the palm of his leather glove, the enchanted orb pulsed with a soft blue light that pointed east. It would lead him to her. When the empress had faced the dark-haired witch in her throne room, she'd cast a spell on her, one that was supposed to make her sleep. It hadn't worked. Somehow the witch had escaped. Still, the empress's magic could be traced by the use of the orb. The witch had been here once, although judging by the muted glow of the blue light, he suspected it had been some time ago. Aborella, sorceress to the crown, had explained that the orb was but a tool to move him in the right direction. Finding the girl would fall on his shoulders, on his training as an assassin.

Hungry and weary, he staggered toward a collection of lights. The twisting branches of strange trees curled under a single yellow moon. He slipped through the darkness toward what must be a road, the headlights of oddly designed carriages speeding past him, and strode at a fast clip, drawing on the magic of the cat's-eye stone in his ring to translate the street signs.

Magazine Street. The orb pulsed faster, its light continuing to point in the same direction. When he neared a small, brightly painted cottage with a sign that read THE THREE SISTERS, the orb stopped pulsing, its steady blue glow still muted but unbroken. The girl had definitely been here once, although the dull thrum in his palm suggested she wasn't anymore. He slid the sphere into his bag and crossed the street.

Inside the pub, Scoria finally gave in to the fatigue waging war on his muscles and sat down at one of the tables. The place reminded him of the Silver Sunset in Paragon, and he hoped he could sup here before carrying on his search.

And then she was there, at his table! Dark hair, eyes the color of lapis, olive skin, and a graceful neck he could snap with little effort. But no, when he looked again, he could see it wasn't her. This woman was heavier, and the orb in his bag remained cold to the touch when he reached for it.

"Can I get you started with something to drink?" the woman asked. Her name tag read Avery.

"Is there another one who looks like you?" Scoria asked.

The female laughed. "Oh, you're thinking of my sister, Raven. She doesn't work here anymore."

"Where is she now?"

The woman made a sound like a snort and ignored his question. She thrust a menu into his hands. "We have Tanglewood jambalaya on special tonight. If you haven't had it before, ours is made with duck and andouille and tends to run spicy. The locals love it."

Scoria's stomach growled. He wasn't sure what the dish was, but if humans could eat it, surely he could as well. "I would like that dish and a glass of..." He scanned the bar, his eyes falling on a large mug of dark, thick ale. "That."

"A Guinness. Good choice. I'll bring you water too."

The female turned to walk away, but he grabbed her wrist. "Where is Raven?"

She cast him a pointed look, tearing her arm from his grip. "Look, dude, I'm not sure what you want with my sister, but you should know she's engaged to be married. She's with her fiancé right now."

He leaned back in his chair, trying to remember the lessons in human culture he'd studied before leaving Paragon. "You have misinterpreted my intentions. I simply need to speak with her about a misunderstanding between her and my... employer."

Looking confused, Avery said, "Does this have something to do with Blakemore's?"

Scoria had no idea what she was talking about, but he nodded evenly.

"Well, Raven and Gabriel are out of town for a few weeks, but the shop is still open. I'm sure Richard or Agnes can help you."

Scoria had to concentrate to keep his expression impassive. "You say *Gabriel* is out of town with Raven?"

She laughed. "Uh, yeah. He's her fiancé. I'll get you that beer and the jambalaya."

Scoria stared at his ring, his mind reeling. The light at the center glowed, and he brought it close to his lips under the guise of rubbing his chin. "You were right, Empress. The girl is in league with the Treasure of Paragon. She is with your eldest son at this very moment."

The cat's-eye blinked at him, and then her voice came, soft as a whisper from somewhere deep inside the stone. "Find them, Scoria, and bring them to me, dead or alive. Do not return to Paragon without them."

CHAPTER EIGHT

Chicago

"This, Artemis, is a litter box." Sitting cross-legged on the floor, Raven stroked the cat's fur and pointed toward the fresh litter she'd made available in the room Tobias had given them to stay in. It was clear the feline refused to use the one he'd set up for her in the basement of the brownstone, but then it was cold and drafty down there. Raven thought the cat might need a new box in a more welcoming location, and it didn't hurt that Tobias's scent was weaker here. Artemis, she'd discovered, did not seem to enjoy Tobias's company.

"Wouldn't it be better to set that thing up in the mudroom?" Gabriel's nose wrinkled in distaste.

"Back up. You're making her nervous. She needs to feel safe." The cat arched her back beneath Raven's scratching nails. "I don't think she likes dragons. Or maybe it's men in general."

"Nothing safer than a room at the humane society," Gabriel mumbled.

Raven gasped and covered the cat's ears. "She can hear you, Grumpy Gus. Stop being so negative. This is going to work."

The *Wonder Woman* theme song blared from Raven's phone, and she swept it off the carpet behind her to bring it to her ear.

"You'll never believe the dress I found to wear in your wedding," Avery blared in her ear. "It's navy blue and strapless. It makes me look like a princess."

"Sounds perfect." Raven glanced at Gabriel and mouthed, *Avery*. He smirked and left the room.

"I also reserved the church for October thirteenth. I know you haven't set a date yet, but it's hard to get Saint Patrick's. We can cancel the date if it doesn't work out."

Raven raised an eyebrow. What would Father Ian think of her if he knew she was a witch? She supposed he didn't need to know. Then again, Marie Laveau was a voodoo priestess and a lifelong Catholic. Perhaps it wouldn't be an issue.

"Thank you, Avery. I appreciate your doing this."

"How are things in Chicago? When will you be back?"

"I'm not sure yet. Gabriel and Tobias haven't seen each other in a long time. I want to give them a chance to reconnect."

"Why can't they reconnect here? Invite him to New Orleans."

"He's a doctor. A pediatric cardiologist, actually. He's needed here."

There was a stretch of silence and then a giggle. "A doctor, huh? When can I meet him?"

Raven groaned. "He's not your type."

"He might be my type."

"He's ultraconservative, likes things meticulously clean and orderly, and almost always follows the rules."

"You're right. He's not my type."

"Thought not. How's Mom?"

"She's good, but oh, some weird guy stopped by the bar looking for you yesterday. He was very persistent. He said something about needing to talk to you... I think it was about the antique store maybe? Something about a misunderstanding with his boss?"

Raven narrowed her eyes. "I never worked on the floor at Blakemore's, Avery. That doesn't make sense. What did he look like?"

"A big guy. Like Gabriel's size big; you know, the type of big you notice. He had this tattoo around his eye—a double crescent. Long, scraggly hair. Dark... not dark skinned but like dark hair and eyes. You know. His clothes were bizarre, even for here. Expensive looking, but like from another country. Oh, and the weirdest part, he paid for his dinner with a diamond. I thought he'd stiffed me, but Mom took it to a pawnshop and it was worth nine hundred bucks."

Raven bristled. There were two physical traits that distinguished Paragonians from humans. One was a double crescent-shaped discoloration around the right eye. The other was three vee-shaped ridges at the base of the skull. New Orleans was brimming with people who loved to celebrate their individuality, often augmenting their physical forms in a number of ways from piercings to silicon injections, but she doubted it was coincidence this visitor resembled a Paragonian. Not when he'd paid the bill with a jewel.

"What did you tell him, Avery?"

"Do you know him? I told him you were out of town

with Gabriel and he should go to Blakemore's and talk to Richard or Agnes."

Raven closed her eyes and cursed under her breath. "If he comes back, don't give him any information about me or Gabriel or anything else. Whatever you do, don't tell him where we are. And if you can, get one of the other employees to serve him. He's dangerous."

"O-okay. Did I do something wrong? Who is this guy? Why is he looking for you?"

"He's a..." Raven looked down at Artemis whose tail was flicking left then right in annoyance. "He's a disgruntled ex-employee of Gabriel's. He's got a history of violence, so be careful."

"Oh my gosh, really? That's so scary. I'll tell Mom too, in case he comes in again. He might. He loved the jambalaya. Ate every last bite, and you know we serve enough for four."

"If he knows you're my sister, he might try to get more information out of you. Protect yourself, Avery. This guy is trouble."

"I have a gun behind the bar and the cops on speed dial."

"Good girl." Raven wished she were there to place a protective ward on the Three Sisters, but it would have to wait. "I'll call you when I know more about our return date." Raven exchanged goodbyes with her sister and hung up the phone. Seeming to pick up on Raven's energy, Artemis let out a disgruntled meow.

Raven climbed to her feet and scrambled into the hall. "Gabriel?"

She found him in the kitchen and relayed everything Avery had told her.

"Based on her description, it sounds like Scoria,"

Gabriel said. "My mother and Brynhoff have not given up on finding you. This is bad, Raven. If a member of the Obsidian Guard is here, they will stop at nothing. They are lethal hunters."

"But *how* did he find me?"

"I'm not sure." Gabriel frowned. "But I'll keep you safe."

"My sister told him I was with you. She didn't know any better."

He inhaled through his teeth.

Raven frowned. "We need to tell Tobias."

"We will when he gets home. He doesn't like me to disturb him at the hospital." He pulled his phone from his pocket. "I'll call Richard and Agnes and give them a heads-up."

Raven slid into his arms. "I'm scared, Gabriel."

He kissed the top of her head. "Scoria doesn't know where we are. No one has this address. You'll be safe here."

She pulled back and looked up at him, a wave of fear passing through her. "But what about them? We're not there to protect them."

He rubbed her shoulder but didn't respond. Richard had answered his call, and Gabriel was already barking orders into his phone.

❧

THE NEXT DAY SABRINA COULDN'T GET TOBIAS OUT OF her head. She couldn't wait to see him again, to feel the way she always felt in his presence, like she belonged there and was valued by him. It made her shift at the hospital downright painful. Patient after patient, she had to check herself to stay focused on the task at hand.

Although she tried not to think about it, her thoughts of Tobias circled back to her coven. She understood why her father had executed the three werewolves the way he had. This was war. A good leader had to think about the morale of the coven. Vampires bonded over a shared win.

But it also made her worried for Tobias. The execution was meant to send a message to the other supernatural creatures in surrounding areas to stay out of the city. Stories about the brutal fall of the Racine shifters would undoubtedly reach other shifter packs, a clear message that Chicago belonged to the Lamia vampires. Outsiders would not be tolerated.

There was nothing more outsider than a dragon.

Still, she'd worked with him for years and had never known he was supernatural. If they were going to be together, she needed to make him understand that his safety depended on them keeping his secret. It could be done, if they were careful.

She prayed to the goddess that he would understand her need for discretion. The memory of his lips, the taste of his blood—it sent shivers of pleasure down her spine. For years she'd assumed he was a stoic and reserved human. Now everything about him intrigued her. When he'd blocked that bullet for her, she'd seen who he really was, a male with a heart as big and broad as that chest she couldn't get off her mind. He was warm and far more generous than any of her kind. And when she was with him, she didn't feel quite so *alone*.

"Hey!" Katelyn yelled.

Sabrina snapped back into the moment. She'd been drawing blood from the young patient. The tube was full, but she'd been so distracted she hadn't withdrawn the needle.

"Sorry." She pressed a piece of gauze over the hole the needle left behind and taped it into place. "That's it. I'll send this to the lab."

"No one can believe I'm getting better. They're afraid to send me home," Katelyn said.

"Yeah. The doctors need to do a few more tests." She tapped the girl on the nose. The doctors thought the recovery was temporary, but Sabrina kept that part to herself. "No more oxygen tube though. Your body is incredible. A miracle."

"It wasn't a miracle. It was Dr. Toby." The girl covered her mouth with both hands and giggled.

"Dr. Toby made you better?"

Katelyn whispered behind her cupped hand, "He put a mermaid scale around my neck and it made me feel all warm and fuzzy inside. When he took it off, I started getting better."

"A mermaid scale, huh?" That was cute. It seemed like it was always mermaids or princesses with this age. And she loved that Tobias allowed his young patients to call him Dr. Toby. So much more personable than the formal Dr. Winthrop.

"He told me I wasn't supposed to tell anyone, but I can tell you, right? You won't tell."

Sabrina paused. "Dr. Toby told you not to tell anyone?"

"He put it on me in the middle of the night. He said the necklace was our secret and that I shouldn't tell anyone about it, not even my parents."

She nodded even as her stomach clenched. "Um. I see. Well, Dr. Toby is a good doctor, and if he asks you to do something, you should do it. I'll keep this a secret, but please don't tell anyone else, okay?"

"Okay."

She forced a smile and squeezed the girl's hand. "I'll send your parents back in."

As Sabrina left the room and told Katelyn's parents that she was done, all she could think about was Tobias. He'd become quite the hero of late. Mermaid scale, her ass. This was exactly the type of thing that could draw attention to him and scrutiny from her coven over what he was. She needed to talk to him soon. One slip could ruin everything.

❧

SABRINA SWORE TO HERSELF THAT SHE'D ASK TOBIAS right away about Katelyn and the mermaid scale. She couldn't put off telling him about the werewolves being executed or about her tenuous position as the heir to the Lamia Coven any longer. But when she met him outside the Field Museum that afternoon, her mouth couldn't form the words.

I'm not just a vampire but also a vampire princess whose father is known for executing werewolves and other shifters, she thought. But the words never left her head. She didn't want to ruin this. A real date with the sexy, mysterious doctor. Her promise to herself dissolved into a distant thought, a shadow cast out by the light of his smile. Not today. Today she'd enjoy being with him.

"When you said you wanted to show me something, I wasn't expecting dinosaur bones," Sabrina said.

Tobias offered her his hand and she took it, threading her fingers into his. "I like it here. Learning about the past has always made me feel hopeful, a reminder of all the things this planet has overcome." Tobias moved closer as they strolled toward the gigantic skeleton of a titanosaur in the main hall.

She raised an eyebrow. "That's an interesting way to look at it considering we're standing beside a creature that is now extinct."

He laughed. "You have a point." He gestured toward the stairs. "The rest of the dinosaurs are on the upper level."

"Is that what you wanted to show me? The dinosaurs?" It tickled her soul that he did. He was like an eight-year-old boy, excited about the adventure of an archeological dig. Unexpected. His blue eyes flashed in her direction, playful and flirtatious. He squeezed her hand. She breathed deeply as the scent of almonds and cinnamon grew stronger.

"The other day, when you were taking care of my shoulder, you asked about where I come from."

"You told me. Paragon," she offered. "Although I'm still trying to get my head around the idea of that land being in a different dimension."

"Harder to believe than the existence of vampires and dragons in the Midwest?"

"Touché." She followed him up the worn marble stairs. "What do dinosaurs have to do with where you come from?"

He grinned mischievously. "Patience is a virtue, Ms. Bishop."

"So is perseverance." She bit her lip and tugged on his hand. "Why can't you tell me now?"

"It's easier to show you."

He led her to an exhibit entrance labeled GRIFFIN HALLS OF EVOLVING PLANET. Sabrina followed him into a room filled with monster-sized skeletons. The hollow, dark holes that were once a triceratops's eyes gave her pause. She felt tiny and oddly like she was standing in a cemetery. She'd been here before, of course, but it had been years ago. The world-class museums of Chicago were something she had taken for granted for decades. She was wrong to do that. This exhibit was breathtaking, and she loved that an immortal like Tobias was still interested in its charms.

Tobias's gaze shifted in her direction. "When I first came here from Paragon, I didn't think my kind had ever been to this realm before."

She laughed softly. "I admit I didn't think you existed before Maverick's."

Tobias gazed up at the bones of a brontosaurus. "My first clue that my people might have a shared history with humans was when I read a book on Greek mythology at university. The mythology of my kind includes many of the same characters as your Greek mythology, although some of the specifics are different."

"Greek mythology? Zeus, Hera and the like?"

"Yep."

"Not what I would associate with dragons."

"Oh, but our origin story includes Greek figures. As the story goes, a daughter of Helios named Circe made the first of what I am. Legend has it that the first dragon was woven from the fabric of the universe by the titans. Back then, dragons were carnivorous beasts filled with magic and unable to shift into this form." He pointed at himself. "At that time, dragons were hunted for their hides and for the magic they carried in their blood, flesh, and bones, not to mention for the treasure that all dragons hoarded. Our numbers dwindled. Dragons were forced into hiding, into caves and remote places. That is how the first dragon, Balthyzika, ended up on an island called Aeaea, an island where the goddess Circe made her home."

Sabrina tucked her hair behind her ear. It had been a long time since she'd studied Greek mythology, but she remembered a little about Circe. "She was a prisoner there, wasn't she?"

"Yes. An outcast of the gods. Aeaea was her island, protected by her sorcery, and therefore an ideal place for a dragon to hide. One day, the goddess Circe asked Balthyzika for a single scale to use as an amulet to protect her son. Dragons can make themselves invisible. A dragon's scale when worn around the neck can render the wearer invisible as well. Circe had powerful enemies, deities who'd sworn to kill her firstborn. Balthyzika was a wise dragon. She agreed to help Circe, but in exchange for her scale she asked the goddess for one thing in return."

He stepped up to an alcove showcasing a smaller set of bones, but Sabrina's attention was locked on Tobias. "What did she ask for?"

"Balthyzika knew that Circe was a talented witch, especially gifted at transformations. She asked that all dragons and their progeny be able to take the form of those who hunted our kind. This form." He pointed to his chest.

"Human form."

"Yes. But in Paragon, there are no humans. This form is also the form of elves, witches, gods, and goddesses. So in our mythology this shape is simply referred to as *soma,* which means our two-legged form. I was fascinated how closely this story mirrored human stories of Circe. Still, I thought it was a coincidence, until I found this." He pointed at the exhibit they were standing in front of: a large flat fossil with an imprint of a skeleton in the stone. The dinosaur itself was about the size of a duck and had... feathers. She read the plaque mounted near the exhibit.

"Caihong juji *was discovered by a farmer in northeast China. Although small in stature, this newly discovered species of dinosaur from 161 million years ago had perfectly preserved bones and feathers. Analysis revealed that* Caihong juji *had a crested head and brightly colored feathers that shimmered iridescent in the light. Its name means 'rainbow with the big crest' in Mandarin."* She shifted her gaze to Tobias. "I didn't know dinosaurs could have feathers."

"When I first came into this exhibit, it was disturbing to me how similar your dinosaurs' bones were to dragon bones, but I found one huge difference. All your carnivorous dinosaurs are theropods. They walked on two legs. Dragons are four-legged carnivores. If we are related to these beasts, it's a distant relation. But this"—he pointed at *Caihong juji* —"this *still* exists in Paragon."

"Excuse me?"

"I know this creature. It lives still in the jungles of my homeland. My people sometimes keep them as pets. We call them *kalitoos.*"

"Oh my goddess."

"This is proof that at some point, millions of years ago, our dimensions, our histories, intersected."

"That... that's incredible." What he'd revealed to her suddenly made her eyebrows shoot up. "Wait, are you saying that if you shift into your other form, you're as big as a dinosaur?"

He nodded. "Roughly."

"Holy shit," she mumbled under her breath. She took a step back despite herself.

"Sabrina..."

"It's a lot to take in."

He placed a hand over hers on the railing. "You're the first person I've shared any of this with."

"I am?"

"Yes, you are. Who else could I trust? Who else would

believe me?"

She took a deep breath and blew it out slowly. "You *can* trust me." Her eyes locked with his, and his energy was so strong she could feel his heat against her skin. It would be rude for her to drain off that energy without permission, but she was tempted. Even the roasted-almond scent of it made her mouth water. She swallowed.

He leaned toward her, his sapphire-blue eyes growing darker until she thought if she tripped she might fall right into their depths. "I wanted to share this with you because I like you, Sabrina. I want to give whatever this is between us a chance."

She took a deep breath and smoothed her hair behind her ear. Now was the time to talk to him about who she really was. All she had to do was tell him that she was vampire royalty and they needed to be discreet. "I..." The word petered out on her tongue. Why couldn't she speak?

His lips were close, his shoulder brushing hers as they leaned on the railing in front of the exhibit. She parted her lips, ready for him to kiss her.

Quite suddenly his gaze shifted away from her and his full lips curved into a scowl.

"Tobias?" She followed his line of sight to a shabbily dressed man who was staring in their direction. The vibe coming off him was nothing short of deadly, but it was the tattoo on his neck that made her skin prickle.

"Isn't that the man from Maverick's Café?" he whispered. "The one who shot at us?"

Sabrina's memory flashed to the shaman on his knees in front of her. To the identical triangular symbol he'd worn tattooed on his neck. Why hadn't she put two and two together? She grabbed Tobias's hand. "We need to get the hell out of here. Now!"

CHAPTER NINE

Nostrils flaring, Tobias took in the scent of the man
with the neck tattoo as he tugged Sabrina by the arm,
weaving between the exhibits. The stranger was a werewolf,
no doubt about it. Tobias hadn't noticed before in Maverick's because the scent of roasted coffee had masked his
odor, but now the stink of wolf was unmistakable. He'd
already shot at Sabrina once. Tobias didn't plan to give this
asshole another chance at hurting her.

His dragon roused, his protective instinct causing him
to put his body between her and the stranger. He guided
her deeper into the exhibit. "There. The tour group."

Tobias remained pressed against her protectively as
Sabrina blended into a large group of elderly tourists.

"No. We need to get away from people." She tugged at
his hand. "I don't want anyone else hurt."

"What does this guy want?" Tobias dodged behind a
man in a heavy wool coat and glanced over his shoulder.
The shifter glared at him through the sea of gray hair.

"He wants me dead."

He tugged her arm. "Why?"

"There's something I need to tell you. I... My coven retaliated against an attack by his pack. We wiped them out. As far as I know, he's the last of them."

"Fuck." Tobias broke into a jog, leading Sabrina toward the exhibit exit. "So he's out for revenge?"

"Yes."

"Their tracking abilities are legendary. We need to go somewhere to cover our scent."

Sabrina shook her head. "We will never lose him. Were-wolves can smell a cheese doodle at the bottom of a tar pit."

Bounding down the hall, Tobias dodged into an area labeled PLANTS OF THE WORLD. "There's a stairwell in the back," he whispered.

Thankfully, this exhibit was almost empty. His footsteps fell in time with Sabrina's as they weaved in and out of the models of exotic plants. He stopped short when he saw the door to the stairwell.

Sabrina swore.

A sign was posted on the door, CLOSED FOR MAINTENANCE. Tobias jiggled the handle. Locked.

"Where do you think you're going, Princess?" The man with the tattoo stood behind them, holding a dagger in his hand like he knew how to use it.

Tobias slid in front of Sabrina and growled. He'd never been a warrior. Even in Paragon, he was a sparring partner for his brothers, nothing more. He'd never won a match in his life. Gabriel could knock him on his ass with one swipe of a bo staff by the time they were teenagers. No, Tobias had always been the quietly speculative one, a trusted confidant to his siblings and occasionally a trickster. As dragons went, he was far more confident in his wit than in his abilities as a fighter. Still, at the moment, he was sure he could tear the man to shreds. His inner dragon had his teeth bared, and although Tobias hadn't shifted in decades, he was ready to do so.

The man's nostrils flared and a laugh started deep in his chest. "You're a shifter. Not a wolf. Something else. Something exotic."

"Don't come any closer. You don't want to find out." The roar that thundered from Tobias's chest could have come from a T. rex, and his throat felt hot. He was close, very close, his body trembling with the need to protect. Sabrina's hand landed on his back. Worried he'd hurt her in the shift, he tried to rein the dragon in but couldn't stop a set of talons from slowly extending from the first knuckles of his hands.

"You don't know what she is, do you?" the man said. "Her coven would cut off your head and bathe in your blood. Vampires don't like shifters. Chicago vampires don't tolerate them within coven boundaries."

"Shut up," Tobias said. He didn't recognize his own voice.

Sabrina moved around Tobias's outstretched arms. Her fangs dropped and she looked positively feral. "What do you want from me?"

"Retribution."

She scoffed. "Your pack murdered my mother. My coven retaliated. You got what was coming to you."

He snorted. "Is that what your dear old dad told you? I hate to break it to you, Princess, but that blood debt was paid decades ago. Not only did we excuse your father's beheading of Frenwald in payment for his crime, we turned over his father to pay off the blood debt, and then we left your territory. It was your father who broke the treaty and slaughtered our kind on our own land." The dagger trembled in his hand. "I am the last of my line. I will avenge my pack."

"Liar."

"Am I?" the man said through his teeth.

Tobias glanced between Sabrina and the werewolf. She was staring at the man's dagger, tears forming in her eyes. It wasn't fear he saw in her expression but something else. Something he didn't fully understand.

"You want your revenge? Then have it!" To Tobias's horror, she spread her arms wide and stepped forward.

"No!" Tobias lunged for her, but it was too late. The werewolf stabbed the dagger into Sabrina's chest, then withdrew it quickly like he might repeat the motion.

Heat tore through Tobias, tore him in half, and then he was standing over her, looking at the werewolf from a perspective only possible in his dragon form. His jaws snapped, his teeth impaling the wolf's shoulder.

"Let him go." Sabrina's soft, pained voice came from between his paws.

Tobias flung the wolf away from her and he disappeared at superspeed. He tried to see how critically Sabrina was injured, but in this form his body was too big. He stilled out of fear he might inadvertently crush her. He needed to shift, but it had been so long and his dragon didn't want to go back in its cage.

He was still wrestling with his inner beast when a family of three rounded the corner. Tobias froze. He tried not to blink.

"Damn, that one is realistic," the dad said.

"Looks like a dragon," the mother said.

"It's a nodosaur," the boy said, rolling his eyes. He stuck a Slim Jim between his teeth and tore off a piece. "They found it in Alberta, Canada."

"Oh, that's right. Looks like the display is under construction." The father pointed toward the sign on the door to the stairwell behind him.

"Do you want to get some lunch?" the mother asked.

The family wandered off toward the exit. As soon as they were out of sight, Tobias closed his eyes and willed his heart to slow. *Back in the box,* he thought. He concentrated on his human form—it was in there, somewhere. A flash of searing heat flowed through him, and then he had the distinct feeling of turning inside out. It wasn't exactly painful, but when he was finally in his humanoid form, he was naked and covered in a slick of mucus. He turned himself invisible.

"Tobias?" Sabrina pressed her hand against the wound in her chest.

"I'm here. Covering our tracks." He dug his cell phone and wallet out of what remained of his pants. There was nothing else identifying about his clothing. He shoved the scraps into a garbage receptacle.

"Get me out of here. There was something on that blade. I'm not healing."

He looked back at her, at the flow of blood oozing through her fingers.

He scooped her into his arms, casting his invisibility over her, and kicked open the locked stairwell door. Ignoring the tools and paint cans lining the stairs, he descended and raced for the exit.

SABRINA COULDN'T REMEMBER LOSING CONSCIOUSNESS. She'd blinked on the stairwell in the Field Museum and awoke in a soft white bed in a spotless room remarkable only for its clean, uncluttered decor and contrasting dark furniture.

"She's waking up," a woman said beside her.

"Thank the Mountain." She turned her head to find Tobias, dressed in jeans and a fleece, leaning over her. He slid his hand into hers and brought his lips to her ear. "I know you've been trying to get into my bed since you met me, but don't you think this is a little extreme?"

A laugh bubbled from her chest, and it hurt so bad it brought tears to her eyes.

"Knock it off, Tobias," the woman beside him said. Her piercing blue eyes assessed her as a doctor would a patient. "Sabrina, my name is Raven. I'm a witch, and I'm helping Tobias heal you. Where does it hurt?"

Sabrina didn't miss Tobias's grimace when Raven called herself a witch. She understood the reaction. On any other occasion she would question the witch's presence in vampire territory, but currently she was in no condition to bite the hand that fed her. If the woman could stop this pain in her chest, she'd take the help. Besides, the one called Raven had a kind face. Maybe she was being naïve, but Sabrina trusted her.

Sabrina opened her mouth to try to relate that her chest hurt and that she was having trouble breathing, but no sound came out. Black dots circled in her vision.

"The amulet isn't working." Tobias reached for her throat and removed a white disk that shone in the light with rainbow colors like mother-of-pearl.

For a moment she wondered what it was, then the pain distracted her from wondering anything. She closed her eyes tightly against the searing wave that burned in her veins. When she opened them again, Raven was peeking under the bandage on her chest. The dark-haired woman frowned.

"What's going on, Raven?" The muscles in Tobias's jaw twitched.

"I'm not sure. You say she was stabbed with a dagger. Do you know what it was made of?"

"No. It looked metal, silver colored. Maybe it was silver?"

"Silver might slow healing in a vampire. I'm not familiar enough with vampire anatomy to know for sure, and I wouldn't know where to start to research effects on a vampire hybrid like Sabrina. It's festering worse than it would if she were human."

"What if there was some left in her?" Tobias asked. "Maybe he poisoned the blade with liquid silver."

Sabrina wished she could speak. Silver didn't hurt her. Not like this. Thanks to her human side, she could wear silver jewelry without irritation. Even full-blooded vampires could tolerate some silver, although it did weaken them. This was more than weakness. Whatever the wolf had stabbed her with was killing her.

As Sabrina watched helplessly, the witch dug in a bag on the nightstand and retrieved a glass vial. She pulled out the cork, then lowered the glass to her wound. Sabrina cried out as Raven dug her finger in the lesion and scraped a sample of the blood, ooze, and grit into the container.

"You're hurting her." Tobias rounded the bed and pressed a clean piece of gauze over the oozing lesion. His worried face came close to Sabrina's. "Shhh. You'll be okay. We're going to take care of you."

"There's something poisoning her, Tobias, and I don't have the spell to determine what it is."

"What do you mean, you don't have the spell?" Tobias asked over her.

Sabrina closed her eyes because the black dots were getting more persistent.

"I mean I absorb magic and none of the spells in my memory are right for this task. Is there an occult shop in Chicago? I need to research this. Maybe ask for help."

Tobias frowned. "I... I don't know."

"You don't know?"

"I've been living as a human for hundreds of years. The occult is not a hobby of mine."

Raven rolled her eyes. "It is now."

Sabrina swallowed and willed the words over her lips. "Bell... and... Candle. Edgewater," she rasped. The witch there was a friend of the coven. She was on the payroll. No witch knew vampires better than her.

Tobias smoothed her hair back. "Shh. We'll take care of it."

"Does that mean anything to you?"

Tobias nodded. "Yeah. Edgewater is a neighborhood here. Bell and Candle must be a shop. I'll find an address. I'll stay with her while you go." He pulled his phone from his pocket and started typing furiously.

"I'll take Gabriel."

Tobias made a guttural sound deep in his throat. "I just forwarded the location to you. Please hurry. Raven, look at her arm."

Although she couldn't see what Tobias did, Sabrina could feel it. Pain branched from the wound in her chest all the way down to the fingers of her left arm. She closed her eyes against the pain. Her body began to shiver, her teeth clacking as the icy poison flooded her veins.

"I'll find a way. I promise," Raven said. Sabrina heard footsteps retreat into the hall.

A moment later, she smelled Tobias's roasted-cinnamon-almond scent grow stronger. The bed dipped beside her, and then the heat of his body swaddled her. Her muscles relaxed, soothed by his dragon warmth. Her body was ailing, but beside him, she felt safe.

"I don't know why you let that wolf stab you, Sabrina, but I'm not going to let you die. I swear to the Mountain, we'll figure this out. Stay with me." His fingers threaded into hers, and then she drifted to sleep.

CHAPTER TEN

Raven held her scarf to her face as she entered Bell
and Candle, a tiny occult shop in the Edgewater
neighborhood of Chicago. Gabriel entered right behind her,
so close that she gave him a cautionary glare. She understood he wanted to protect her, but that didn't mean she
needed to wear him like a sweater. It might intimidate the
employees here.

Gentle warmth surrounded her as she passed the
threshold, and a citrus-scented zing of energy filled her
nose. Another witch was here. A good witch. Her power
was a balm, a fresh-baked cookie, a vanilla-scented candle.

"Mmmm." Raven removed her scarf, unzipped her coat,
and rolled her shoulders. Sabrina's message hadn't led them
astray. This place was brimming with magic.

"I'll take that to mean this is the right place," Gabriel
whispered.

"Can't you smell the magic?"

Gabriel shook his head. "I can feel it though, like a
tickle at the back of my throat."

A woman appeared in front of them, no bigger than a

child, with a hunched back and two abnormally short arms, her malformed hands turning in toward her chest. One of her eyes was cloudy and didn't move in conjunction with the other. She had the most beautiful aura Raven had ever seen.

"Oh," Raven said. "You're powerful. A witch and something more."

The woman grinned. "I am of druid blood. What a pleasure to have a visit from a natural witch. Most who come in here think I'm nothing more than the cashier."

Raven laughed. "Is this your store? It has the most wonderful energy. It feels like a cup of tea."

"Thank you. It's a custom spell of essential oils and ancient enchantments. But you didn't come here to ask me about my store." Her good eye flicked to Gabriel. "I can see you have serious business. What can I do for you today?"

Raven pulled the vial of blood and grit she'd taken from Sabrina's wound and held it up between her fingers. "I need to know what the silvery substance is suspended in this blood. It's keeping my friend from healing properly."

The old woman narrowed her good eye on the vial, her nostrils flaring. She glanced toward the front window. "Come to the back. Out of sight."

Raven followed her through the shelves of books and carefully curated crystals to the checkout counter.

"Remove the cap."

Raven obliged, unscrewing the vial. A foul odor wafted from the tube.

"Your friend has been assaulted by a vampire," the old woman said. "I smell both vampire and human blood."

"Our friend is a vampire. Half vampire, half human." Raven held the sample closer to the woman's nose.

The old woman's bushy gray eyebrows rose. "Are you positive about that?"

"Her mother was a necromancer," Raven explained. "She's the only one."

A harsh, gritty sound came from the witch's throat. "What is your name, sister?"

"Raven."

"You seem like a good person and I sense you are a powerful witch, so I will give you a warning. Your 'friend' is the heir to the Chicago vampire coven, and I highly doubt an actual friend at all. Her coven is well-known for being intolerant of other supernaturals. I am the last practicing witch in this city with any real power, and the only reason they allow me to stay is because they believe my disability is a hindrance to the magic I am capable of. You, however, they will kill the first chance they get."

"Kill me? Why would they kill me?"

"Fear. Vampires are terribly afraid of other supernatural creatures due to their daytime vulnerability. This coven especially will not tolerate outsiders. If I were you, I'd let this poison do its dirty work."

Raven glanced at Gabriel. The firm set of his jaw echoed her feelings precisely. They couldn't trust this witch, not without talking to Tobias, but she seemed to be telling the truth. "Do you know what that is in her blood?"

"This is very rare. I didn't think any existed anymore."

"What is it?"

"The only thing that can make a stab wound lethal to a vampire other than a wooden stake to the heart. The last vampire hunter of Chicago discovered it by accident while investigating the Holmes murders. A vampire, by definition, is dead—a reanimated corpse. This solution is made from the crystallized bodies of a type of African dermestid beetle mixed with the sap of *Mancinella dendrocnide,* a deadly plant from the same region. Decades ago, a scientist named Wulfrid Keetridge, who also happened to be a werewolf, discovered the substance during an exploration of the Congo. Native locals used the concoction to break down the bodies of their dead.

"Keetridge brought the substance back to Chicago where it was used to successfully turn the tide in the war between the vampires of the South Side and the were-wolves of the North Side. When used to coat weapons, the crystallized sap will break down the body of a vampire faster than it can heal itself. It's more effective than a wooden stake. A stake must be applied to the heart. Keetridge Solution can be injected into a vampire anywhere and it will fester until the poison reaches the brain. It is absolutely lethal."

"Is there an antidote?"

She laughed. "No."

Raven narrowed her eyes. The scent in the air shifted. Her gut told her Madam Chloe wasn't telling the whole truth. "There must be something that can be done."

"Dear witch, I can see this vampire means something to you. Fear not. If you are as powerful as I think you are, there is a way for you to cure the vampire. Though it will not be easy."

Raven lowered her chin. "If there is a spell, I can do it. I promise you."

The old woman toddled to a bookshelf and a large tome floated down from the top row. "There is no antidote, but you can extract the substance if it hasn't reached her brain. I'll warn you, the longer you wait, the more difficult it will be and the more potentially deadly."

Raven snatched the book out of the air and placed it on

the counter. She held her hand above it. The pages flipped themselves, the magic feeding her as the spells turned under her fingers. When she'd taken all it had to give, it closed itself with a thunk.

The witch clucked her tongue. "This isn't a library, dearie. That will be $149.95."

Gabriel pulled out his credit card.

"I'll need a dozen white candles, a bone dagger, and a live rat," Raven said.

"The candle and dagger I can do. You're on your own for the rat. May I suggest a pet store?" Candles floated onto the counter along with a curved, bone knife. The witch smiled. "The new total will be $395.98."

Gabriel handed her the card, and Raven watched in wonder as the woman used her crippled hands to promptly ring them up as her items bagged themselves. Raven gripped the handles of the recyclable paper sack. She smiled warmly at her fellow witch. "Thank you for your help."

"You may call me Madam Chloe." She hopped down from the stool behind the register. "I wish you luck, but I will warn you. Vampires are not your friends. Be wary, sister. You may find yourself in dire circumstances if you refuse to acknowledge her risk to you."

"Understood."

"You'll find a containment spell in that book that neutralizes the supernatural powers of the one you use it on. It may come in handy if she turns on you."

"Thank you, Madam Chloe. I'll keep it in mind."

She zipped her coat and wrapped her scarf around her face before following Gabriel out into the winter cold.

"I don't think Madam Chloe was lying," Raven said. "Do you think Tobias knows?"

Gabriel growled. "If he does, he's thinking with his dick. He has no idea the kind of danger he's put us in. If this woman is truly vampire royalty..."

"Be prepared if all this is as much a surprise to him as it is to us. I doubt he'll take the news well."

Gabriel's head came around quickly to face her. "No? Why not?"

"Because he loves her, Gabriel! You must see it. The look in Tobias's eyes when he talks about Sabrina is the same as the look you used to have when people talked about me."

Gabriel opened the door to the car and helped her inside, looking every bit the dragon she knew him to be. "A lot of good that will do if she gets us all killed!"

❧

IT HAD BEEN A LONG TIME SINCE TOBIAS HAD experienced the level of dread that burned in his torso. Over three hundred years to be exact. The last time he'd felt this way was the moment his uncle's blade had severed the neck of his oldest brother Marius on his coronation day. That day a wave of his mother's hand had sent him and his siblings tumbling through a tear between dimensions. They'd been cast out, exiled from Paragon.

As he watched over Sabrina's unconscious body, holding her hand, that familiar dread made his heart ache. Why had she let the wolf stab her? Had she known what she was doing? Known the consequences? Known that she might die?

He ground his teeth. *Unacceptable.*

His dragon wanted her. Deep inside, a part of him he'd forgotten existed had chosen her the moment she'd kissed him in that stairwell. Oh, Tobias had desired her long before that. He'd admired her for years. She was quirky and caring, the type of nurse he'd always wanted by his side if he could get her. He'd suppressed those feelings when he'd thought she was human. The kiss simply unveiled what was already there and made her accessible to him as a fellow supernatural. She'd awakened the dragon. Now he needed her. Needed her like he needed a home.

Damn, where was Raven? Whatever poison was on the blade the wolf had stabbed into Sabrina's heart was working its dark magic. Spidery black veins spread from the wound down her arms, torso, and legs. They hadn't marred her beautiful face yet, but he could see the poison spreading, creeping like death across her collarbones.

Her hand, ice-cold in his, was limp, helpless. He couldn't lose her. Not now.

"We have it." Raven entered the room looking far more grim than when she'd left. Behind her, Gabriel mirrored her expression. "I can fix her."

"Thank the Mountain." He did a double take when Raven didn't move. "Why do you two look like this is bad news?"

"The witch we got this from shared something with us, something you need to know," Gabriel said.

"What?"

"She said that Sabrina's coven does not tolerate other supernaturals in their territory. She suggested that if Raven saves her, she or her kind will kill us all." A dark cloud passed behind Gabriel's eyes. He leaned a shoulder against the doorway as if the conversation was draining him.

Tobias shook his head. "That's bullshit. Sabrina would never hurt you or anyone else."

"But her coven would, wouldn't they?" Raven shot him a knowing look.

"I... I don't know." Tobias wished he could forget the wolf's face when he'd accused Sabrina's coven of slaughtering his people. That wasn't her. It might be her kind, but it wasn't her. "She is not her coven."

"Sabrina gave us the name of that occult shop. The witch there knew her." Raven's tone was heavy with concern. "She swore to us that supernaturals in this city are either working for the vampire coven, driven out by it, or murdered by it. Sabrina knows what you are. She knows what I am. What if the witch is telling the truth? What if Sabrina intends to force us out of the city?"

"I don't give a shit. You will fix her." An icy chill ran the course of Tobias's body, and a deep growl bubbled from his throat. "Fix her now, before it's too late."

Tobias watched his brother start at the ferocity in his voice. Good. He should be afraid. Tobias was going to lose his shit if Raven didn't get moving on the cure.

"Consider what we are telling you—"

"No," he said through his teeth. "You told me you need to stay here for a while, that it isn't safe in New Orleans for you. This is the price. Do this or get out." He pointed at Sabrina.

Raven lowered her chin. She glanced at Gabriel, who gave her a stern nod.

"Okay, but I'll need your help. This isn't going to be easy." Raven approached the side of the bed. "She's infected with a rare poison designed to eat dead flesh. Vampire flesh. If she weren't half human, she would likely already be dead."

Tobias growled, his lips peeling back from his teeth.

Raven glared at him. "That shit isn't helping anyone. Are you going to help me or wait outside?"

"I'll help you," Tobias said. Gabriel rounded the bed. "What's he doing?"

"I'll have to perform a spell to draw the poison out of her system. I can do it, but it's going to hurt. Wherever this stuff is in her body, it's going to work its way out via the shortest route possible."

"Tear through her skin." Tobias swallowed hard.

"Yes, and whatever other organs are in the way. As a vampire, she'll heal, Tobias. It won't kill her. But it will hurt."

"There's no other way?"

Raven shook her head. "No. She's dying. We need to do this quickly."

He nodded. "Okay. What do I do?"

"You hold her arms. Gabriel will take her legs."

Tobias obeyed, but seeing Gabriel touch Sabrina sent him into a mental tailspin. He choked back a growl and looked away, directly at Sabrina's face.

Raven's emerald ring glowed to life. Candles flew from her bag and placed themselves on every surface around her. With a snap of her fingers, their wicks blazed to life. The scent of burning cloves bloomed within the room.

"Artemis, if you please," Raven said.

The cat appeared beside her, then jumped onto the bed. A small rat squirmed in her teeth.

"Where did she get that?" Tobias asked.

"She's very resourceful." Raven gave him a cross look. She drew the rat from the feline's mouth and held it over Sabrina's chest. "Ready?"

Tobias met her eyes. "Please save her, Raven."

She nodded sternly, then turned her attention to the

task at hand. Raven's blue eyes filled with light, and she snapped her fingers over the struggling rodent. It went limp in her palm. Extending the rat's body over Sabrina's torso, she yelled, "*Antallagi!*" She stabbed the rat in the gut with a bone knife. Blood dripped. Power flooded the room in a tidal wave that blew Tobias's hair back. The candles flickered. His nostrils flared as the scent of cloves grew stronger.

Suddenly Sabrina's eyes flew open. Raven dropped the dagger and helped Tobias hold Sabrina's arm down with the hand that wasn't holding the rat. Tipping her head back, Sabrina shrieked. Bloody silver globs broke from her flesh—the poison leaving her system—and traveled through the air to the rat, where they buried themselves in the creature's gut. Sabrina cried out again, arching off the bed, her eyes wild with agony, her breath coming in pants between screams as a thousand pinpoints of red exploded across her skin. Tobias held her wrists to the mattress, feeling torn in two. He desperately wanted to save her from the pain but was entirely helpless to do so.

"Shhh. Shhh. It's going to be okay," he said, but he had no idea if he was telling her the truth.

She screamed again.

"Is this normal?" he yelled into the enchanted wind that swirled in the room. His eyes locked on Raven. "You're killing her!"

Sabrina's screaming reached a crescendo. And then it stopped. The black veins receded and then disappeared. The last pieces of silver floated from her skin and invaded the rat's body.

"Sabrina, I'm here. Stay with me," Tobias said.

Ever so slowly, her breathing evened out and her back lowered to the bed. She was covered in dozens of open wounds, but they were healing, closing themselves up. Her limbs relaxed.

"You're okay. We got it out of you," he said. He wanted to hold her hand but was afraid to let go of her.

"It's done. You can release her," Raven said, pinching the rat closed with both hands.

He freed her wrists. Gabriel moved to Raven's side from where he'd been securing her legs.

"She'll need rest and to feed." Raven nodded toward her bag and Gabriel retrieved a unit of blood from its depths.

"I used my invisibility to procure this for you. It should be enough to get her home," Gabriel said.

Tobias nodded. "I'll take care of her."

Raven gestured toward the door. "Gabriel, come help me burn this in the fireplace." They left together and closed the door behind them.

All at once, Tobias's knees turned to water. He staggered to Sabrina's side and sat down beside her, taking her hand in his. He thought it felt warmer, but he couldn't be sure. Maybe he was just colder, weaker from exhaustion.

Her eyelids fluttered.

"Sabrina?"

Tears streamed down her cheeks and then her eyes were open, red-rimmed, staring at him.

"I'm sorry Raven hurt you. It was the only way to save your life," he said.

"I know," she said softly.

Tobias told himself he wasn't going to ask. Not until she was stronger. But he couldn't hold it in. None of it made sense. "Sabrina, you need to tell me... Why?"

CHAPTER ELEVEN

Everything hurt. Sabrina rolled her head on the pillow. It was the perfect time to tell Tobias the truth. This was what she'd wanted, a chance to tell him who she really was and explain why they needed to be more careful. But she hesitated. The truth was that she was greedy, selfish. She was afraid he'd push her away.

It had become real for her when she'd seen him shift. Nothing about the transformation was easy, but he had become the beast for her. Although she'd been almost blinded by pain at the time, she remembered his dragon was absolutely lethal. She'd seen herself in that beast, realized that she and Tobias shared much more than an interest in healing. She wished things were different. She wished...

Her gaze fell on the bright red blood dotting the white cotton covering her. "I'm sorry about your sheets."

He shook his head. "I don't care about the sheets, Sabrina. Answer me. Why? Why did you let the wolf stab you?"

Oh, how her heart ached to see him like this. Or maybe the ache she felt that cut to her bones was from what she'd been through. She was hungry. Her fangs descended, and she ran her sandpaper tongue across her lips.

"I've put your life in danger twice now," she rasped.

"I'm not the one who was almost killed today. Given a battle between werewolf and dragon, the dragon always wins. Why didn't you stay behind me?"

She wrapped the corner of the sheet around her finger. There was no turning back. She must tell him, and she must tell him now. Her voice was barely a whisper as she answered, "Because I realized he was right."

Tobias stilled. "Right about what?"

"I told you I was half vampire," she began, her vision going blurry with her tears. "What I didn't tell you is that my father is master of the Chicago coven. I am the heir to his throne. I will become master at the end of the month, when my father moves to Racine to manage our new territory, the territory we took from the wolves."

"That's why he called you princess. You're a vampire princess." Tobias drew back, his expression turning impassive.

"Yes." Sabrina licked her lips again. "Vampires are extremely territorial. It's true what I said, that the wolves started it. Frenwald murdered my mother in cold blood."

"I remember." Tobias's voice was tender.

"My mother was a necromancer, and her magic was what allowed me to be born, but the wolves thought I was an abomination. Frenwald came for me. My mother got in his way and ended up dead. Her last act was to raise my father from his day rest. He saved my life. Slaughtered Frenwald where he stood. I was five at the time. I remember it. I remember the blood."

"Oh, Sabrina."

"Don't feel sorry for me. This is the life of a vampire, Tobias. We are born to be killers. We are predators."

His jaw tightened. "If that's true, why did you let the wolf stab you?"

She sighed. "After my father killed Frenwald, he demanded additional restitution for my mother's life. The Racine pack turned over Frenwald's father. They said the attack was his idea. My father killed him as well."

"Justice," Tobias said.

"The wolf today, he was telling the truth. It should have been enough. But my father's lust for revenge wasn't quenched. A few days ago, I watched the alpha of the Racine pack, his mate, and the pack shaman die brutally at the hands of my coven. We'd already slaughtered the rest of them. Every wolf dead but the one who stabbed me. We took their land. We took their lives. My father could have stopped long ago, but he wanted them all dead. Dead shifters do not retaliate."

Sabrina watched Tobias's throat bob on a swallow. His face paled. This was it. This was when he would know and he would leave her.

"It was cruel and senseless." Her voice trembled, both from the pain still pulsing in her body and the torment overwhelming her mind. "But I can't say that to anyone but you. Vampires who don't have human hearts rarely feel compassion. Vampires who are destined to be masters cannot show mercy. It is not our way. It would be suicide."

"You let him stab you because you felt you owed him?" Tobias scoffed.

"Yes," Sabrina said. "He had a knife, not a stake. I didn't know the blade was poisoned. I wanted to give him closure. If my suffering made him feel like the people we slaughtered are somehow avenged, then I did the right thing."

Tobias reached out, his hand hovering near her face for a moment before stroking the hair over her ear. "I need to ask you something, and I need you tell me the truth."

She lowered her chin. "Anything."

"The wolf said other supernaturals are not allowed in vampire territory. I'm gathering that's true. So, what did you plan to do with me? Force me from your territory or kill me?"

She couldn't stand the disappointment in his eyes or the dejection in his voice. And still his fortitude made her heart swell. Given what she'd just shared, if he'd been a vampire, he might have killed her, ripped her head from her shoulders. He knew she was too weak to defend herself. But he was spreading his arms wide, waiting for the dagger.

"Neither," she said, and she loaded the word with all the promise she could muster. "I planned to keep your secret forever. I planned to pretend I never learned you were a dragon. No one knows but me, and if we're careful, no one will ever find out."

"You'd keep my secret."

"Yes. But the wolf who stabbed me today, he saw you. He saw what you are. He saw your face. And the amulet you used on Katelyn... Tobias, the coven has eyes everywhere, and now there's a werewolf out there that might want to finish the job he started. I think we should stop seeing each other for a while, until I know it's safe."

"Not see each other anymore outside of work at all?"

"Right."

"I'm not okay with that," he said immediately.

"Please. It's the only way. We've been lucky so far, but—"

"But nothing. You just told me the vampires in your coven are a bunch of heartless murderers. I'm not going to let you go back to that. Not when you are the kindest and bravest woman I've ever met. You're not like them, Sabrina. You don't belong with them."

❧

IF TOBIAS COULD HAVE REACHED OUT AND SNATCHED his words from the air between them, he would have. It was clear he'd offended her. By the look on her face, he'd plunged another dagger into her heart. By the Mountain, she was pale, almost as white as the sheet that covered her thin flesh. Her red hair was dull and her eyes heavy with the need for sleep. And now tears. Fuck, she was crying.

"All I meant was you are exceptional," he said. "Special. Your human side makes you better than them."

"No." Sabrina shook her head, her voice thready. "You don't understand at all."

Tobias noticed for the first time how dry her lips were. He retrieved the bag of blood Raven and Gabriel had left for her. "Drink this. You need it."

Her pupils took on that haunting silver quality he'd first seen in the stairwell. Their gazes caught as her fangs extended, and then she struck, quick and sharp as a snake. She closed her eyes, her throat working. The bag emptied. She crushed the plastic in her hand, drawing out the last drops in a matter of heartbeats. The entire process was brutal and feral.

"I am a vampire," she said, handing him the remains of the plastic bag. "I love my father, and even though I am not like him and I have all the wrong instincts for one of my kind, I love my people. They're my family."

"So, you accept what your coven did to the werewolves."

113

"No... Yes..." She shook her head. "I would not have done what they did. Do you think that means I'm too weak to rule?"

Tobias reached out and ran his thumb across her cheek. "You are tough and strong but capable of compassion. Compassion doesn't make you weak, Sabrina; it makes you wise."

"It is a weakness." She shook her head. "I shouldn't have done what I did today. I have been tapped to take over the largest vampire coven in North America. How will I ever lead and protect a coven when I can't even kill what is trying to kill me?"

Dumbstruck, Tobias simply stared at her. Was she truly convinced her savage heart, the one he'd always both feared and respected for its soul-piercing intuitiveness, was a weakness? He rose from the bed and paced the room. "Your humanity is an asset."

Her body leaned heavily against the pillows. The blood had helped, but she still looked like a wrung-out dishrag. "Those are nice words, but that's not how it works. A giraffe can't lead a pride of lions."

He narrowed his eyes on her. "A giraffe? Are you saying you don't feel like one of them? That deep down, you don't even feel like the same species? If that's true, say no. Don't become master."

She looked exhausted, and he immediately felt guilty for pushing her. Her wounds had stopped bleeding, but they were still there, barely crusted over.

"When you let that wolf stab you today, you didn't know if it would kill you or not, did you?"

She licked her lips. "I don't want to die. I'm not suicidal. I wanted to do the right thing."

Tobias had never considered himself to be exceptionally

intuitive, but of all his siblings, he was the one the others came to with their problems, the one they trusted. He wasn't afraid to call someone out on their bullshit, and when he kept a secret, he might as well have dropped it to the bottom of the ocean for how locked down the info was. Right now he saw the truth peeking out from behind a wall so thick it might have been his own.

"You don't want to be coven master, do you?" As soon as the question had bridged his lips, Tobias wanted to slap himself. It was intrusive and presumptuous. It was too much.

"It doesn't matter what I want." She shook her head. "I am my father's daughter. I've been groomed for this from the day I was born."

"You shouldn't have to do something you don't want to do."

Her gaze met his. "If I don't do it, someone else will. The next in line is Tristan. Believe me, none of us will enjoy the results if he rises to master."

"Tristan?"

"Second in line for the throne. He would love to find a way to usurp my role. He's been trying for years."

"Let me guess, Tristan has no problems with exercising too much compassion."

She shook her head. "He has no conscience, even for a vampire."

Tobias winced. Her coven had slaughtered an entire pack of werewolves. How much worse could it get?

"Tobias?" Sabrina rubbed her arms as if she were cold.

"Yes?"

Her gaze locked on his. "I know you have questions. I want to tell you everything, but... I'm still hungry."

He glanced at the door. "I'll get you something from the

kitchen. What are you in the mood for? Soup? A sandwich? I can run out for something."

Her eyes flicked to his lips. "I don't want a sandwich."

It took him a second to realize what she was talking about. He pointed to his chest. "You want to feed on me?"

She nodded.

"Last time, my blood made you pass out."

She licked her lips. "Not blood. Energy. Like in the stairwell. The blood helped, but I need more."

A slow, distinctly male grin spread his lips. He sat down beside her on the bed. "Do you want to kiss me, Ms. Bishop?"

Her green eyes pulsed silver around the edges. That look was predatory, almost frightening, but he didn't pull away as she scooted toward him. He'd removed her bloody outer clothing to clean while she slept, and now the sheets slid from her black lace bra and pooled around her hips. When he reached out a hand to steady her, his fingers met the cool, smooth flesh of her back.

"Please."

There was no way he could deny her. He ran his tongue along his bottom lip and leaned in. They were face-to-face, a breath away from touching. He arched a brow. "It's the least I can do. I'm a doctor. I live to heal."

His next breath was cut off when her lips met his. Soft. Wanting. He gathered her into his arms and settled her on his lap, brushing his fingers down her spine in long, easy strokes. The moment she began to feed, he felt it. Energy flowed over his lips and into her mouth in a hot rush, like a warm breath of air, an exhale of sunlight that kept going and going. The sensation was erotic, tingling. Draining, but in a good way, like the beginnings of a runner's high.

As an immortal, Tobias had energy to spare. He reveled

at the way her skin warmed under his touch. The thought of feeding her like this, of giving her what she needed, it made him hard. He adjusted her on his lap so she could feel what she'd done to him.

"Mmmm." She moaned into his mouth, her tongue sweeping in. "Tobias..."

She shifted to straddle him on the bed. He hooked his hands behind her knees and pulled her closer, where she ground herself against him, hip to hip.

"I don't want to hurt you," he whispered into the kiss.

"You won't hurt me. It's helping."

He tangled his fingers into the back of her hair, relishing the feel of her pert breasts pressed against his chest, her nipples mounding like pearls behind the lace of her bra. By the Mountain, she was lovely, perfect, a rare gem his dragon wanted badly to have and to hold.

"Be mine," he said into her mouth.

The flow of energy stopped and she pulled her head back to look at him. He held her gaze.

"What?" She laughed a little.

"Be mine. Only mine."

A breath caught deep in her throat and she pushed off of him. "We've been on a couple of dates, both of which have gone terribly wrong." She ran her thumb along her bottom lip. "We are nowhere near a place where we can or should be exclusive."

He stood, his attention fully on her. She was still covered in blood, and he had the urge to carry her into the bathroom, strip her the rest of the way down, and give her the bath of her life. "Why not? Are you denying this thing between us?"

CHAPTER TWELVE

Everything slowed for Sabrina. The energy she'd taken in from Tobias made her head spin as if she were tipsy, but even half-drunk her heart was screaming, warring with her brain, which was sending up all sorts of warnings. Tobias's feelings were not one-sided. He'd awakened things inside her she'd never thought possible. Hell, she'd never admitted her reservations about leading the coven to anyone else. She had hundreds of vampire friends and a handful of human ones, but none of them knew her as well as he did. It was strange. She'd always liked him, even when she'd thought he was human, but now... This was so much more. Now he was the one, the only one, who knew exactly who she was and accepted her anyway.

Only, could she say the same? Did she truly know Tobias?

Not yet. Not enough to make some harebrained commitment at the first whiff of romance.

"Tobias, you haven't been listening. I will take over the Chicago coven from my father at the end of March. It's done. Those vampires are my responsibility."

"And?"

"And I can't be yours, whatever that means, because I have to be theirs."

Tobias backed off and held up his hands. "What if it was just us? What would you say if it were just you and me and the coven didn't exist?"

Sabrina didn't answer him. She didn't know. It was too much, too fast. "Where are the rest of my clothes?" she asked. "I need to get out of here."

He frowned. "They're in my washer. You were covered in blood."

"Can I borrow something to wear? I don't think I'm strong enough to dematerialize all the way back to my apartment, and it's too cold to risk it like this."

"Don't you want to take a shower? Get cleaned up? You should stay. Rest."

She shook her head, her hands coming to rest on her hips. The motion reminded her she was standing in his bedroom in nothing but her underwear. *Fuck.* "If I stay here, I might do something we both regret."

His gaze bore into her. "I would never regret a moment with you."

For a time she couldn't move. The weight of his full attention was like a tractor beam. She fought the pull, the unwavering desire to fling herself into his arms and do something about the ache that had formed between her legs. All she could think about was the way the length of his cock had felt against her, how it might feel inside her.

His nostrils flared. She smelled it too. Her arousal was a perfume in the air, her vampire pheromones revealing her need for him.

"Please," she said. "Please let me go, Tobias. I need to process what happened today. I made a mistake. There's a wolf out there who wants everyone in my coven, me included, dead. I should have ended him when I had the chance. Instead, I let my human emotions get the best of me. Now I need to decide if I should warn my father or hope the knife in my chest was enough for the werewolf to feel avenged."

"If you want to track him to know for sure, I can help you. If he's left town, we let him live. If he's still here, I'll take care of him even if you can't."

"You'd do that?"

He stepped toward her. "Yes."

The heat was building between them again. He hadn't even touched her.

"Please, Tobias, a change of clothes."

He started as if waking from a dream and nodded slowly. After digging in a drawer, he sighed. "Everything of mine is going to be too big. I'll go ask Raven. She's closer to your size."

"Who is she to you anyway?" Sabrina wondered if the witch was a friend, an ex-lover, or if he'd called on her specifically to help her.

"She's my brother's fiancée."

"Your brother? I thought you said you were alone here."

"In Chicago, yes. He's from New Orleans. Just visiting."

Sabrina frowned.

"What's wrong?"

"Please be careful, Tobias. I've told you the truth. My coven is not accepting of other supernatural beings. One dragon might be overlooked. A family of dragons is harder to hide. If my coven suspected anything, you'd be in terrible danger."

"But not from you. You wouldn't do that to me..."

"No."

He drew back, an invisible chasm forming between them. The smile faded from his mouth. "Against my better judgment, I'll find you something to wear." The words fell flat, not his usual teasing. "Feel free to clean up. The bathroom is through that door."

Sabrina watched him leave the room and felt a crack deep within her heart. It was so real she torqued forward and caught herself on her knees. This was goodbye. It had to be. Tobias must understand now how dangerous it was for them to be together.

Rubbing her aching chest, she made her way to his bathroom. Dried blood streaked her hair and peppered her body. She scraped a blotch off her arm. Now that Tobias's roasted-almond scent wasn't overwhelming her, the stench of blood was. Like death. She'd never get a brush through the dried clumps in her hair without a shower.

Reluctantly, she turned on the water and let it heat up. She hadn't intended on staying long enough to clean up, but she couldn't go anywhere like this. Stripping out of her bra and underwear, she noticed a silvery scar under her collarbone. A quarter inch to the left and that poisoned dagger would have lodged directly in her heart. That might have been the end of her. Even Raven and Tobias couldn't have resurrected the dead.

She climbed into the spray. By the goddess, it felt good. And there was shampoo, rosemary mint, and a roughhewn chunk of soap that smelled of the ocean. She scrubbed herself until her skin pinked, watching the blood swirl the drain until she was squeaky clean. Once she turned off the water, it occurred to her that she hadn't been quick about it. As she wrapped a fluffy white towel around herself, she looked at the clock on the counter. Two a.m. The middle of the night. She'd better go soon. She had to work in the morning.

A knock came on the door. Tobias handed her a pile of clothes, yoga pants and a long-sleeved tunic T-shirt.

"Thanks."

"There's an extra toothbrush in the drawer." He pointed toward the sink. "Feel free to use it. I buy them in bulk."

"Thanks," she repeated softly.

He turned on his heel and left. No flirting. His eyes did not drift down her body. Good. She'd told him the truth, and she'd scared him away. So why did it feel like her heart had dropped into her stomach?

She brushed her teeth and dried her hair before dressing in the clothes he'd given her. Comfortable and they fit. Thanks, Raven. She emerged from the bathroom and stopped short. Tobias had changed into a pair of flannel pajama bottoms and a gray T-shirt that looked so soft it begged to be touched. He was watching TV. She hadn't even noticed the device was on the dresser opposite his bed before. Her gaze dropped to the remote in his hand.

She couldn't help herself. She laughed.

"What's so funny?"

"I saw you turn into a dragon today."

"Yeah?"

"And now you look like every human man in America."

"Don't vampires watch TV?"

"Sometimes. Most of the time vampires feed or obsess over who to feed on next. They're also quite fond of sex." He raised an eyebrow and flashed her a crooked smile. She looked away. "For most vampires, every channel is the Food Channel."

He chuckled at that. "Do you read?"

"I love to. Just finished Diana Gabaldon's latest."

He clicked the remote and selected a channel. "I have *Outlander*."

"First season?"

"All of them."

"I like the first one the best."

His eyes locked with hers, and then he tossed back the covers on the opposite side of the bed and beckoned her with his hand.

"I should go. I have to work in the morning."

"Me too."

"What I said before, it all still applies."

"It's TV, Sabrina. I'm not expecting you to sleep with me." His lids lowered. "But I would like your company. This has been one hell of a day."

She took a deep breath and blew it out slowly. Everything felt heavy, and the bed looked so clean and soft. He'd changed the sheets. Caving to the temptation, she crawled into bed and stretched out beside him. He scooped an arm behind her head and pulled her closer. Cheek against his chest, she allowed everything to be swept away. All her worries about the coven and the wolf were drowned out by the steady beat of his heart. Damn, the shirt was as soft as it looked.

He clicked the remote, and the opening sequence of *Outlander* started to play. Her eyes were closed before it ended. The last things she remembered before she drifted off were his lips in her hair and his gentle voice in her ear.

"Rest. You're safe with me."

❧

TOBIAS OPENED HIS EYES TO A SCENE STRAIGHT FROM heaven before recognizing it as what it was, a vision from hell. The heaven part had everything to do with Sabrina. Beside him, she slept, her red hair fanned out around her on the pillow, young and whole again. He had her vampire constitution to thank for that. What a blessing and curse that was.

He'd held her until she'd fallen asleep last night, then turned the TV off and drifted away himself. He couldn't remember sleeping more soundly. He breathed in her scent, honey and moonlight, and tamped down the urge his dragon was sending him to mark her as his own. He wanted her. Not for one night but for always. Wanted to mate with her. Make her his.

The scariest part—he was already hers. And she was something he knew little about. A hybrid: half vampire, half human. As far as he knew, there was no history of a dragon mating with someone like her. He'd be lying to himself to say it didn't turn him on to think about how rare she was, what an extraordinary and precious woman lay next to him in bed, but that was not why he loved her. Yes, he did love her, didn't he? He'd started his descent into that mad rush of insanity when he'd still thought she was human, her compassion as a nurse and quirky idiosyncrasies intriguing him to the point of distraction. And when she'd kissed him, his interest in her had gone from casual to intense.

It was her intelligence and compassion, though, that had ruined him for all other women. The way she'd healed him after he'd taken the bullet for her, the way she'd sacrificed herself for her coven, a coven of vampires that didn't truly know her or respect her for the right reasons. She was strong and wicked smart and as kind as anyone he'd ever known. And now he understood that she was a leader who wore her power lightly. If there was anything he could pinpoint, it was that. He was in love with the way she wore her strength like armor she hoped never to use, her wit like a quivered arrow, her compassion like an offered hand and well-worn smile.

She opened her eyes. Blinked. It was early morning, still dark. Their shift started at six a.m. Both of them needed to get up, get dressed, and drive to her home so she could change before they were due at the hospital. Only, he couldn't move. He stared at her, memorizing the slope of her green eyes, her pale, freckle-less skin, her full, rose-colored lips.

"We should get ready and go," she said softly. "It's almost five."

"How do you know that?" The clock was on the nightstand behind her head. She'd just opened her eyes. She couldn't have seen it.

"It's a vampire thing. The sun will rise in a little over an hour. I can feel it in my bones, in my blood. Even though I don't have to go to ground, my instincts still tell me to. They tell me how much time I have to get out of the sun. Once the sun rises, the feeling goes away."

"Interesting."

"You're not moving."

"Neither are you." He reached for her, tracing his fingertips over her lips. Full, plump lips. Down her long, graceful neck. He placed a kiss along her pulse and she arched against him. Over her T-shirt, between the mounds of her breasts. She had perfect breasts. Full and luscious. He paused to look her in the eye before tracing her curves. A shaky exhale escaped her lips. He completed the circle, his thumb flicking her nipple through the thin layer of cotton. A perfect round pearl strained the fabric. He brought his lips to it and warmed it with his breath before teasing it through the cotton with his teeth. She moaned and dug her fingers into his hair.

His touch trailed lower, stroked down her stomach and toward her waistband.

She caught his hand by the wrist before he could go any lower.

"You're trembling."

"I can't. I'm sorry. I want to, but I can't." Her voice cracked.

He retracted his hand. Internally, he chided himself. She wasn't a dragon. She didn't feel the driving need to mark and mate like he did. If he pushed her too hard, he'd scare her away. Clearly, she needed time. "I'll take you home."

They were in the car in less than twenty, speeding toward Marina Towers. After a quiet ride, he parked in front of her building.

"Can we go back to how it was before? Until I know it's safe?"

He forced himself to smile. "Of course."

Without a word, she dematerialized from the seat beside him.

"Faster than the elevator." He shrugged, feeling like an empty husk. Was that it? Go back to how it was. He was supposed to pretend that every cell in his body didn't long for her. Fat chance. Possible for her maybe, but not for him. Not anymore.

He was about to pull away from the curb when his phone dinged. A text. It was Sabrina's number.

Someone was here.

Tobias left the car double-parked and cloaked himself in invisibility. It would have been faster to fly to her balcony, but that would require removing his coat and shirt. Not how he wanted to face whatever was happening up there. He shadowed an owner into the building, hopping on an elevator behind him. It was easy enough to get to her forty-ninth-floor condominium. He waited until the hall was empty to knock. The look of confusion when she opened the door was quickly remedied when he slipped inside and dropped his invisibility.

"Thanks for coming up," she said, her voice choked.

The apartment was ransacked, furniture toppled, everything in the kitchen drawers overturned and dumped on the floor. Without saying a word, he strode to each of her two bedrooms. No one there, but he confirmed they were in the same state of disrepair.

"Who would do this?" he asked her.

"At first I thought it might be the werewolf, but I don't smell wolf."

"No," Tobias said, inhaling deeply. "I smell vampire. Not you. I know your scent. This was done by a pureblood."

"I smell it too." She frowned and pointed at the far wall. "I think someone doesn't like the fact that I was chosen as the new coven master."

Tobias followed her gaze. UNWORTHY was painted in blood on the taupe wall.

"Get changed. I'll drive you to work," Tobias said, his protective instincts kicking into high gear. He started righting the dining chairs. As soon as she was out of the room, he was going to scrub that shit off the wall.

"Really Tobias. You don't have to do that. The sun is rising. I'll be okay."

"Please." He growled, closing his eyes and shaking his head. When he opened them again, she was staring at him. She sighed.

"I'll be out in a minute."

CHAPTER THIRTEEN

The werewolf, Sabrina thought, was just the beginning. What Tobias didn't realize as he cleaned up her living room—a gesture she found overtly romantic—was that messing a vampire's bed before sunrise sent a message far beyond "unworthy." In vampire culture, over-turning furniture and drawers, tearing curtains, and other-wise ruining a vampire's sleeping place could be a death sentence. Anyone in her coven would know that she would not be harmed by what was done to her apartment tonight. She was a daywalker, after all. But it didn't matter. The message was the same.

Someone wanted her dead.

What's more, whoever had been here tonight was likely now aware that she had not been. Questions would be asked. If not here, where had she been? It was paramount that no one know she'd spent the night with Tobias. Under the best of circumstances, her father would assume he was human and send a vampire to wipe his mind. Under the worst of circumstances, he'd order Tobias dead, an act that would more than likely reveal the truth he was a dragon shifter and seal his fate.

She changed into her scrubs, thankful for her nursing job. She couldn't wait to bury herself in her work. She loved caring for the sick. It was when she felt the most human. By the time she put her hair up and brushed her teeth, Tobias had righted the main room of her apartment and even washed the bloody message from the wall. She didn't bother saying he shouldn't have. She appreciated it, and she told him so.

"Thank you." A heavy weight settled on her chest. "I'll deal with the rest of it later. We need to go."

His jaw tightened. "I can ask Raven to put wards around this place. You need more protection. I'll have her do it while we're at work." She didn't miss the way the offer came with some reluctance. If Tobias and Raven had a strained relationship, it might make what she needed to tell him easier.

"That's not necessary." She shook her head. She couldn't accept more help from the witch. "You need to ask your brother and Raven to leave Chicago. If my coven learns what Raven did for me—"

"I think it *is* necessary. Whoever did this is dangerous. The wolf who stabbed you is still out there." He placed his hands on her shoulders and pulled her in close. "I'll keep you safe until we can get something in place."

"No," she said. "Tobias, you haven't been listening to me. You can't protect me. You need to protect yourself *from* me and my kind. You need to protect your family. At least until I take power. This is only going to get worse until that crown is on my head. Please. You have to go. I'll drive myself to work."

"Sabrina..."

Her eyes prickled with unshed tears. She held up her hands. "I'm sorry."

Before she lost her nerve, she donned her coat, grabbed her purse off the hook, and held the door open for him. Pain radiated through her chest as he gave her one more lingering look before heading for the elevator. She let him go and willed herself not to cry.

It had to be this way. Relying on Tobias put him at risk. She couldn't do it anymore, no matter how much it hurt.

***

Tobias slipped out of Sabrina's apartment, turning himself invisible before reaching the elevators. Silently, he waited. She'd pushed him away to keep him safe, but Tobias had no intention of going anywhere. Whether or not she realized it, she needed him. In the past few days she'd been stabbed in the chest and had her apartment ransacked. No way was he abandoning her to save his own hide.

When she emerged from her apartment, he followed her to the parking garage, hoping his scent wouldn't be a dead giveaway. Then again, he'd just left her place. It would make sense that his smell would still be in the air. Admittedly, he bordered on full-blown stalker at the moment. He didn't make a habit of following women. But he had to make sure she made it to her car safely. Whoever had wrecked her apartment was likely still out there. Anyone who would do such a thing would want to see the results of their effort.

He stopped behind a concrete pillar. Thanks to his invisibility, she couldn't see him anyway, but the spot gave him protection from the other cars pulling through the garage. Plus it gave him something to hold on to when he saw a stocky, greasy-haired vampire appear beside her vehicle.

"You stayed out last night," the vampire said. "All night. I was afraid something had happened to you." The low male voice was definitely too quiet to be human, but Tobias had no trouble detecting the venom in his words. He trained his ears in the direction of the conversation.

"That is none of your business. Why did you wreck my apartment?" Sabrina's accusation made Tobias clench his fists. So she had suspected someone. Who was this prick?

"Who said anything about wrecking your apartment? Are you in danger, Princess? We should notify your father."

"Stay out of it."

"I think you owe me an explanation. Out all night. Condo is ransacked."

"I don't owe you anything, Tristan. Stay away from me," Sabrina said.

Tristan? Who was Tristan to her? Wait, she'd mentioned him before. He was the vampire who would be master if Sabrina stepped down. She'd said he was nothing short of evil. Tobias's skin prickled. The male had the flat, soulless eyes of a snake, and his scent matched what he'd smelled in her apartment.

Without thinking, Tobias lurched toward the two, wanting desperately to place himself between her and Tristan. His toe caught on an empty Coke can, and it rattled across the parking garage. He squeezed his eyes shut and cursed. A vision of Gabriel sweeping his legs with a bo staff and sending him crashing to the practice mat filled his head. Of all the times for his lack of stealth to rear its ugly head, did it have to be now?

He froze as the two vampires looked directly at him. It would not go over well if Sabrina knew he'd been watching her. She'd told him in no uncertain terms to back off. Thankfully, when the vampires' search came up empty, their eyes refocused on each other.

"I want you to stop following me, Tristan."

"Or what?"

"Or I'll tell Calvin."

"Okay, let's tell Calvin. I think he'd be interested to know his daughter is spending the night with a human male."

A growl pierced the early morning quiet, menacing enough that Tobias could hardly believe it came from Sabrina, but she'd moved on the other vampire and had her hand wrapped around his throat. "How many times do I have to tell you? It is none of your concern what I do with my free time, whom I feed on, or how."

"It is if you are becoming romantically entangled. There are rules, Sabrina. The master of the largest vampire coven in North America can't be shacking up with her lunch."

"I'm not shacking up with anyone."

"Good." Tristan stepped out of her grasp and smoothed his clothing. "Interspecies relationships are forbidden among vampire royalty for a reason, Princess. They make us vulnerable. Your one and only priority should be the coven."

"I was raised at my father's side and have participated in his rule from the time I was a young. I do not need a lesson in duty from you." Her fangs were fully extended now, and Tobias dug his fingers into the sleeves of his coat against a chill that had nothing to do with the weather.

The other vampire backed away from her with a slow swagger. "No. No, you do not."

"Stop following me."

"No."

"Tristan, let me put this as plain as I can. In less than a month, I won't need Calvin to punish you for disobeying a direct order. If you continue to defy me, my first order as master will be to have your heart torn from your chest and burned at my feet."

Tristan's eyebrows shot up. He scoffed at her and circled two fingers above his head as he took an exaggerated and elaborate bow. "Yes, Your Majesty."

In the next breath, he was gone, his body twisting into a whisper of darkness before disappearing entirely. Sabrina cursed, climbed into her blue Nissan, and peeled out of her space, tires squealing.

Mine. The dragon inside Tobias stirred, scales pressing and twisting against the inside of his skin. He tried to rein in the protective instincts that raged, foreign and unwanted, behind his brow. He shouldn't have underestimated her. As caring and soft as Sabrina could be, she'd handled herself well with her adversary. Still, he needed to keep her safe. He wouldn't forgive himself if he didn't, and neither would his inner dragon.

CHAPTER FOURTEEN

The truth was that medicine was more of an art than a science. Sabrina had always wondered at the miracle of it, how people could be at death's door, their skin gray, their breath as shallow as a whisper, but with the right drugs, the administration of oxygen, or a medical procedure, they could be brought back to life again. Her kind were immortal and her father expected she'd be as well, despite her human blood. Certainly she healed like an immortal. She'd never been ill and had stopped aging in her early twenties. Until the poisoned dagger, she'd never been seriously injured.

The thought made her realize that what Tobias and his friend Raven had done for her yesterday was what she did for humans on a regular basis. They'd healed her, cared for her when she couldn't care for herself. Her heart ached. Tobias deserved better than her, better than how she'd treated him the past twenty-four hours. He deserved a woman who would throw her arms and legs around him and absolutely rock his world after the kindness and selflessness he'd shown her. Truth was, she desperately desired to do just that. But after learning it was Tristan who had destroyed her apartment, she knew she was doing the right thing pushing Tobias away. Tristan was dangerous, and he knew she'd spent the night with a human. If he found out that human was Tobias, he'd do something horrible to him to get under her skin and force her to abdicate the throne. She would for him. But stepping down would be counterproductive. Only by rising to power could she protect him by rule of law.

Staying apart was the only way to keep his secret.

Sabrina concentrated on her work, resolved to try not to pine for Tobias. It was almost noon when she took her first break and jogged down to the cafeteria for lunch.

"Let me guess, your favorite is alphabet?" Tobias handed her a bowl from his place in the soup line directly in front of her. Damn it. How was it that in a hospital this size, she kept running into him?

"Why would my favorite be alphabet?"

"You can spell out EAT ME with the noodles. Gives you a sense of accomplishment when you do."

She laughed and shook her head. "Chicken noodle is my jam."

"Oh?"

"What do you eat when you're sick? Chicken noodle. If I eat it, I'm curing the illness before I even get it."

"You can't get sick because of what you are, not what you eat."

"How do you know? It might be the soup."

"That makes no logical sense."

"Logic is highly overrated, Doctor. You should ditch the logic in favor of magic."

"I think I've heard someone say that before." He winked

at her over a half smile and slowly poured himself a bowl of chicken noodle.

She filled her bowl and passed him by to sit down near the windows. He waited a beat and then sat down across from her.

Dropping her spoon, she rubbed her temples. "Tobias, I don't think sitting together is a good idea. Every second we spend together just makes it harder."

"I understand that you believe we need to stay apart, but I need to tell you something. It's important."

She sighed. "What's going on?"

"I owe you an apology." The steam from the soup kissed his cheek, and she thought the resulting blush of his skin was the most enticing thing she'd ever seen.

"Why?"

"I followed you today."

"What are you talking about? When?"

"I saw you talking to Tristan in the parking garage."

She narrowed her eyes. "The Coke can. That was you?"

"Yes."

"You had no right spying on me."

"I know. You're right. I'm sorry." He looked down at his bowl. "Why do you think Tristan ransacked your apartment?"

"It was him, wasn't it? He denied it, but I picked up his scent."

Tobias nodded. "It was definitely him unless, of course, he has recently been a guest in your home?"

She scoffed. "Never."

"Then it was him."

"As I mentioned to you before, Tristan is my father's trusted advisor and the next in line for coven master after me.

He's highly respected and has a following among my coven. He's been gunning for me since I can remember. He wants to intimidate me so that I step down from the position."

"He wants to be master, huh?"

"It's more than that. He's a misogynist and thinks humans are barely a step up from animals. I threaten everything he believes in."

"Because if you became master, he'd report to a half-human female?"

"More than that. A vampire coven is a lot like a hive of bees or maybe a colony of ants. It's in our genetics to follow our master. Once I become master, he will all but have to obey me. It will become uncomfortable for him to not follow my lead."

"How uncomfortable?"

"He'll feel sick to his stomach. It's not impossible for vampires to disobey. It happens. And he can break from the coven and suffer no illness. But my father always said when it came to vampires, it was easy to find defectors—just look for the ones hurling their lunch."

"So not only is Tristan hungry for power, he's desperate to not have to obey someone he hates, namely you."

"Exactly. Which is why I'm worried about him finding out about you." She lowered her voice. "About us. He's following me. He knew I spent the night with a human last night. If he finds out who you are, he will use you to get to me. He might even hurt you." She placed her hands on the table and lowered her voice to a whisper. "I wouldn't push you away if I didn't think it was absolutely necessary."

He nodded but didn't leave.

"Did you hear what I said, Tobias?"

Lowering his voice to a whisper that would have been

impossible for a human to hear, he asked, "Do you think he sent the werewolf?"

Sabrina paused. "No. There's no reason to believe that. The werewolf would have wanted me dead for more reasons than Tristan."

"Maybe, but how did the wolf find you? Not once but twice? During the day. In places your kind does not frequent."

Her eyes widened. "Places *I* don't frequent. I've never been to Maverick's before, and it's been years since I visited the museum. But it couldn't be Tristan. He sleeps during the day. How would he know where I would be?"

"He could be paying someone to follow you. Or working with the wolf directly. If Tristan is working with the werewolf, he might have supplied your workplace and address, told him how to track you. I assume he knows where you work."

Sabrina looked over her shoulder. The cafeteria was full of strange faces. Was one of them working for Tristan?

She shook her head. "Tristan knows if he hurts me, my father will kill him. No questions asked."

"Only if your father believes Tristan did it. Much easier for him to blame a rogue werewolf."

Damn, she couldn't argue with his logic. Tristan wanted to hurt her. Would he go so far as collaborating with a werewolf? *Are you in danger, Princess?* When Tristan had said those words, there was an inflection in his tone as if he'd known the answer. Sabrina frowned. She wouldn't put it beyond the slimeball.

"Collaborating with our enemies is low, even for Tristan. But it's possible."

Leaning across the table, the hot soup steaming between

them, Tobias met her gaze. "Move in with me, Sabrina. I can protect you."

"What? No. That's ridiculous."

"You're worried your nearness will put me in danger, but it is far more dangerous if we are apart. Together we can protect each other."

"No." She lowered her chin, a nervous laugh bubbling up in her throat. "We are not a couple. We don't owe each other protection."

"One word from you and that could all change. Everything would change. The only one keeping us from being a couple is you."

As hard as it was, she simply shook her head and raised an eyebrow. "I've been to bed with you twice, Doctor. My goddess, what more do you want from me? Blood? Oh wait..."

He leveled a sultry male stare in her direction. "Oh, I have some ideas."

Sabrina shifted in her chair and took interest in her soup. All they could have was this, their working relationship. She had to make him understand. "Everything changes once I take my place as master, Tobias. We need to bide our time, keep our distance until it's safe."

He shook his head. "If Tristan is targeting you like we think he is, it's going to get worse before it gets better. I can't protect you if we're apart."

She buried her face in her hands. "You don't need to protect me. I'll protect myself."

The look he gave her said it all. She hadn't ended up with a poisoned dagger in her chest by protecting herself. She shook her head and picked up her spoon.

"I think they're skimping on the chicken in the chicken noodle."

His brow furrowed. "Yeah. I'm pretty sure they dunk a leg in and call it a day."

Without another word, she started eating. He followed her lead. There was more he'd wanted from her, but thankfully, for now he let it go.

⁂

THE FIRST TEARS BEGAN TO FALL THE MOMENT Sabrina materialized in her apartment at the end of the day, a bottle of wine secured in her grip. Every time she thought about Tobias, she felt torn in two, like one arm was chained to her coven and the other to her desire for him, and both had become semitrucks traveling at top speeds in opposite directions. Despite the risk, she'd enjoyed seeing him today. After lunch, they'd managed to bump into each other again in the break room. Perhaps the energy she'd absorbed from him played a part in the crazy need she felt to be in his presence. Had her taste of dragon blood been addictive?

The pain that was happening in the general region of her heart might have been withdrawal, but she was apt to believe it had more to do with the way he made her feel every time he looked at her, like she was everything. Like she was *worthy*. All she wanted to do was dematerialize to his home and take him up on his offer to live with him.

That would be a tragedy. The intense twinge of longing Sabrina fought to deny was too close to a bond to flirt with. Bonded vampires within the species had to be treated as a unit in every regard. The attachment was so complete it was considered cruel to separate them. The mates of vampires who died in battle were known to walk into the sun rather than live without their partner. She'd made light of bonded couples in the past, questioning the sanity of anyone who would willingly enter into such a relationship. Now she could feel the attachment building within her, a tug deep inside her bones drawing her to Tobias even when she knew Tristan was watching her every move.

She threw her parka on the sofa and shuffled into the kitchen to pour a glass of the cabernet she'd procured to drown her sorrows. It was times like this that she was glad she was half human. Full-blooded vampires could not get drunk from alcohol, and she planned to tie one on until the edge was off this reckless crush.

No sooner had she raised the glass to her lips than a knock came on her patio's sliding glass door. Definitely a vampire. Anyone else would have come to the main door of the apartment. She couldn't see who it was thanks to the glare from the kitchen lights bouncing off the glass, but she set her wine down and hurried for the door. If a vampire was visiting her here, she'd be expected to receive them. Aside from Tristan, she'd welcome anyone from her coven inside.

"Father!"

Calvin Bishop stepped into her apartment and shook the excess snow from his hair and shoulders. He wasn't wearing a coat, and his skin was luminous in the darkness. "Sabrina, I'm glad you're home. We need to talk." His gray eyes flashed as she slid the door closed behind him.

"Come on in. Have a seat." She pecked him on the cheek, and he encircled her in a tight embrace.

"I hope I'm not interrupting anything." His eyes scanned the room, and his nostrils flared. No doubt he could sense the recent turmoil, smell the blood. Everything was back in order, but her father had a sixth sense about these things.

"Just having a glass of wine."

"I don't know how you can drink that swill." He eyed the glass on the counter. "Aren't you afraid it will dilute your true nature?"

She swept the full glass off the counter and placed it in the sink. Out of sight, hopefully out of mind. "It actually tastes delicious if you have human taste buds."

He frowned. "I have no doubt, considering the way the humans are always gulping it by the gallon. But you are a vampire, Sabrina, the daughter of a master and soon to be master yourself. Appearances are important. That's why I'm here."

Her stomach clenched. This was an unexpected conversation. Had Tristan said something to him about her condominium being ransacked? Was that the real reason for her father's visit and inspection of the room? She'd kill the sleazeball. "What's going on?"

"You're ascending to master of our coven very soon. This is no small thing. You will be only the third female in the position and the first hybrid."

"I'm honored. I take the responsibility seriously."

"Good. Then you will understand why things have to change."

"Change how?"

"You have done the coven a great service providing us with blood from the hospital for our stores. Many sick vampires have been saved with that blood. New vampires have been introduced more gently to the vampire world with the help of that blood."

That was one way to put it. Normally new vampires woke up so hungry that it wasn't uncommon for them to kill a few humans before mastering responsible feeding habits. Those odds had greatly improved with the introduction of a bag feeding before they were allowed to hunt. "I am happy to do it."

Her father took a seat at her table and crossed one leg over the other. "When you are master, you won't have time to perform your human job at the hospital and also devote yourself to a coven of this size."

"Why not?"

"It's time for you to resign, Sabrina, to start living like a vampire full-time."

Sabrina's cheeks turned cold as all the blood seemed to drain from her head. Was the room spinning, or was that her brain whirling desperately for something to say? She forced a smile. "It won't be any problem. I've always been able to balance my work at the hospital with my responsibilities to the coven."

His jaw tightened. She had the oddest thought that he looked like a mannequin just then. His back was unnaturally straight, his skin and hair flawless, his dress pants and shirt perfectly smooth, as if no wrinkle would dare mar her father's appearance. It was odd having a parent who never aged but even odder to have one who rarely if ever changed. Calvin was a product of the Renaissance, old-fashioned and patriarchal. The look on his face was one she'd seen before. He was laying down the law, and there was no room for negotiation.

"Although your contributions in this regard were acceptable before, when you take on my responsibilities, it will be necessary for you to be more accessible to your charges. You must stay underground with the others. There are no days off from being master. You know that."

An invisible vise squeezed her chest. Sabrina swayed on her feet. "Of course... Yes." The words formed of their own volition. Everything in her, her very blood, urged her to agree with her father. He was master. No one argued with Calvin Bishop. "Obviously the coven will need me to be accessible to them."

He placed his hands on her shoulders. "Not just accessible. You must become one of them, fully and unequivocally. It is time for you to embrace your true vampire identity."

She took a deep breath and let it out slowly. "I thought I had. What else do you want me to do?"

"You will sell this place and you will move into my quarters in the tunnels. You will resign from your job. You will eat, sleep, and work with the others."

"But... but what about the bagged blood?"

"Another vampire has been hired as a late-night janitor. He is exceptional at compelling humans. He will take over your duties."

Deep inside her, the thought of sleeping in the tunnels all day festered like an old wound. She cleared her throat. "I wonder, though, if my talents of being a daywalker would be better leveraged here. It could be a way to establish dominance over our enemies, something they aren't expecting. It's what makes me strong. It's an advantage."

He shook his head. "Maybe in time, once you've proven yourself as a vampire. You can't allow the coven to question your loyalty."

"But—"

His expression hardened. His hand slashed through the air between them. "Enough. The decision is made. The real estate agent will be here this week to list this place. I suggest you tender your resignation at Lurie Children's Hospital as soon as possible."

For a long moment, she tried to think of an excuse, some reason that would be acceptable to him that would allow her to keep her home, her human life, and her only safe way to see Tobias. But she knew her father, and she understood why he was doing this. It all made sense now. Tristan was the one who had drawn *unworthy* on her wall and also the one who'd told her father it was there. He was trying to break her. Trying to get her to relinquish her crown. She wouldn't do it.

"Yes, Father." Her heart broke to say it.

He stood from the sofa and spread his arms. She accepted his embrace.

"Change is always difficult, but this will be for the best. Trust me." He pinched her chin and offered her a wide smile.

"Yes, Father." As soon as he was out the door and had disappeared into the night, the tears came, and this time they didn't stop until she was fast asleep.

CHAPTER FIFTEEN

It took energy not to worry. As Raven sat in front of the fire, her hand stroking Artemis's back, Gabriel at her side, she tried not to dwell on what she'd just learned. The act of worrying was too exhausting, too pointless. Richard had called. A man fitting the same description her sister had given them—definitely Scoria—had come into Blakemore's Antiques looking for her and Gabriel. Richard and Agnes had been ready with the story they'd agreed upon: Gabriel had sold the store and decided to travel with his new bride. Last they'd heard, Gabriel and Raven were in New Zealand.

She hoped the Obsidian Guardsman would fall for it. She prayed he'd give up and return to Paragon.

"We can't go home to New Orleans," she said. "Not until we know he's gone."

Gabriel didn't answer. He looked into his mug and mumbled. "What's the deal with Chicago coffee? This stuff is strong enough to melt paint off the walls."

"Gabriel? Are you listening to me?"

Her love's face looked like stone, half his features dark,

the other half flickering in the firelight. "Tobias wanted us gone last week. Technically, we were only supposed to be here one night. Yes, after I cured Sabrina he said we could stay, but who knows how long she and her coven will allow us to remain here? I don't trust her, not after what Madam Chloe told us and with what I know about vampire nature."

Artemis hissed loudly, jumped down, and ran away.

"I agree," Raven said to the cat. She stood and paced to the mantel where she stared into the fire, her anger burning as hot as the flames. "Tobias needs to come to terms with the fact that his girlfriend's coven considers other supernaturals the enemy. He's in danger here."

"You're right." That wasn't Gabriel's voice.

Raven slowly pivoted to find Tobias standing behind the two wingback chairs in his living room. She thought he looked older than the last time she'd seen him. Sadder.

"I have been unfair to you, and for that, I apologize. Sabrina confirmed that you were telling the truth. She insists we stay apart for my protection. She warned me that her coven might be watching us. Regardless, she promises she won't tell her coven about any of us."

"Oh, Tobias. I'm sorry. I know you care for her."

"It is what it is." He looked absently toward the fire. "We're on good terms. Still have to work together."

Raven winced at Tobias's tortured expression. She searched for the right thing to say. "I read in the paper today that one of your patients has been miraculously cured and will be released from the hospital soon."

He scoffed. "Thanks to both of you. It was the amulet. A little girl named Katelyn is alive because of you."

Raven and Gabriel exchanged glances. "Oh. Well, if it weren't for you, it wouldn't have found its way to her."

Tobias hung his head. "So, it sounds like the two of you will be staying longer than expected?"

"We have a situation," Gabriel said. "There have been two sightings of an Obsidian Guardsman in New Orleans. We think Scoria followed Raven back from Paragon."

"Scoria? The captain of the Obsidian Guard?" Tobias laughed. "You must've made an impression for Brynhoff to send the big guns after you." He arched a brow at Raven.

"He's actively hunting me," Raven said. "I can't go back there."

Tobias sighed. "I knew returning to Paragon was a bad idea." He cursed.

Raven braced herself. With everything going on with Sabrina and her coven, it was natural Tobias would want them to leave.

"You can stay here for as long as you need," Tobias said.

Raven breathed a sigh of relief.

"On one condition."

Raven looked at Gabriel, who seemed as surprised as she was. "What condition is that?"

"I need you to place protective wards around this house and Sabrina's apartment. Her place was ransacked last night. And if what I suspect is true, she's been followed. We're being watched. We all need protection."

"By the Mountain, that woman seems to have a target on her back," Gabriel said. "Who did she piss off?"

"There's another vampire. Tristan... He's second in line for the throne and a real asshole."

Gabriel sucked air through his teeth. "That could get ugly."

"What am I missing?" Raven asked.

Gabriel's dark eyes locked onto her. "Vampires, at least the ones in Paragon, are community oriented in a violent

149

way. She's going to be the queen bee of a swarm capable of draining every human in this city. Once she is crowned, she will have dominion over them. From now until her coronation, she's at great risk. If... What was the vampire's name?"

"Tristan," Tobias said.

"If Tristan can kill her or force her to step down before her coronation, he can grab that power for himself. Once she is crowned, the coven will be sworn to protect her. Tristan would have to overthrow the entire coven to take charge."

Tobias frowned. "Sabrina said something about that. She thinks the answer is us staying apart. I think she needs my help to get her to the finish line. Thus the wards." He nodded at Raven.

Gabriel glanced at Tobias. "You can lay the protective wards yourself. When it comes to protection, dragon magic is just as effective as that of a witch. We've had to protect our treasure for our entire existence."

Tobias shook his head. "I don't trust myself. I've used more dragon magic this past week than I have in decades. I'm out of practice."

"Maybe, given the danger we are in, it's time to dust off your ring." Gabriel looked pointedly at the large sapphire on Tobias's finger. "When was the last time you spread your wings? You are a dragon, after all. How can you deny what you are?"

Raven held up a hand. "Gabriel, give it a rest!"

The two brothers turned surprised expressions toward her. It wasn't like Raven to lose her temper, but she couldn't take a moment more. She turned back to Tobias. "If you don't feel comfortable casting the protective spells, I'm happy to do it."

"Thank you." Tobias looked genuinely relieved.

"You're welcome. And thank you for letting us stay."

Tobias shrugged. "To be honest, it's refreshing having you around. It's been a long time since I had any sense of family in my life. Considering what's going on with Sabrina, it's a comfort to not be alone. You were right. We're not in Paragon anymore. It's silly for us to act as if we are. Gabriel is right too. I've denied what I am for far too long. If this thing with Sabrina has taught me anything, it's that."

Raven thought Gabriel's eyebrows were going to shoot through the roof. She gave him a warning nudge to keep his I-told-you-so to himself.

She placed her arms around Tobias's slumped shoulders, brushing off Gabriel's jealous glances. "We're here for you, Tobias. We'll help. Any way you want us to. I'll lay the wards tomorrow."

"Thanks," he said, pulling back from Raven's embrace. "And if you don't mind, please keep this on the down low. Sabrina wasn't exactly keen on the idea. And we don't want to gain any more attention from her coven."

"Done," she said. "It will be our secret."

"There's one more thing," Tobias turned toward Gabriel.

"What's that?"

"I need your help tracking a werewolf."

CHAPTER SIXTEEN

March roared in like a lion, and Chicago loomed, a city of steel and ice on the horizon, the wind becoming a sharp edge that made everything more difficult. Tobias disliked both the cold weather and the distance that had formed between him and Sabrina. Sure, he'd occasionally bumped into her in the hall or in the break room, but she'd kept their conversations painfully short. He took to leaving her animal crackers at the nurses station. Those she never turned away.

At least he knew she was safe. Raven had placed protective enchantments around her apartment and balcony. No one who meant her harm could make it past the barrier.

The space between them did have one major benefit. He'd had time to try to track down the wolf who'd stabbed her. Gabriel had helped him return to Maverick's and then to the museum. The werewolf had been bleeding the last time Tobias had seen him. His scent should have been easy to track. But the trail ended at the street. Someone had helped him. And all of his leads on the triangular tattoo the wolf was sporting had ended at the museum. The werewolf hadn't been seen in Chicago since.

Dragons were excellent trackers. Two dragons were almost impossible to elude. Two dragons and a witch? Tobias was not only sure the werewolf had left the city, he was certain that the car used to take him there hadn't come back.

Good news when it came to keeping Sabrina safe, his top priority. If he didn't keep her safe, who would? For as long as he'd known her, she'd never put herself first. Not with her patients. Not with her coworkers. She wanted to keep him safe and to be the best coven master she could be. In her mind, both of those things meant staying away from him. But no amount of time or space would ever dull his need to protect her.

Funny, he'd never realized the power the vampire community held over Chicago. In all the years he'd worked here, their existence had never been an issue. Then again, his life was about as mainstream and human as a supernatural's could get. If it hadn't been for the kiss he'd shared with Sabrina, he would have gone on admiring her from a safe, detached distance.

But he *had* kissed her, and his inner walls had crumbled. She'd won his heart and enchanted his dragon. With one kiss, she'd awakened his inner beast.

To numb the pain, he threw himself into his work. On this day, he found himself again in room 5830, under far different circumstances than when he'd put the amulet around Katelyn's neck. The girl was going home. Every doctor on her case had run every test imaginable and could find no reason to keep her. The humans called her a walking miracle. In some ways, Tobias agreed. His coming across Maiara's healing talisman was a miracle in a way, and it warmed his heart to have put it to good use.

"I just want to thank you," Katelyn's mother said. "The official story may be that this was the result of spontaneous healing, but we know your exceptional care had something to do with it." She pulled him into a hug, her wiry arms and bone-thin fingers strong against his back.

Often Tobias had seen the woman hunched over Katelyn's bed, her human body sagging under the weight of the bad news that had seemed to flow from the walls at the time. Today she was better. Eyes brighter, spine straighter. Although the older woman was painfully thin, she had always struck Tobias as being solid, as if she were made of bricks instead of flesh, a tower of strength wrapped in cardigan sweaters and bolstered by hospital coffee. Her hair had grayed over the course of her daughter's illness, but the rest of her seemed impervious. The experience had galvanized her. Pulling back from the hug, she had tears in her eyes. It was the first time he'd seen her cry.

"I don't think I can take the credit for this one," Tobias said. "Sometimes there are forces greater than ourselves at work in our lives. All we can do is be thankful, cherish the days fate is merciful enough to give us. Katelyn is a great kid. It makes me happy to know I played a small part in her recovery."

"We won't forget you," Katelyn's mother said.

Katelyn herself walked to him, her body growing stronger by the day, and he bent to accept her hug. She'd grow again now that she was well. He hoped he'd have the chance to see her again years from now, a normal teen with normal problems.

"Thanks, Dr. Toby." She cupped her hand around his ear and whispered, "I won't tell our secret."

"What's that?" her mother asked.

Tobias stood and guided Katelyn toward her. "A game we used to play to pass the time." The smile he flashed was both meant to put them at ease and end the conversation. "I'll call someone to escort you out. You get one last ride in a wheelchair."

He slipped out the door to notify the medical assistant at the desk that Katelyn was ready to go. He'd cheated death with this one, but he didn't care. He'd do it again a thousand times. Only he wondered in the back of his mind if there would be repercussions. Would fate ask him for payment in the future for the death he'd stolen from her? If so, he'd happily pay the price.

He finished signing Katelyn's discharge papers. When he looked up again, he started. Sabrina was there, and she didn't look happy.

"It's good to see you," he said, moving around the desk. "It's been a while."

"I'm sorry, but I told you..." She brushed her red bangs from her forehead. All vampires were pale, but Sabrina's complexion was even whiter than usual. And she seemed sad somehow. Something was wrong. She was dressed in street clothes and still wearing her coat. "You know why I had to stay away."

"There's something I have to tell you. It's important." He looked at his watch. "Can we conveniently bump into each other in the break room later?"

She shook her head. "I'm not here to work. Actually, I just tendered my resignation." Her voice cracked. He could tell she was trying to hide it, but he heard it loud and clear.

"Why?" It didn't make sense. For as long as he'd known Sabrina, he had never questioned her love for the job. For her sake, he carefully sanitized his expression to one practiced and impassive, his doctor's mask: analytical, practical, no-nonsense. It was also a lie. Tobias felt ripped apart. His inner dragon coiled and hissed, urged him to throw her over his shoulder and take her somewhere he could force her to stay near him. He kept that part of himself carefully under control, hid it as well as he could from those piercing green eyes that he swore could see right through him.

She pulled a Kleenex from her pocket and blotted under her eyes. "I can't tell you that. Not here. Not now."

"When?" Too much emotion. The mask was slipping.

They were interrupted when Katelyn, pushed in a wheelchair by one of the volunteers, emerged from her room with her mother following behind her. The family headed for the elevators at the end of the hall, disappearing out of sight.

"How did you do it?" Sabrina whispered. "You never told me how you healed her."

"I'm still waiting for your explanation of why you're resigning. I think this is a case for quid pro quo."

She turned away from him, but not before he saw a tear roll down her cheek.

"Talk to me."

"It's too risky." She looked over her shoulder.

"Sabrina, please..." He rested his hand beside hers on the nurses' station, not touching but close enough that the space between their fingers seemed to carry an electric charge. Would a shock ensue if he touched her?

She wiped her cheeks. Their eyes met, and for a long moment he resisted the strong desire to kiss each of her eyelids. Kiss away the tears.

"It has to be somewhere secret and in full daylight," she whispered, her eyes darting over her shoulder.

Tobias frowned. What had happened to her? Had

Tristan done something terrible to her? He'd kill the vampire. "Lincoln Park Zoo. Polar bear exhibit. Noon tomorrow."

She nodded once, pulled her coat tighter around her, and left. Everything in him screamed not to let her go, to haul her off to his treasure room where he'd hoard her like the wealth he kept there. Only, he hadn't maintained a treasure room in a century and he wasn't a monster. As much as he wanted to act like a beast, he forced himself to let her go. And counted the seconds until he could see her again.

ᘛ

Sabrina materialized in the tunnels, completely alone. It was the middle of the day. The coven was sleeping. At least she'd have this when she was master, a few stolen hours of alone time when she didn't have to worry about Tristan or anyone else following her. Then again, that wasn't entirely true. She would always have to look over her shoulder. Maybe not because of Tristan, but they had other enemies.

Jaw clenched, she made her way to her father's chambers. It would be another hour before he was up and there was something she needed to do before he woke.

"Good morning, Sabrina," Paul said, his Chicago PD uniform looking a bit crumpled at the end of his long shift. "You're up early."

She held up the notebook in her hand. "I wanted to inventory Dad's apartment for decorating purposes before I move in. I thought it would help if I did it while he was sleeping. He doesn't get much privacy during the night."

Paul laughed. "Ain't that the truth. I just want you to know, I'm willing to stay on as your security detail once your father is gone. I like it here. You people have been good to me."

And you don't want us to eat you, she thought.

"Of course. You have the most experience." She placed a hand on his shoulder and gave him her most convincing smile.

He unlocked the heavy vault door, opening it for her. "You're one of the good ones, Sabrina. Have a good night."

She nodded her head and entered her father's chambers. Flipping on the light, she removed her booties and padded across the main room in her socks. Avoiding her father's bedroom, she made a beeline to his office. Aside from the mahogany desk and plush leather chair that were typical of an executive office, the place resembled a library more than a workspace. The walls were lined with books and scrolls that detailed the history of their race, her royal lineage, and the laws of her coven.

The tomes she was interested in rested on the top shelf, dusty and unused. Vampire reference manuals about other species. There was one on witches, another on the fae, and another labeled creatures of the sea. But it was the shifter volume she was interested in. She used one arm to hoist herself up and select the massive book from the shelf, cradling it as she returned her feet to the floor.

Positioning the book on the desk, she carefully opened it, the smell of aging parchment thick in her nostrils. Werewolves... shifters... bears... she skimmed the entries in the table of contents at the front of the book. All the way at the bottom, she found what she was looking for.

"Dragons," she whispered, flipping to the referenced page. Before she said goodbye to Tobias forever, she had to know for sure that she didn't have any other options. If she could have given her heart a voice, it would have sang its hope that somehow dragons were the exception to the rule, the one supernatural species vampires could coexist with. She tried not to get her hopes up as she flipped to the page specified.

She was surprised to find the entire section was only two pages long. She began to read, translating the old language in her head.

Although dragons are now thought to be extinct, the most ancient vampires remember a time long ago when they lived among us. Thought to be the most dangerous form of shifter, dragons hold the distinction of having originated as beasts, blessed with the ability to transform into men by the Greek goddess Circe. This is in sharp contrast to the werewolf, for example, whose species originated from humans cursed to become beasts.

Having evolved then from magical beasts, dragons share qualities of inherent magic similar to natural witches. Due to their potential for insurmountable power and their latent magical abilities, it is said that dragons were forbidden from mating outside their species.

Folklore from before vampires kept written records suggests the dragons left Earth for a new land before the great flood as a concession to Hera who did not approve of Circe's creation. In any case, a suspected dragon should be considered dangerous to any coven and should be reported to the Forebears immediately.

Sabrina's blood froze in her veins. She shut the book and took a step back. Forebears. Only the most serious threats to vampire kind were referred to them. One did not simply submit a form or send an email. The Forebears were the supreme ruling body for vampires, the eldest ones, the originals. Many rarely emerged from their underground castle, having chosen to sever their relationship with the outer world rather than veil what they were to adapt to modern living. They ruled from the center of a heavily forested and largely abandoned part of Eastern Europe, plucking villagers from the surrounding area at will. Reporting to the Forebears meant going to that godforsaken place in the middle of nowhere and risking life and limb to convey one's message, possibly waking a vampire who'd gotten bored and decided to sleep for a year or two. She'd heard stories from her father about them. A tremble ran through her as if the ground beneath her feet were shaking.

Hastily, she returned the book to the shelf. Law or no law, she would never report Tobias to the Forebears or anyone else. She'd go to her grave protecting him. Once she was master, if any vampire suggested even an inkling of suspicion about what he was, she'd squash the idea immediately, even if she had to threaten, imprison, or kill them to do it. It was part of the reason she'd decided she must become master. There was no other way to protect him and his family but to rule.

It was the only way to deal with this mess. Tomorrow, when they met at the zoo, would be the last time she'd speak to him. She'd explain the situation and say her goodbyes. And then she would watch over him from afar, using her pull as master to keep him safe. It was the only way to keep him out of harm's way and ensure he could continue to do what he'd been born to do—cure sick children.

She checked that everything in the room was exactly as it was when she came in and then returned to the sitting room, drawing her notebook from her pocket and beginning to sketch. Her father emerged from his bedroom a few moments later, dressed in only a robe.

"Sabrina, I didn't know you were stopping by."

She held up the notebook. "Sketching my new digs. I

have a question about your office. Are you leaving the books?"

"No. I'll be taking my personal library with me. Some have sentimental value. I can have copies made if you like."

"Please. They would be invaluable."

There was a knock at the door and her father crossed the room to open it. Sabrina watched a gorgeous human woman sashay into the room, her curves straining a low-cut red dress.

"Will you be joining me for breakfast?" her father asked.

Sabrina fidgeted when the dark-haired beauty met her eyes and pulled her hair off her neck. "I can feed two, if you want some. As long as you don't take too much."

Her father stared at the pulse under the human's pale skin, his fangs elongating slowly. This was natural vampire behavior, but the feeling in her stomach wasn't hunger. The room felt too hot suddenly. She got to her feet and strode toward the door.

"I already ate." Her eyes flicked to her father. "I'll be in the Star once you've fed."

He didn't respond to her. He couldn't speak around his fangs. Instead, he struck, sinking his teeth into his willing victim.

Sabrina slipped out the door, leaving her father to finish his meal.

CHAPTER SEVENTEEN

The day was sunny. Cold, snow-covered, but sunny. It was amazing what a difference a blue sky made. It might be thirty degrees outside, but with no wind and the bright rays baking his face, Tobias thought he could sense spring on the horizon like a song in the distance that was growing closer.

Sabrina arrived then, in front of the polar bear exhibit, her hood up, sheltering her face from view and also from the sun, he supposed. He'd seen her outside during the day before. Now he wondered if those times had been uncomfortable for her.

"Should we go inside?" he asked, glancing toward the nearest building.

"No. It's safer here. The sun makes me weak, but it will kill other members of my coven, and there's no place for a human spy to hide." She looked around at the abandoned walkways and leaned up against the polar bear enclosure.

Tobias understood. It was noon on a Friday but cold for humans. They might have been the only ones at the zoo by the looks of things.

"Tell me what's going on, Sabrina. Please." He tried to keep his voice neutral, but emotion slipped through despite his best efforts.

"My coven is called Lamia. I don't know if I told you that before." She shrugged in her puffy coat. "You should probably know that. It's the largest coven in North America."

"The largest..." He couldn't keep the surprise from his voice.

"Next weekend, I'll take over as master. I had to resign because it's a full-time job leading a coven of that size. I can't be a nurse and a master."

"No?"

"No. And I sold my place. I'm moving into the tunnels after my coronation."

"The tunnels?"

"My coven lives in a network of tunnels under the city. It's important that I'm there for them, that I'm one of them." Her voice trailed off.

"It doesn't sound like this is something you want to do. You love being a nurse, Sabrina. You love the daylight. You have a life. Are you sure you want to do this?"

Her chest expanded, and he heard a rush of breath flow from under the hood. "I am, Tobias. I... I feel this is something I have to do, not just for them but for us."

"How could this possibly be for us?"

"I've been groomed for this since I was born. My father made sure the coven feared me so that my human side would never be questioned. This is my crown to take up. Once I rise, I'll have the power to make sure the coven leaves you and your family alone. If I don't do it, Tristan will. I can't give the coven any reason to doubt me before my coronation."

"Because Tristan will use anything he can against you."

"You were right about him. He was having me followed."

His eyebrows shot up.

"After our conversation in the cafeteria, I noticed a face in the crowd. A human. Someone who ordinarily I would never notice. But I noticed him when I was leaving work, and then again, later in the day when I was shopping on Michigan Avenue. I intentionally bumped into him. Easy enough; humans are dreadfully slow. Once I had him in my grip, I compelled him to tell me the truth. You were right— he'd been following me and reporting back to Tristan on the regular."

"And is this spy now at the bottom of Lake Michigan?" It made Tobias's skin crawl to think Sabrina had been followed this entire time.

She laughed. "No. Instead of breaking his neck, I decided to leave him to do what he was sent to do. Then I avoided you and focused all my time on coven business. Let the man report my virtuous vampire behavior. It was as close to a *fuck you* as I'm going to get until I become master."

"That's why you've been so distant?"

"Yes." She shook her head. "Nothing has changed. I want to be with you, Tobias. I wouldn't have avoided you if it wasn't absolutely necessary. There's no reason we can't be friends once I become master, as long as no one suspects you're not human."

"Friends." He didn't like the sound of that.

"And more, eventually. If we're careful." She moved her hood back on her head, and her eyes sparkled in the light. "Our coven has ties to everything in this city, things you see and things you don't see. We live under the surface, pulling the strings. We can either be a force for good or a force for evil. If I become master, I make sure the coven stays a force for good. In time, I'll be able to carve out a safe place for us."

"In time..."

"It's the only way."

"So, the only future you can see for us is one where we sneak around, surviving on stolen moments?"

She laughed sadly under her breath. "There's something else I have to tell you. If any vampire finds out what you are, they're supposed to immediately report you to the Forebears, the council of ancients that oversees all vampires. Vampires hate shifters, and dragons are thought to be extinct. If they learn what you are, Tobias, they will see you as a threat and they will want you and your family dead."

Tobias ground his teeth, the news of Scoria's arrival dancing through his head. "Wanting my family dead seems to be an epidemic lately."

"Who else wants your family dead?"

He waved a hand dismissively. He refused to worry her about anything else. "I'll wait for you, Sabrina. Forever if I have to."

He didn't miss the tears that formed in her eyes. "It already seems like forever."

"There's something you should know," he said. "I tracked the werewolf who stabbed you. He's left the city."

"Are you sure?"

"Positive. We know he had help. Someone got him out of the city. But he's gone."

"If Tristan was working with him, the men he has following me know nothing about it. I compelled them to within an inch of their lives—they told me everything."

A gust of wind blew between them, and Sabrina hugged herself against the chill. He took a step toward her, wanting to share his natural heat. She didn't back away. "In my life-time, I've been flung across the universe, ridden a ship across the Atlantic to come to the New World, and trekked the wilderness with an indigenous guide to settle in Chicago. My life has not been easy, Sabrina, and that's not even scratching the surface of what I've endured on this planet alone. I've never met anyone quite like you, and I thought maybe I could love you. That's a hard thing too. To be so close to something you thought you might never have, to briefly feel the warmth of the sun on your face and then have it snatched away."

"Oh Tobias...." He smelled her tears on the wind.

"I can wait for you, but I don't want to." A growl rumbled in his chest, and the polar bear darted deeper into his habitat.

She sighed. "You come from a different world... Paragon, right?"

"Yes."

"So, if you had the opportunity to be the leader your people needed, to go back home and fix whatever went wrong that made you escape to this world, wouldn't you do it? I know it's hard for you to put yourself in my shoes. You weren't raised to be royalty. But I have to do this, for so many reasons. I owe it to my people."

He stilled. He'd never told Sabrina he was Paragonian royalty. Who was he kidding? He barely qualified. As third in line, he had never had a chance of sitting on the throne and never would. It wasn't even worth mentioning. "I think I get where you're coming from. I just wanted you to know how I feel."

She paused and looked down at her gloved fingers. "So, how did you cure Katelyn?"

"I used a magical healing amulet that my brother recovered from our Native American guide, Maiara. I helped Gabriel with something in exchange for it. I tried to use it to heal you too, but it didn't work."

"I remember. I saw it. White and iridescent."

"Yes."

"You told Katelyn it was a mermaid scale." She laughed.

"That was actually her hypothesis. I just didn't tell her she was wrong." He gave her a wry grin.

"You know if you ever use it again, people will suspect you. One little girl is explainable. More and the coven will grow suspicious."

"I know. It's locked away now. It was a onetime thing."

They stared at each other in the cold, bright sun, and he thought at the right angle her skin looked translucent, like she was carved from ice. He squelched the desire to take her into his arms and watch her melt in the heat of his embrace.

"I am sorry it has to be this way," she said, her voice breaking. When she spoke again, he could hardly hear her. "I felt it too, the warmth, almost like I'd found something I never knew I'd lost. But that's not how the world works. Life isn't about our happiness, is it? It's about survival and expectations and doing the right thing even when it's difficult."

He stepped in closer to her, the saline scent of her tears filling his nose. "World be damned." In one motion, he brushed her hood back, braced his hand on the back of her neck, and kissed her. It was not a gentle kiss. It was filled with longing and passion and need. He was a boy staring at the moon, knowing his feet would never leave the ground.

Only they did. One moment he was kissing her in the zoo and the next his molecules had broken apart and were traveling over the city at her command.

Sabrina re-formed in Tobias's bedroom and toppled into his arms. Dematerializing during the day was mentally and physically draining, but she'd had to get out of there. As abandoned as the zoo seemed and as much as she'd taken precautions by sending her human shadow on a wild-goose chase in advance, someone might have been watching. And while she should have stopped kissing Tobias and pulled away, she couldn't bring herself to do so.

"Whoa," he said, catching her in his arms. "You shouldn't have done that. Not during the day." His eyes darted around the room.

"No shit." Her eyelashes fluttered. "Couldn't stay. Someone might see."

She leaned heavily into his chest and he rearranged her in his arms. He was still wearing his winter coat, a heavy, camel-colored cashmere, soft and cool beneath her cheek.

"I'll be fine in a minute," she said.

He held her tighter. "Take your time. You're safe here. Raven has wards around the place."

"I'm surprised I got through."

"They only keep out those with malicious intent. You must not want to kill me."

"Not at the moment." Her eyes drifted to his lips.

She blinked. The bed was made. Everything in its place. Same Tobias. "Did I tell you the last time I was here that this room is exactly what I expected it would be?"

"What does that mean?" Tobias laughed. "What did you expect?"

"It's... meticulous. Like when you do surgery. Everything in a row. Neat. Orderly. Thought out for practicality. Just like everything else in your life."

"My bedroom is meticulous?" The corner of his mouth twitched.

"Impeccably made bed, white walls, shiny dark wood, clean lines, not a speck of dust on any of the furniture..."

"I like things clean."

"You like things perfect." She straightened and took a step back from him. "I'm not perfect, Tobias. I never will be. Right now my world is a mess. I'm being followed, forced to quit my job, made to live underground and lead a coven of vampires." She swayed on her feet and took a deep, cleansing breath as the tears threatened to come.

"You're perfect to me." Tugging off his hat and gloves, Tobias stripped out of his coat and reached for hers. She let him remove her it as if she were a child.

"I shouldn't be here right now." Pulling off her hat, she ran her hands through her flattened hair and tried not notice the way his biceps stretched the sleeves of his white dress shirt. She failed miserably. The open collar revealed a deep recess between his neck and collarbone, the muscles of his chest and neck pronounced enough in that small window to cause her insides to turn electric and alive. With his coat off, his heady cinnamon-almond scent pervaded her senses.

"I might as well tell you, Raven warded your place as well."

"I thought I told you not to do that."

"I didn't do it; Raven did."

She gave him a withering look.

"I'm sorry to go against your wishes, but I couldn't leave you unprotected." He shook his head. "It was enough of a burden to leave you alone. It would have broken my heart if something happened to you."

"You're forgiven." She meant it. In truth, she was relieved to hear he'd done it. With the Realtor showing her apartment to strangers throughout the day, she'd been worried Tristan or someone else would leave her a booby trap.

"Are you still drained?" he asked. "You can feed on me."

"No. I'm fine." His blond hair was mussed and her fingers itched to right its silky strands. She wanted to curl against his side, caress the hard muscles of his chest and stomach. She wanted him. The hyperfocused attention of his sapphire-blue eyes, the feel of his body, his energy, over her. Over her, yes that's how she wanted him. She didn't want to think, just feel. She wanted him in control.

It was a revelation to feel this way. Her entire life, her father had trained her to be a predator, a killer, a ruthless leader, but as she looked at Tobias, all she wanted to be was *his*. Even if it was for one night. She wanted to hand everything over to him and let go.

"Sabrina, please don't cry. What is it? What do you want?"

She wiped under her eyes. "I want you," she said. "So bad it hurts."

His eyes widened and his nostrils flared. "Then be mine."

"Yours? What does that even mean?"

"It means, whatever else you are—a nurse, a master, a human, a vampire—that you're mine too. Give yourself to me."

She shook her head and backed away a step. "How am I supposed to do that? Think about what you are asking. In a matter of days, I will be master. The coven will own me until I can get a support system in place that I can trust. I am not my own. How can I give you something that isn't mine to give?"

His gaze transfixed her, his eyes fathomless pits of

sapphire that drew her in. "Whatever you give me, Sabrina, it will be enough. You are enough for me."

"The only thing I can give you is tonight. I can't promise you more." Her voice was shaking.

"There's a saying where I come from: dragons do not mate lightly. I can give you tonight and I can set you free tomorrow, but you should know I will never be free of you. I can't go halfway into this."

"You're not bound to me." She said it because she feared it. The vampire bond rose within her and she pushed it down deeper. She could do this, couldn't she? Just have sex. Nothing more.

"I will be. You must know I've fallen in love with you." The words hit her like bullets, straight to the heart.

He was so close now she could feel his warmth. "I love you too." She was breathless, spinning, weightless, falling.

Sabrina knew she couldn't give him what he was asking for, not really. Whatever happened between them now, it would be a onetime thing. She'd have to devote herself to the coven. Still, everything in her wanted him. His energy had fed her, but the gnawing inside her now was a different type of hunger, one that she couldn't deny.

Rushing into his arms, she dug her fingers into his shirt and tore, sending buttons flying. She crashed into him with every bit of passion she'd kept restrained these past weeks. To be a vampire was to notice everything. Her mouth warred with his, a clash of velvet tongues and hard, demanding lips. Eyes closed, she reveled in his intoxicating scent, the bouquet of his blood pulsing beneath his skin. The beat of his heart quickened in her ears. Her fingers traveled over the peaks and valleys of his chest and stomach.

Damn, he was a piece of art, all corded muscle and long, lean limbs. Her hands found his belt and then his fly. And when she lowered his briefs, the magnificent length between his legs made her hiss. It jutted toward her, long and proud, making her instantly wet between her legs. When his touch skimmed the waistband of her pants, she thought the brush of his fingers against her belly might make her combust.

"Be mine, Sabrina," he said again. The low purr had started in his chest again, a pleasant buzz that did wild things to her insides. She inhaled deeply, the scent of his arousal mingling with hers in the air.

"I want you in me." She pressed herself fully against him. His skin was hot now, like he'd stood too close to an open flame. She panted with need.

He grabbed her by the shoulders and backed her against his dresser. "Say you are mine. I need to hear it."

She was. She knew she was. Her vampire side was pounding on her inner doors, begging for her to let go, to drown in this love he was pouring over her. It broke her heart to see him tremble. Could she throw out the lasso of her bond and tie him to her forever?

His fingers found the hem of her shirt and hoisted it over her head. For a second she was embarrassed to remember that the bra she was wearing was nothing special, old and white. He didn't notice. It was off her in the next breath. His hand cupped her breast, bolstering it as he bent to take her nipple into his mouth. The hot feel of his tongue on her flesh made her toss her head back and moan.

"You're mine." Possessive was the only word for the look he gave her, his hooded eyes slowly scanning every inch of her exposed skin.

She could fight it no longer. "Yes," she gasped. "I'm yours."

CHAPTER EIGHTEEN

Tobias understood that when Sabrina said yes, she meant yes for tonight. She'd told him as much. Her first priority was her coven. He wanted more than tonight. He wanted forever, and forever between two immortals was a very long time.

"I'm yours."

Her words echoed in his head. On some level, it would be wise to stop, to push her away. But he couldn't bring himself to follow his own sage advice no matter the consequences.

Once he took her to bed, there would be no escaping a strong and permanent bond to her, and if she did not share that bond, it could drive him insane. It had happened to his brother. He'd mated with their guide, the healer Maiara, before a rival tribe had murdered her in 1700. He'd gone insane after she died. To this day, Tobias had no idea what had become of him, although he'd heard rumors that he lived like an animal in the caves of Sedona.

Would that happen to him? If Sabrina left him, would he recede from the world and become something that couldn't possibly be mistaken for human? He feared losing his mind, but as he looked at Sabrina, he was helpless to deny himself.

He drew back and stared at her in all her naked glory. No makeup, yet her prominent cheekbones carried a well-fed blush and the bright green of her eyes needed no embellishment. Her silky hair fell in soft red waves around her shoulders. Her torso was long and lean with graceful limbs and creamy skin that reminded him of milky glass. Her wounds had completely healed, and her sex... He swallowed. By the Mountain, her sex was smooth, hairless.

"It's a vampire thing," she said. "Something about our biology."

"You're beautiful. Every part of you."

Her gaze raked over his body. "What about you? How are dragons... different?"

"Well, I don't have the fangs of a vampire."

She laughed, her cheeks darkening with her subtle blush. "You know what I mean."

Anxiety twanged behind his breastbone, and he swallowed hard against it. He was a dragon and a male. He'd lost his virginity centuries ago while he was still in Paragon. He'd had other women since then, human women, only all those times he'd kept his true nature hidden. He didn't have to do that with her.

"There is one thing."

Without a word, she lowered her chin, her eyes twinkling in silent encouragement.

He tightened the extra muscles in his abs, surprised they still worked after centuries of disuse. Long-dormant muscles between hip and deltoid stretched to life. It felt good, as did the unraveling of his wings from his back. He extended them above his shoulders, scraping the ceiling before folding them again behind him.

Sabrina's green eyes turned wide and wet, her mouth gaping. Did she find him grotesque? Would she run from the room? Had he frightened her?

"I can put them back. Just give me a minute. It's been a long ti—"

"Don't you dare." She moved closer.

Wrapping her arms around his neck, she pressed her breasts deliciously into his chest. Her skin was cooler than his own, and the doctor in him wondered if her core temperature was always on the cool side. Then her lips met his and he stopped thinking altogether. Her mouth was a wonderland and he explored every corner, staking his claim as his fingers traced delicious patterns over the soft skin of her back. Muscle shifted beneath his touch. She straddled his leg and reached for his right wing. Her nails tickled delightfully along the underside and the feeling flooded his body with heat and made his cock twitch. He looked at her through his lashes and stretched the wing to give her better access. She stroked him again.

"When you shifted in the museum, I couldn't see you very well. I was lying at an angle and in excruciating pain. But I remember this color. Your scales are like moonlight on freshly fallen snow. There's a blue tint. Like your ring."

"I've rarely studied my full reflection as a dragon, of course—when I shift, my dragon self has other priorities— but in my home in Paragon, the floors of the palace where I used to play were made of polished obsidian, and I remember..." He looked at her. "What's wrong?"

She'd backed away and crossed her arms over her chest. "You played in a palace as a child?"

"Yes..."

"I have so many questions." Her fingers stroked along the edge of his wing, and he closed his eyes. "What is that sound?" she asked. "It's heavenly. Almost like a purr."

"Mating trill. It's a dragon thing. It's supposed to draw you to me. Is it working?"

"Oh yes." Her lips were on his again, and all that was left happening in his brain was a carnal need to be inside her. Lucky him, she must have felt the same way considering how her mouth and vampire strength were pulling him against her. And then her hand worked between them and palmed his length.

He hissed. "By the Mountain, Sabrina, I won't last long if you keep that up."

When she pulled back to look at him, her fangs had dropped. "Good. I think we've waited long enough."

One beat of his wings and her back was against the wall. Her arms wrapped around his neck, her legs lifting to hook over his hips in one fluid movement. It was as if she could read his mind.

"I can feel your emotions," she said into his mouth. He gave her room to speak. "My human side, the side that feeds on energy, can also read it like the written page. Your desire for me is... oh God...."

"I need you, Sabrina. Like a bird needs the sky." His voice cracked.

"Then take me."

He repositioned himself and entered her slowly, her tight flesh gripping his own. He had to measure his breaths to keep from finishing before they started. Supporting her weight, he pulled out partway and slammed into her again, pleasure riding him like an animal.

"Oh," she growled out, in a gritty, sultry voice that made his blood sing. Her head tipped back. "I see now how dragons are different." And then her hips were moving, fast. By the Mountain, he'd never had sex like this. A human couldn't move like this. He felt himself nearing the brink and tried to slow down, to make it last longer.

She dug her nails into his scalp. "Now. Don't stop. Don't you stop."

He thrust into her, her back slamming hard into the wall as the force of her release collided with his. Lightning-hot intensity coursed through him again and again until all he saw was light and all he felt was the grip of her soft, cool flesh asking him for more.

And so he gave her everything.

❦

SHE WOULD NEVER FORGET THE WINGS. NO MATTER what happened tomorrow, Sabrina would dream about those breathtaking silver wings working over her until the day she died. She had plenty of material for her dream world. They'd made love at least four times last night. She lay next to him now, face-to-face, his fingers stroking back and forth over the curve of her spine even though his eyes were closed and his breath was even.

The feeling was mutual. She'd drifted in and out of sleep, waking only to burrow closer to him. Thankfully, it was Saturday morning. Watery light sifted through the window. The sun was rising. The coven would be under-ground by now and she hadn't closed on her apartment, so they wouldn't be expecting her. Not yet anyway. Plus she'd quit her job, so she didn't have to work. She had a few hours before she had to go.

"Tobias?"

"Hmm."

"I don't mean to wake you, but it's almost six. Do you have to work today?"

"No. Took off." One sapphire-blue eye blinked open.

"You did?" She smiled wide enough to show her back teeth.

"Don't get too excited. I promised to give my brother and Raven the full Chicago Saint Patrick's Day experience. We're going to view the green river, watch the parade, and have corned beef and cabbage at the Curragh."

She sighed and lifted onto her elbows. "I'm overseeing the process. It's witchcraft, you know. Vampires have a hand in all the unions. We provide the materials to make this happen. I'm not sure what's in the bulk of it, but it's magic that turns the orange powder to fluorescent green. We have a witch from Edgewater on our payroll who does it every year."

"Madam Chloe?" Tobias asked.

"Yes. The one and only." Sabrina stopped short. Tobias was grinning up at her like he'd just found the toy at the bottom of the cereal box. "What's that look for?"

"Your cheeks are pink."

Tobias was responsible for her flush. She'd fed on his energy all night long. "I guess being with you literally warms my heart."

His strong, sinewy arm scooped her against his chest. "When will I see you again?"

Her smile faded. "I don't know. We need to be careful. My coronation is a week from today. Tristan will be doing everything in his power to undermine me. We need to stay apart until then. Don't call attention to yourself. If he doesn't know about you, he can't use you to get to me."

He rolled her onto her back and settled between her

knees, burying his nose in her hair and inhaling deeply. Her pulse began to race again.

"A week, huh? I waited a lifetime for you. I suppose I can wait a little longer."

She pressed her lips against his. "Once I'm master, I'll figure out a way for us to see each other. My father has dozens of secret rooms and passageways throughout this city. We'll find a way to be together. All you have to do is keep these"—she stroked his wings—"tucked away for my pleasure. As far as my coven is concerned, you'll be one of my human staff. They'll never suspect a thing."

He bit her bottom lip gently. "Are you saying you'll sell me as your walking blood bag?"

Her expression turned serious. "I think it's the only way."

There was a long silence as Tobias rolled onto his back and rested his head in a nest of his fingers. He looked up at the ceiling. "I wish it were different, but I'll take what I can get."

She rolled on top of him, spreading her knees and sinking into him. She feathered her lips against his. He answered with a long, languorous kiss.

When he finished, he asked, "But... are you excited about becoming coven master? Every time you talk about it, you get this look on your face. Sometimes I think you're going to cry."

She rubbed sleep from her eyes and tried to answer honestly. "I think anyone might feel overwhelmed. Since I was a child, I've been groomed to take over. I'm ready. Of course I'm ready. It just came on suddenly."

"But you love being a nurse. It's your calling. Aren't you sad you have to give that up?"

"Yes. Life is like that though—we don't always get what

we want. Or maybe it's that we have to choose between the things we want. I want to be a strong leader for my coven. I also don't want to change anything about my life. I can't have both."

"Is this where you quote Voltaire and say 'With great power comes great responsibility'?"

"Power is more of a cross to bear than most people understand. This is my fate. It is who I am, and it is who I will be. You need to know that."

A shadow passed through his expression. "I think I understand."

"But?"

"I was just thinking you're a healer, like me. You prefer feeding on energy instead of blood because you don't want to hurt anyone. Although you've been trained not to react to it, you gain no pleasure from violence. When we were in the museum, you sacrificed yourself and took a knife to the chest rather than hurt a sworn enemy."

"So?"

He stroked her hair. "You are a kind, gentle, and selfless woman. You can force yourself to be a brutal mob boss like your father, but will you be happy? I want you to be happy."

A long silence passed between them, and Sabrina's head was flooded with the shaman's words. *You will never be like them.* She frowned. Her voice sounded small when she answered him. "I guess we're going to find out."

His arms wrapped around her and she rested her cheek on his chest, enjoying the simple comfort. "All great leaders lead reluctantly. It wouldn't be normal for this to be easy for me. I'll have to change. My father didn't have it all figured out when he took the helm, but he rose to the occasion."

She felt him kiss the top of her head. "You are like no other woman I've ever met. If anyone can do this, it's you."

Pushing herself up, she rubbed her body against the length of him. The way he looked at her made her feel like a goddess. Like she could do anything.

"A week, huh?" he said.

Lowering her forehead to his, she reached between them. He was ready. She slid herself down until he was inside her again. "Let's say goodbye in a way that will last."

CHAPTER NINETEEN

The truth rarely received a warm welcome. To some, it cracked across the cheek like a slap. To others, truth's knock was ignored like an unrecognized stranger's. Tobias had underestimated Sabrina. Yes, she was sad to leave her human life behind, but he'd seen something else in her today. When it came to her people, she was fiercely loyal and willing to sacrifice her own happiness for them.

He pondered that and more as he, Gabriel, and Raven neared the east side of the Michigan Avenue Bridge.

"Gabriel, look!" Raven pointed at the water beyond the railing, dyed bright green for the occasion. "It matches your ring."

It *was* shocking the first time you saw it. The Chicago plumbers' union had been dyeing the river green since 1962. He used to come watch the boats spread the dye every year until questions regarding the environmental friendliness of the coloring caused him to lose his enthusiasm over it. Now that he knew Sabrina and her coven were behind it and that it was magic, not chemicals, he took it in with a whole new appreciation. And Raven's excitement was infectious.

"How do they do it?" Gabriel asked.

"Witchcraft," Tobias said.

Raven paused among the crowd to look at him as if he might be joking.

"The same one you visited for the cure," Tobias said, intentionally cryptic.

"Madam Chloe?" Raven looked delighted.

Tobias pressed a finger over his lips. "Top secret."

The sidewalk was crowded and Raven gripped the brown railing and stared out over the winding green river. "Sabrina's certainly concerned about keeping us all a secret, isn't she?"

Tobias winced at her harsh tone. That was unlike Raven. "She has her reasons. It's okay."

"Okay? Is it really okay that her coven thinks it's better than everyone else? It sounds to me like she's an ungrateful, self-centered bitch."

Tobias held up his hands. He'd never seen Raven act like this before. "Chill—there's no need for insults. Let's go back to the house and talk this out." Tobias could hardly believe his ears or the way the air around them began to crackle with Raven's ire.

He glanced at Gabriel whose mouth was hanging open in shock. His brother gave him a half shrug and then placed a hand on his mate's back. "Raven?"

Raven's face was bright red and covered in a sheen of sweat.

"Gabriel, what's wrong with her?" Tobias muttered but his brother just shook his head.

"I saved her life." Raven pointed her finger at Tobias's chest. "I warded her home to keep her safe. We are here hiding from an assassin, and I still found enough compassion to put my neck out for her, and she thinks we're lesser than her stupid vampires? I don't think so!"

Tobias reacted, trying to cover Raven's mouth. "Raven, stop!"

An electric shock blew him back a step.

Gabriel's expression tightened as purple fireworks zinged off Raven's exposed skin and popped in the air around them. He looked as perplexed at Raven's sudden bout of rage as Tobias.

"Perhaps Tobias is right. We should continue this conversation in private," Gabriel murmured.

"Perhaps I should end this right now." Raven raised her ring. It glowed like a star between them. She focused on Tobias, her entire body shaking.

Tobias held up his hands. "Whoa, whoa, whoa... Where did that come from? Let's all take a beat and talk about this civilly." His eyes drifted to the crowd around them. Thankfully, no one seemed to be paying much attention to their quarrel. This was Chicago on Saint Patrick's Day. The crowd was already getting rowdy.

Raven pitched forward, her body undulating.

Gabriel's eyes went wide. "Raven, are you okay? You look like you're going to be sick."

The witch hurled. Tobias watched in horror as vomit spewed from Raven's mouth in a color that almost matched the green river. But the sick seemed to make Raven's magic tantrum worse. Flashes of light popped and spiraled in the air around her, and light shimmied across her slick skin in waves.

"Gabriel, what's happening to me?" Raven's eyes rolled back in her head and she collapsed.

Gabriel caught her unconscious body and pulled her

into his arms. The crowd pointed and murmured to each other. That was going to be a bitch to deal with if it ended up on video. Sparks of purple and emerald-green magic zinged off Raven's skin like it was the Fourth of July.

Suddenly, a familiar face pushed through the crowd and grabbed his shoulder. Sabrina, and she was furious. "You have to get her out of here, Tobias. She's drawing too much attention."

He gave her a nod and turned toward the crowd, smiling and spreading his hands. "Happy Saint Paddy's Day, everyone!" Tobias clapped twice and waved his fingers. "We're a performance art troupe from Columbia. Looks like someone drank too much green beer." He waved a hand at his brother and Raven. "Enjoy your morning."

Sabrina helped clear a path as they navigated the crowded walkway. By the time they reached the street, Sabrina had already hailed a taxi.

"I'll take her to my office. I need to examine her. She's sick," Tobias said to her.

"Just get her out of here." They climbed in and Sabrina slammed the door behind them.

CHAPTER TWENTY

A short Uber later and they entered the austere surroundings of his medical office building across from the hospital. Thank the Mountain Tobias didn't have office hours today. Gabriel ushered Raven into the elevator. She was awake now but still flushed.

"It's so hot." She tugged at the collar of her coat.

"Has anything like this ever happened before?" Tobias asked.

The two looked at each other. "When I first came into my magic, symbols used to glow along my skin anytime Gabriel touched me, but they went away after I absorbed the magic of my ancestors. I've never had anything like this."

Tobias unlocked the door to his medical office and ushered them both inside to an exam room. "Put her on the table."

There was a tornado of dark smoke and Sabrina appeared beside him. "What the hell is going on, Tobias? Do you know how many people saw the human fireworks show today?"

Tobias turned to her, "She's sick, Sabrina. Something's wrong. Really wrong."

Sabrina took one look at Raven and snapped into nurse mode. She grabbed Tobias's stethoscope from his neck.

"Get her out of that coat, Gabriel," Tobias said.

Sabrina started taking Raven's vitals. "Her blood pressure is high, and so is her temp. Really high. One hundred and three."

Tobias frowned. "We can add that to puking fluorescent green and sending off magic sparks." He pulled out his penlight and started examining her.

"Ugh. I feel terrible," Raven said.

Gabriel rushed from the office and returned with a plastic cup Tobias recognized as coming from his waiting room. "Try to drink something."

"What have you had to eat today?" Tobias asked. "Maybe it's food poisoning."

"Fluorescent food poisoning?" Sabrina spread her hands.

"I didn't eat *anything*. I haven't felt good in the mornings lately, so I've been skipping breakfast."

Tobias stared at Raven, assessing her overall condition, then felt a cold suspicion worm up through his gut. When Sabrina's eyes met his, he knew she suspected it too. "Gabriel, my personal office is the second door on the right. There are packets of peanut butter crackers in the top drawer of my desk."

As soon as Gabriel had left the room, Tobias addressed Raven directly. "We need to talk."

"Why? What's going on?" Raven asked. "Tobias, after everything that's happened today, just give it to me straight. I can't take much more of this."

"I, uh, I was just wondering... you said you were sick in

the mornings." Tobias swallowed hard. "And I know you thought you were barren, but... could you be pregnant?"

❧

"Pregnant?" Raven said breathlessly. "No. I can't be. I mean I really can't be. Remember the chemotherapy? My eggs are fried." She ran a hand over the swollen mound of her abdomen. Sure, she'd been a little bloated lately and hungry all the time, but she couldn't be pregnant.

Her mind raced back to Crimson's temple, to the fertility ritual the voodoo queen had forced her to participate in. The bright white lines of the circle came back to her, the offerings of fruit and eggs. Gabriel had made love to her in the center of that spell—a quick animalistic coupling they'd been helpless to resist—to save their lives. It couldn't have worked, could it?

Today was the seventeenth of March. The spell had taken place on Mardi Gras, February thirteenth. About five weeks. Wasn't that too early to be having symptoms?

"What's going on?" Gabriel asked, charging into the room with a handful of peanut butter cracker snacks. She reached out and plucked one from his grip.

"We were wondering if Raven's nausea might be due to pregnancy," Tobias stated.

"I told him it was impossible. I'm barren. Dr. Freemont told me that the chemotherapy I was on had completely destroyed the functioning of my ovaries. I haven't had a period in years."

Gabriel's face turned stony, his eyes flicking down to her abdomen. "Impossible in human terms."

"Brother, is there something you need to tell me?"

"Raven and I were forced to take part in a voodoo queen's fertility spell," Gabriel murmured.

"But she's dead," Raven added quickly. "I killed her. And come on, a spell can only do so much. Right? Right?"

"You need to test her," Sabrina said.

Raven had almost forgotten the vampire was there. She was right beside her, her hand very close to hers on the examination table. Close but not touching, as if she wanted to be there for Raven but not overstep her bounds.

"I'm a pediatric cardiologist. I don't have pregnancy tests in the office."

"But you do have an ultrasound machine," Sabrina said.

"An ultrasound!" Raven protested. "This is ridiculous. I can't be pregnant. I can't be."

Gabriel exchanged a look with Tobias that Raven couldn't read.

"Let's give it a go," Tobias said. "We'll prove you're not pregnant, and I can check out your other organs while I'm at it."

Raven didn't feel like herself. Her skin was hot. A headache pulsed at her temple. She had an urge to tell Tobias to go to hell and leave her alone.

"Raven, please," Gabriel said. He looked concerned.

"Okay," she said reluctantly.

"Come this way. I'll show you to the room." Tobias helped her off the examination table and led her to the ultrasound room where he left her and Gabriel so that she could change into a paper gown.

"Honestly, Gabriel. I'm feeling fine now." She fought to make her voice chipper. "This is entirely unnecessary. We're missing the parade."

Gabriel folded her clothes and stacked them on a chair. "Might as well let Tobias get it out of his system. He's a healer. He won't feel right until he knows exactly what's going on."

"I'm just so angry. Everything is pissing me off." She held up the peanut butter cracker she was eating. "Why do they use crumbly crackers in these things? We can send a man to the moon but can't make a cracker that doesn't go everywhere when you eat it?" She scootched back on the table, patting down the paper gown with more gusto than necessary,

A scowl flattened her mate's mouth. "We will figure this out. Tobias will know what to do. He's very smart."

"Then what is he doing with Sabrina? I put our lives in danger to save her. She's a vampire mob boss. He knows she wants us out of the city." Raven's ears felt hot, and she had the sudden urge to hit something.

"He said we could stay and she's here, helping him take care of you." Gabriel took a seat beside the examination table and took her hand.

"But it's the principle. Doesn't anyone else see that it's the principle of the thing that these vampires think they own the city?" She shoved another cracker into her mouth.

Gabriel cleared his throat. "Don't take this the wrong way, Raven, but it seems unlike you to carry this much anger over something like this. You are usually the one tempering *my* anger."

"I'm consumed with it. I can't remember ever feeling like this before." She rubbed her temples. "I must be sick. It must be the illness."

A knock came on the door, and Tobias entered with Sabrina at his side. They were both wearing gloves. Gabriel's hand came to rest on her shoulder. She leaned back and stared at the ceiling. After a few minutes of machine adjustments, Sabrina squirted a glob of lube on Raven's lower belly and applied the wand to her skin.

"It might be too early to see anything this way. Normally with early pregnancy we do an internal ultrasound, but Tobias doesn't have the right equipment for that," Sabrina said.

The sound of her voice was sandpaper against Raven's ears. Shit, she needed to get a handle on this. Why was she so angry?

The wand glided under her belly button, curled, and stopped.

She heard Sabrina gasp. "Tobias. Do you see this?"

"What? What is it?" Raven asked.

Tobias replaced Sabrina by her side and his face was as grim as Raven had ever seen it. He reached across her body to turn the screen to face her. A steady, intermittent whooshing sound met her ears. Raven wasn't sure what she was looking at. There was a round white shape inside her abdomen. Beautiful in a way. Oval with a texture like a mound of pearls. It almost looked like... It looked like...

"An egg," Tobias said. "You're carrying a dragon egg."

CHAPTER TWENTY-ONE

O f all the things Tobias had thought might happen today, seeing a dragon egg inside a human uterus was not one of them. He'd believed Raven when she'd said she was barren. There was no reason to think she was lying. Not to mention, the side effects of her chemotherapy were familiar to him. Only, he hadn't considered the magic factor.

First, there was Gabriel's tooth, capable of healing her cancer but also capable of healing the damage caused by the chemotherapy. Second, there was the fertility spell. Tobias wasn't familiar with voodoo, but magic could accomplish strange and mystical things. Even as he looked at the egg, he couldn't wrap his head around what he was seeing. He'd presumed that the copulation of a dragon and a witch would result in a human fetus that might shift into a dragon after it was born. Never had he suspected the young would form in the same way it would if Raven were a dragon.

"Tobias?" Gabriel grabbed his elbow and shook. "What does this mean?"

"It means Raven is pregnant with a dragon." Tobias

repositioned the ultrasound and looked at Gabriel out of the corner of his eye. "Congratulations, brother, you've accomplished the most forbidden act of our species."

Gabriel shook his head. "No. No. Not an egg. She has a human body. We have to get it out."

"Get it out?" Raven sat up, wiping the lube from her belly with a wad of tissues from the box next to the monitor. "You aren't touching my baby. Neither of you."

"You don't understand, Raven. It's a dragon." Gabriel spread his hands as if what he was saying was obvious.

"Dragons lay eggs and then keep them warm until they hatch. You don't have a dragon's body. The egg will be too big and intractable to pass through your birth canal," Tobias said. He was trying his best to remain clinical and detached, but inside he was reeling. This was bad. So bad. "Chances are you and the youngling will both die if you try to deliver it."

"What a load of crap." Raven's face reddened as she spoke.

Tobias frowned. "No wonder her blood pressure and temperature are raised," he said to Gabriel. "The dragon inside her is heating everything up."

Raven wrapped a hand around her opposite fist and brought it to her forehead. "Here's what we're going to do. We will allow the egg to develop to the typical size and then take it out via cesarean section. Obviously I won't be able to sit on it like I assume a dragon would—"

"Oh, the dragon mother doesn't sit on the eggs. She's not a chicken," Gabriel said with a chuckle. One look from Raven and he sobered up. "Normally the eggs are placed near the heart of the volcano inside the mountain."

Raven ground her teeth. "We'll buy an incubator." She

said the words slowly, and Tobias cringed at the venom in them.

Gabriel stopped talking and turned statue still, staring at the picture on the monitor. A muscle in his neck twitched like it had a life of its own.

Tobias tried his best to explain the dangers to Raven. "A fully formed dragon egg is about the size of human triplets. It might be possible for you to carry it to term, but it won't be comfortable for you, and removing it will require an experienced ob-gyn. Whoever does it will have to understand what he's doing. You will have to introduce a human doctor to dragon physiology." He rubbed his head. "And hope they're crazy enough not to tell our secret."

"*You* can do the surgery," Raven said, looking him directly in the eye. "You're a talented doctor, and we have magic and the healing amulet to use if there's trouble."

"Ooooh, no. I want no part of this." Tobias waved his hands and shook his head. "This would be enough to get us all beheaded if we were in Paragon. It's said that the offspring of a dragon and a witch will have the power to flatten cities. It could be the most powerful supernatural being this world has ever known."

Gabriel's hand shot out and caught his brother by the shoulder. "Folklore. Nothing more. We are not in Paragon, brother, and you owe Raven for saving your girlfriend's life."

"I'm allowing you two to stay under my roof in exchange for that, remember? Debt already paid."

Raven narrowed her eyes and bared her teeth. "Then I guess I'll trust Mother Nature and hope my body knows how to lay this thing when it's time."

"Be reasonable," Tobias said. "Mother Nature didn't do this. Magic did. There is nothing natural about this whelp."

She glared at Tobias as if she could knock him down with a look alone. "Baby. *My* baby."

"Relax. I wasn't being insulting. A whelp is what we call a baby dragon in Paragon," Tobias said. "This could kill you, Raven. What happened today, it won't be the last time. Your human body isn't designed for this."

"I'm willing to take that chance."

Raven turned toward Gabriel, but he was stunned silent. His face had paled to roughly the shade of the paper lining the examination table, and his eyes were far-off and vacant.

"Gabriel?" Tobias cleared his throat. Damn, if this had happened a few weeks ago, he'd have sent both of them packing. But now Tobias found himself staring at the monitor and questioning everything he used to believe. The steady whoosh, whoosh of the whelp's heartbeat replayed in his head and he caught himself growing wistful, wishing things were different, longing for family.

It was Sabrina, he knew, that had changed him. She'd made him accept what he was because she accepted what he was. And accepting his dragon nature meant reconnecting with this, the reality of being a dragon, here and now, in the crazy city of Chicago.

Raven rubbed Gabriel's hands between her own.

Slowly his eyes shifted to meet hers and Tobias watched the corners of his mouth lift upward. His eyes wrinkled at the corners. "We're having a whelp."

"Yes. A baby."

"An heir. A boy... or a girl."

"Yes!" She smiled wider.

"Gabriel?" A chill ran the length of Tobias's spine. He couldn't believe they were actually considering going through with this. Then again, he couldn't imagine doing anything else.

Gabriel embraced Raven, almost lifting her off the table. When he set her down again, Raven's eyes roamed the room behind Tobias.

"What happened to Sabrina?"

Tobias started and spun around. She'd been standing right behind him only a few minutes before. Now Sabrina was gone.

CHAPTER TWENTY-TWO

Tobias left Gabriel and Raven and exited the ultrasound room. "Sabrina?"

"In here."

He found her in his office, her face in her hands. "What's wrong? Have you been crying?"

"I asked you for one thing, Tobias. One thing." Her voice broke. "I asked you to lie low. To not call attention to yourselves."

"You saw the egg. She had no idea. It's not her fault. She's having some kind of reaction to her fetus."

Sabrina's shoulders slumped. "No. It wasn't her fault. It was yours."

Tobias winced. "What are you talking about?"

"You knew it would be safer for them if they left. You knew I was being followed and that this was a delicate time for me... for us! And you put them on display anyway."

"I wasn't planning on having Raven snap, crackle, and pop in front of a crowd, Sabrina. It was a mistake."

"Well, it's a mistake that has consequences."

"What are you trying to say?"

"Madam Chloe saw you. The humans that work for us saw you. We're lucky that it was during the day and the vampires were asleep, but if anyone recorded it..."

"It happened quickly. I didn't see any phones out—"

"It doesn't matter, Tobias. Don't you see that I can't just sweep this one under the rug? I'm going to have to compel every human I can track down to forget they ever saw you there. Madam Chloe can't be compelled. I'll have to put the fear of the goddess into her. If Tristan learns what happened, the coven will tear apart the city looking for her. They will not stop until she's dead."

"I'm sorry," he said. "But it's not like we did this on purpose."

"Tell that to the torches and pitchforks." Sabrina sighed and stuffed her hands in her back pockets. "Raven and Gabriel need to get out of town for a while. And if you were smart, you'd go with them."

"Hey, I'm doing the best I can here," Tobias snapped. "But let's be honest—if it wasn't for your coven's draconian laws, this wouldn't be an issue. You know, you signed up for that. I didn't. I'm staying and so is my family."

"It's not safe!"

"I'm not caving to a maybe threat from an asshole vampire that may or may not know anything about us."

Sabrina shook her head and headed for the door.

"Where are you going?" Tobias asked.

"To try to clean up your mess."

"Wait? Can we talk about this?" Tobias hated to leave things like this. She was angry. Really angry.

She shook her head. "No. You need to give me space. Don't call me. Don't text."

"You don't mean that!"

"It's not safe, Tobias." Sabrina was yelling now. "It's over. It's for the best."

Before he could say another word, she was gone.

☙

DUTY MADE THE WORLD GO ROUND. PEOPLE HAD responsibilities. It was discipline, not desire, that made a community strong. What would the planet be like if everyone followed their whims?

Sabrina had a duty to report Raven to her father and while she was at it, Gabriel and Tobias. She was days away from being elevated to master. It was her responsibility to protect her fellow vampires. Tobias and his family were outsiders in vampire territory. She knew without a doubt now that Raven was dangerous; she'd heard Tobias say that the youngling would be powerful enough to flatten cities.

Only, if she told her coven, the vampires would tear the witch to pieces, and Sabrina couldn't have that. The truth was, she liked Raven. The witch had saved her life. And she knew how much Tobias loved the woman and Gabriel. She loved Tobias. Which was why she had ended it with him.

She'd indulged her love for Tobias long enough. It was time to focus on doing what she had to do to protect him and his family, even if it did break her heart. She'd tracked down every human on their payroll and eradicated any memory they had of Raven, but there was one person left, and convincing her to keep her mouth shut might not be as easy.

She pushed open the door to Bell and Candle and strode into the occult shop like she owned the place. Nothing less than total confidence would get her what she wanted from the witch. Sabrina had to find out how much

Madam Chloe knew about Raven, the dragons, and Sabrina's relationship with them. She'd have no mercy on the witch if she'd told anyone anything.

"May I help you, Princess?" Madam Chloe hobbled out from behind the counter, her crippled arms tucked uselessly against her chest. She did not smile as she scanned Sabrina, her eyes sharply suspicious. "Was the river not what you expected?

"I have questions. Answer me honestly."

"Of course."

"Did you see anything unusual today by the river?" Sabrina's gaze narrowed on the woman.

"If I did, wouldn't I tell you, Princess? No one would dare keep a thing from your coven."

Sabrina coupled her hands behind her back. "That's not an answer. I'll ask again. Did you see anything unusual today? Has another witch been in your shop, not a human practitioner but one with actual power like yourself? Tell me the truth. I will be master soon, and if you are not honest with me now, you will regret it."

"There was one," the witch said softly. "She said she needed help healing a vampire. I provided that help out of loyalty to you and your coven."

"Which vampire?"

"I do not know." Her eyes shifted away.

"Liar."

Madam Chloe raised her eyebrows at Sabrina. "There is only one vampire who might be stabbed during the day in an area of the city where a witch could find and treat her. That vampire is you, Princess."

"Now we're getting somewhere. Honesty is important. So a witch was here and on the bridge today."

"Yes," Madame Chloe agreed reluctantly.

"I need someone I can trust. Can I trust you?"

"Above anyone."

"Then answer me this. Did you tell anyone about the witch or my injury?" Sabrina focused her full attention on Madam Chloe, using her full power to read her emotional spectrum. The witch was nervous and more than a little angry.

Chloe scowled. "You vampires, the games you play."

"What games?"

"I had to tell him something, you know. He knew you'd been stabbed and wanted an explanation of how you'd survived. There are only so many options."

"He, who?"

"Tristan, Princess."

"How did Tristan know I'd been stabbed?"

Chloe closed her eyes and shook her head. "It isn't my place to speculate, but he was rather knowledgeable about the specifics regarding your wound. The exact specifics."

"Please explain."

"The ingredients to make Keetridge Solution haven't been available in the Midwest for decades. My sources say the werewolves haven't had access to it in even longer. The only place one could obtain it around here would be—"

"My coven. We kept some for executions." Sabrina frowned.

"Tristan knew the dagger that stabbed you was soaked in Keetridge Solution. How do you suppose that could be?"

Sabrina growled. So it was true. Tristan didn't just hate her. He wasn't just following her and harassing her. He wanted her dead. She'd previously accepted that Tristan had tipped off the wolf who stabbed her, perhaps hoping to scare her away from becoming master. But this was far worse. What Madam Chloe was saying was that Tristan provided the wolf with the Keetridge Solution that almost killed her. Tristan, with premeditation and full knowledge of what he was doing, had endeavored to have her killed. Not a scare tactic but an attempt at eliminating the competition. She took a deep breath and blew it out.

"What exactly did you tell him?"

"I told him that a woman who might have been a witch came in for an antidote and that I gave one to her. I did not learn her name and my understanding was that she did not call Chicago home. My assumption was that you called her to the city to treat your wound and that she has gone home now."

Everything inside Sabrina worked to parse out the truth of the witch's statement. Her emotional spectrum was neutral, her heart rate steady. Sabrina's nostrils flared as she searched the witch's scent for any hint of untruth, but as far as she could tell, the witch was being perfectly honest.

"Was there anyone with the witch?" she asked softly.

"No," Chloe said immediately.

This time she was lying. Sabrina detected a gamey aftertaste on her emotional palate, and there was a spike in the witch's pulse. All at once, Sabrina understood.

"You liked her," she said softly.

"Yes, I did." Madam Chloe nodded her head.

"Then I will confirm that this lone witch is in fact gone from the area. And what happened today?"

Chloe nodded. "I don't think anything happened today. The humans are wild this time of year. You never know what you'll see."

Sabrina nodded and offered Madame Chloe a warm smile. "I thought so. I'm looking forward to continuing our arrangement and getting to know you better once I'm in power. You are good at what you do."

"Thank you."

Sabrina pivoted and headed for the door.

"There is one more thing I must share with you, Princess," Madam Chloe said.

Sabrina stopped short and turned back toward the witch, waiting for her to continue.

"The night Tristan came asking about you, he asked me for a containment spell, the type your coven has requested before. When used on the bindings of a supernatural being, it will render the prisoner powerless. I provided it. He did not say how he planned to use it, but I do know this: his thoughts of you were dark, Princess. I do not like him. I do not trust him."

"I will take care of Tristan."

Madam Chloe breathed a sigh of relief and bowed low. "Thank you." When she straightened again, she met Sabrina's gaze. "I was concerned when I heard your father was moving to the new territory. He was always fair and kind to me. I think you will be the same."

Sabrina glanced down at the floor. "If I am half the leader my father has been, I will count my reign as master a success."

Madam Chloe shook her head. "Just make sure you reign. Tristan has it in for you, Princess, and the last thing Chicago needs is him."

CHAPTER TWENTY-THREE

New Orleans

Scoria had a job to do, but finding the witch named Raven had proven difficult. To be sure, he hadn't believed a word the dark-skinned man and elderly woman had told him at Blakemore's Antiques. The loyalty of the two humans toward Gabriel was evident by the way they spoke so warmly of him and the witch, whom he'd learned was called Raven. What he'd reported back to the empress was one undeniable fact: Gabriel, the heir to the kingdom of Paragon, had mated himself to the witch.

Mating with a witch was punishable by death. It was an abomination, a danger to the throne. Allowing the two to persist in this behavior put the entire land of Paragon at risk. As a member of the Obsidian Guard, he had a duty to eliminate the threat, to bring them to his queen, dead or alive.

Now he just needed to find the two lovers. The faster he performed his duty, the better the chance of catching the dragon off guard.

"The price is your blood." The one who had introduced herself as Delphine wiped her wrinkled hands on her filthy apron and stared at him from the door of her hovel. The rumors he'd gathered from the underbelly of New Orleans had called her a Casket Girl, although *girl* was a misnomer. The woman was elderly, her hair almost entirely gray. Still, if the vampire he'd spoken to could be trusted, she and her sisters were the finest oracles in the city.

"How much blood?"

"Only a cup." She smiled, showing all her teeth.

"I agree to your terms."

"Come upstairs and meet my sisters."

He followed her through the filthy, rodent-infested room and up two flights. There, in an equally filthy attic, two other elderly women sat crocheting by candlelight. One appeared so ancient as to be near death, and Scoria hoped she would live through the ritual to find the witch.

Delphine appeared with a chalice and a dagger. "Your arm."

He offered his flesh to her tentatively. Scoria had no qualms about snapping her neck if she tried anything funny, lingered too long, or stabbed him in the wrong place. He watched her carefully as she drew the blade cleanly across his forearm and deep red blood flooded the gold and jewel-encrusted goblet. As expected, his arm healed quickly. He folded it toward his body as soon as it had stopped bleeding.

The old woman brought the blood to her lips and moaned.

"Sister," the other women said in unison. They dropped their crocheting and hobbled out of their chairs. "Save some for us."

A cackle rose up from Delphine's throat, and before Scoria's eyes the woman became young again. Her gray hair transformed to a lustrous black, her skin plumped to pink perfection, and her clothing became new again.

"You are witches?" Scoria hissed.

"No," Delphine replied. "We are something else. Just three girls sent from our homes to this city and cursed with an illness that keeps us alive and in need of blood. Relax, *dragon*. Remember, you came to us."

Now that the other two women had drank his blood, they'd become young as well. Young and beautiful. Their shapely figures swayed to a music he couldn't hear, and they turned and danced before a fire that blazed to life inside a scrying glass at the center of the room. An uneasy feeling ran the length of his spine. Witches could not be trusted, and he did not trust that these women were not witches.

"Who told you I was a dragon?"

"Your blood tastes the same as Gabriel's. One does not forget the taste of dragon blood."

"Gabriel is who I am trying to find! Along with that witch Raven."

Delphine hissed. "Raven is a powerful witch. You must not reveal that we helped you. She would be displeased with us, and we wish not to enrage her."

He nodded his head, although he had no intention of keeping a promise to these foul creatures.

He backed away from the three as their dance grew wild and uninhibited. With long, graceful kicks and majestic leaps worthy of the stage, they arched and spun around the fire, circling, pulsing to the music. As he waited and watched, their eyes turned black as obsidian and their dance became more aggressive until he considered descending to the exit. He glanced toward the boarded window, assessing ways of escape. But he didn't need to take such drastic actions.

Abruptly, all three women stopped. They swayed before him like tall grass in a breeze. An image appeared in the scrying glass between them.

"Watch, dragon. Your mark is there." Delphine pointed at the fire burning within the glass.

An image appeared in the flames, and Scoria moved closer to get a better look. The witch Raven was standing on a bridge in a strange land with bright green water. She became ill and sparks of light circled her body. Gabriel caught her before she collided with the walkway. And wouldn't you know it, the male who comforted them both was none other than Tobias, another heir to the throne and now the enemy of the empress. There was also a female whom Scoria did not recognize. An ally. So the heirs were gathering forces.

He must tell the empress. This was far worse than they'd expected. Her children were uniting.

"Where is this green river?" he asked the strange sisters, trying to mask the disgust in his voice. His skin crawled when he looked into those black eyes.

In perfect unison, the three answered him. "Chicago."

CHAPTER TWENTY-FOUR

The smell of roasting meat woke Tobias. It was nearly six, but he had no desire to get out of bed. After Sabrina had poofed out of his office, he'd tried to reach her, to get her to talk to him. She'd sent him one final text.

It's over. For the best.

His follow up messages had gone unanswered. He couldn't shake the feeling that she'd quit him cold turkey, and the thought hurt like hell. Eventually, he'd crawled under the covers and escaped into much-needed sleep.

A knock came at the bedroom door. "Tobias? Dinner." Raven's voice was steady and sweet. They'd worked it out after Sabrina had left, not that there was any real choice for him to make. Raven had chosen to carry the baby, no matter the consequences to herself or his brother. He would not abandon them. He'd given his word he would do his best to deliver the egg when the time came.

He climbed out of bed and pulled on a shirt before opening the door. His soon to be sister-in-law waited in the hall.

She frowned when she saw him. "Are you okay? I know you're upset about the baby—"

"No." He leaned against the doorjamb. "I'm not upset about the baby." He handed her his phone and showed her Sabrina's text. "Sabrina ended it. It was just too dangerous for her... for us."

"Oh, Tobias..."

He rubbed his eyes. He needed an aspirin... and a fentanyl patch.

"You don't think she'd tell her coven about us?" Raven asked softly.

"No. Never."

"She made it clear she wants us out of the city. Are you sure you can trust her? What if..."

He raised an eyebrow. "What if what?"

"Madame Chloe said she was dangerous. What if she got close to you to assess the danger to her coven?"

Tobias frowned, considering it. "It seemed real though. It was real for me." He shook his head. He refused to believe Sabrina would betray them. "It was real. She won't tell anyone, Raven. She won't."

"I'm sorry." Raven put her arm around his shoulders, her eyes filling with tears. "I shouldn't have suggested she would. I think this pregnancy makes me irritable and has completely destroyed the filter between my brain and my mouth."

For all his education and experience in the operating room, Sabrina was a puzzle he couldn't solve. A dragon's heart was made of stone, but even stone could break. Or shatter, as the case may be, as if it were a Fabergé egg smashed under her heel. He was a doctor, but he didn't know how to heal this break.

"How about you?" he asked her. "How are you feeling?"

"Better than fine. All my symptoms are gone. I made myself a potion of ghost peppers, ginger, and turmeric and the fever came down."

"Ghost pepper?"

She shrugged. "It's not like I could google dragon pregnancy, but I experimented with some spells in my head about combating fever and swelling and it worked. Maybe dragon baby likes things spicy."

"Whatever works."

Raven pointed toward the stairs. "I wanted to do something nice for you, to thank you for everything, for hosting us here and for agreeing to help us with our baby. I made lamb and roasted potatoes. Veggies. Gabriel said it was your favorite, but I suspect it's actually his, isn't it?"

Tobias snorted. "Both. We both love lamb. It's the closest thing to falz on Earth."

"Falz?"

"Falz are a type of mammal in Paragon, like a giant guinea pig with tusks. The meat is delicious."

"Well, the lamb is the perfect temperature, so if you want your falz alternative, you should come now. Also, this is the first time I've cooked a major dinner on my own, so if you don't come down and pretend to enjoy it, I'm going to have to stick my foot up your dragon ass."

He cracked a smile. "Then I guess I better come down. Give me a minute to freshen up."

Raven disappeared. He retreated to his bathroom. Fuck, Gabriel was a lucky bastard. Only now did he realize the magnitude of his brother's mating. Raven had given herself to him, for life. Their upcoming human marriage was nothing compared to the bond they shared between their souls. She was *his*. So in love with him she would die to give him his young. What did Gabriel have that Tobias didn't to deserve a woman like that?

Sabrina had *said* she was his, but it was all a lie. She was no one's but her coven's.

Feeling wretched, he descended the stairs to find Gabriel lighting two white tapered candles on the dining room table.

"Raven said you'd been sleeping. Are you well, brother?"

Tobias took a seat at the head of the table. "I'm here."

Raven appeared with a bowl of potatoes. "His heart is broken."

Tobias did a double take. "Can we not talk about this?"

"Sabrina's smell is still on you, you've been sleeping all afternoon, and you look like someone kneed you in the balls." Gabriel picked up the knife and fork that rested next to the leg of lamb and started carving. "It wouldn't take a psychology professor to draw a few conclusions."

Tobias's mouth gaped uselessly.

Gabriel loaded his plate with a slab of bright red lamb. "It's been a long day full of surprises. Have something to eat. You'll feel better."

Sawing off a corner of the lamb Gabriel had dropped in front of him, Tobias popped it in his mouth. It was delicious, and another pang of jealousy struck him along with a heavy dose of homesickness. He wished for the easy days of his youth when his family would gather around the long ebony table in the Obsidian Palace after a long day of training. The biggest problem any of them had in those days had to do with the males of the village pursuing their sister Rowan a bit too aggressively. He'd been delinquent back then, never caring to finish his studies or practice his weaponry. He'd left the heavy lifting of royal responsibilities to Marius and Gabriel. Maybe that was why he'd overcompensated with his education here.

"I asked her to be mine," he said around a bite of potatoes. The confession spilled out of his mouth and his chest instantly felt lighter upon sharing it. There was a clank as Gabriel released his fork and it clattered against his plate. Their eyes met. Tobias answered his unasked question. "She said she was. She lied."

There was a collective gasp from the couple, and Raven lowered her fork. Their pity dropped on him like a wet blanket.

"That's a big step, Tobias. How long have you known her?" Gabriel asked pointedly.

Tobias leaned back in his chair and crossed his arms. "How long had you known Raven? I seem to recall you mentioning a month? What was it you said about loving her the moment you saw her?"

Gabriel locked eyes with his brother.

"You love her," Raven said. "Love doesn't keep a timeline."

"I wouldn't have asked her to be mine if I didn't. I have worked with her for close to three years, although I only recently discovered she was a vampire. Maybe I never really knew her at all until then."

Gabriel's hand landed on Raven's arm, and Tobias watched something pass between them without a word spoken.

"Please excuse me." Raven left the dining room in the direction of the bathroom.

"Vampires have never been known for their love of dragons." Gabriel threaded his fingers together on the table. "There's a history of violence. Are you sure we're safe staying here?"

Tobias scratched along his jawline. He'd forgotten to shave that morning, and new growth caught on his fingernails. "That was thousands of years ago. In Paragon. Before we were born. It's practically folklore. Paragon has been at peace with the vampires of Nochtbend for generations."

"How many dragon-and-vampire couples did you know in Paragon?"

"None," Tobias said. "But as you are so fond of saying, brother, we're not in Paragon."

"This is different. This is nature. Dragons create fire. Vampires are prone to burning. They fear us, Tobias. You know as well as I do that a vampire's will is dominated by the needs of their coven. They never act alone and rarely take a mate outside their societal group."

Tobias stared down at his half-eaten lamb. Despite the delicious meal, he'd lost his appetite. "Shut the fuck up."

"Excuse me?"

"Gabriel, shut. The. Fuck. Up. You mated a witch and broke Paragonian law. You're having a forbidden baby. You have no right telling me who I can and cannot mate."

"I was only—"

"No. Shut it." He scoffed and pointed at his mouth. "I have all my teeth, brother. Never bound myself to anyone. I haven't even taken an oread into my service, even when two attempted to follow me here from Crete. Do you know why?"

"Enlighten me." Gabriel looked genuinely perplexed.

"We are refugees, Gabriel. We are ghosts of another time and another world. Look what happened to you. A witch cursed your ring and almost killed you and everyone you've ever bound to you. You came within a fraction of an inch of bringing about the end of Raven and those two innocent employees at Blakemore's. I've been here hundreds of years, denying myself any real connections, living as a human, surviving alone. Don't tell me who to love. Don't tell me who I can or cannot mate. You don't get to be a hypocrite. Not with me."

Gabriel returned to cutting his lamb. "Fair enough. I was only trying to be comforting."

Tobias glared at him incredulously until he couldn't help but laugh.

"What?" Gabriel asked.

"You are terrible at giving comfort. A complete failure. If I am ever bleeding from an open wound, please do not try to comfort me."

"Hmm. I mean no offense. You have come to accept Raven. I would do the same for you if..."

"If there was anything to accept." Tobias rested his head on his fist. "Again, not comforting. Maybe you're right about dragons and vampires though. Sabrina suggested we all leave the city."

"What did you tell her?"

"I told her we weren't leaving. Where would we go? You said New Orleans isn't safe."

Gabriel returned to his lamb, his expression growing impassive. He did not make eye contact as he said, "If Sabrina does not appreciate the male she had in you, she is unworthy of you."

For some reason, in that moment, Tobias thought of Killian, their father. He watched Gabriel eat his meal in silence.

"Why are you staring at me?"

Tobias took a sip of his wine. "That last thing you said. It was comforting."

Gabriel shrugged.

Tobias sighed. For as strange a day as it had been, he

had to admit he was glad his brother was here. Family was a feeling he'd lived without for far too long. It was a closeness he hadn't felt in a long time. A closeness he needed.

Raven returned to the table and folded her napkin in her lap. "I hope you two worked things out."

"My brother doesn't deserve you," Tobias said.

Gabriel recoiled, baring his teeth.

Raven winked. "Meh. True, but I took pity on him. We all have our crosses to bear."

CHAPTER TWENTY-FIVE

Sabrina charged into the tunnels, her blood pumping in her veins. She should have been exhausted. After a night of lovemaking with Tobias and a long day that had ended with her visit to Madam Chloe, she was overdue for some serious R & R. But this thing with Tristan had gone too far. She'd always known he was an asshole, but she'd underestimated how murderous his intentions were. Tristan had known she'd been stabbed, and if Chloe was to be believed, he'd expected her to be dead. He'd expected it because he'd arranged it.

"Hi, Paul. Is my father awake?"

The jovial human nodded and reached for the door. "He's practicing. Feel free to wait inside. He's expecting you."

He opened the door for her, and she entered her father's well-appointed great room, the sound of the grand piano filling the underground space. He was playing Beethoven, *Moonlight Sonata*, and she paused to listen, not wanting to disturb his practice. Even so, he noticed her and smiled, his timeless beauty making it hard to believe he was hundreds of years old. Effortlessly, he transitioned into a rendition of Vivaldi's *Storm*. He knew it was her favorite.

When he finished, she clapped and whooped just like she used to when she was a child. "Perfect as always."

He stood and spread his arms, inviting a hug. "Because I practice, my child."

She wrapped her arms around him and placed a tender kiss on his cheek. "And because you were born with perfect pitch."

He bowed slightly. "Now, what did you want to talk to me about? Your text said it was urgent."

"It's Tristan. He tried to have me killed."

Her father withdrew, his lips peeling back from his teeth. "What do you mean, killed?"

"There is something I haven't told you. Three weeks ago, I was stabbed in the chest."

Her father shrugged. "Stab wounds heal, darling. Was it vampire play?"

She shook her head. Vampires were naturally violent. A stabbing that did not result in death would be seen as play or a test. Her father might defend her from either, but it wouldn't accomplish what she'd come for. She needed to neutralize Tristan.

"This wasn't play and it wasn't a test," she said. "There was a necrotic agent on the blade. Keetridge Solution. If I were one hundred percent vampire, I would be dead."

"Keetridge Solution?" Her father scowled. "I thought we had eradicated every source of the substance besides our own."

"I have reason to believe that if you check our stores, you will find some missing."

"That's impossible. Are you sure—"

"I was able to compel a doctor at the hospital to care for

me. He extracted the substance and Madam Chloe tested it for me. She told me what it was."

"And it was Tristan who stabbed you?"

She shook her head. "No. It was a werewolf. The last of the Racine pack."

He hissed. "Sabrina, why did you not bring this to me? Did you kill the beast?"

"I wanted to handle it myself, both to prove to myself that I could and to get revenge for the pain it caused me. But I haven't been able to find the werewolf."

The savage growl that tore from her father made her skin prickle as if it wanted to flee from her body. She'd known he'd be unhappy with her about this part, but it was necessary. She couldn't thwart Tristan if her father didn't believe every word she said was the truth. No doubt Tristan was counting on her fear to keep her silent.

"We need a tracking team on this immediately. Do you have anything with his scent?"

She shook her head. "He took the dagger with him."

"Fucking werewolves."

"But Father, about Tristan..."

"Mmm, yes. What does he have to do with any of this?"

"That's why I came to you now. Madam Chloe told me that Tristan stopped in to her shop this week and accused her of helping me survive. He'd expected me to be dead, Father, and was disappointed when I wasn't. He knew I'd been stabbed with Keetridge Solution. I was cured by humans in a home where Tristan cannot enter. The only way he could have known I was in mortal danger was if he'd arranged it."

Her father's teeth clenched, and a vein in his neck bulged with his anger. "Tristan has access to our stores."

"Yes. There's something more. The day after, when I

returned home, Tristan had ransacked my apartment. I caught him leaving the scene. He threatened me."

"And still you did not bring this to me."

She sighed through her nose. "Father, I can handle Tristan if it is just Tristan. I've been doing it for years. He's had me followed and tried to subvert my position in the coven more times than I can count. Only today did I learn he was involved in the stabbing. I came to you because after what Madam Chloe told me, I now realize that Tristan must have had a relationship with the werewolf and provided him with the Keetridge Solution that coated the dagger I was stabbed with. If I handle this on my own, it will mean knocking Tristan's head off."

Her father became eerily still. "A relationship between Tristan and a Racine werewolf is unlikely to be newly founded."

She crossed her arms over her chest. "My thoughts exactly. Not to mention, stealing Keetridge Solution is treason. Do I have your permission to take him out?"

Her father paced to his bar and poured himself a glass of blood. "If it were any vampire besides Tristan, my answer would be yes."

"But?"

"But Tristan is one of the oldest and most respected vampires in Chicago. He was here before I was, Sabrina, and is powerfully connected. He's respected among the old ones. If we don't have proof of his murderous intentions, the coven could turn on you before your coronation. I'm afraid the others are not going to take the word of a witch."

"So I can do nothing?"

He narrowed his eyes. "Leave it to me. Tell no one of this. I will take care of Tristan."

"Soon, I hope. My coronation is in a matter of days. If

his goal, as I suspect, is to take me out of the equation in the hopes you will name him as my replacement, he's going to increase his efforts."

He kissed her on the forehead. "Trust me. Have I ever failed you?"

"I do trust you. And no."

"Good. Now, would you like to stay here tonight? Paul will keep you safe."

"As tempting as that sounds, I still have a few boxes to pack. Plus I want to start checking in with the club owners this week, make sure they're on board with my transition. I'm not going to let a vampire like Tristan bully me into doing anything I wouldn't ordinarily do."

"Thatta girl."

"Thank you, Daddy. I know I can count on you."

Secretly rejoicing, she let him walk her to the door. Her success was written all over Calvin's face. Tristan had no idea what he was in for.

⁂

"Thank you for coming with me. Gabriel said if he eats one more hot dish he's going to burst into flames," Raven said.

Tobias watched her shovel in another mouthful of pho. She'd covered the stuff in sriracha sauce, and he swore her ears would start smoking any minute, but he smiled and nodded. Dragon pregnancies made the blood hot. What she'd discovered made sense. By eating super spicy food, she was probably causing her body to release endorphins, counteracting the negative effects of her raging hormones. If it worked, who was he to argue?

"It's normal," he said. "If you were a dragon, you'd spit fire. Let's hope that's not the case with you."

She stopped eating and gave him a hard look. "Please tell me you're kidding."

Tobias couldn't hold it in anymore. He laughed openly. "I'm joking. Dragons breathe fire, but it has nothing to do with being pregnant."

She smacked him upside the shoulder. "Damn it, Tobias. I was about to start researching antacid spells."

"Sorry." He forced the corners of his mouth down. Truth be told, he loved teasing Raven. She was good-humored and easy to make laugh when she wasn't pregnancy-raging. She reminded him of his sister, Rowan, in that way. Tobias needed more laughter in his life, especially now that Sabrina was gone. It had been two full days since she'd vamoosed from his office, and he hadn't seen or heard from her since.

"Can I ask you a serious question?" Raven set down her chopsticks.

"Of course."

"How long is the usual gestation?"

"A year. Six months inside and six months outside. I'm guessing that due to your human anatomy, it will be different."

"Different how?"

"Mother Nature is funny. She adapts and evolves. I'm pretty sure a human-dragon hybrid will still have a year gestation, but I'm guessing your smaller size will shorten the number of months you carry the young internally. There's no way to know for sure until it happens."

She scraped her thumbnail against her bottom lip. "More and more since Gabriel awakened this thing in me, this magic, I feel like every day is unpredictable. I used to be a planner. I did well in school, didn't procrastinate, ever. Now, there's no planning. I just roll with the punches."

"Does that upset you?"

"It upsets my sister. Avery has been trying to plan a wedding for me that I sometimes think will never happen."

"It will happen, Raven. You'll have your wedding, one way or another."

She gave him a genuine smile. "You're not so bad, Tobias, you know that? No matter what Gabriel says."

He did a double take. Raven broke into raucous laughter.

"Are you going to finish that?" she asked, pointing at his bowl.

"No." Tobias had eaten a late lunch and wasn't actually hungry. He'd only come to give his brother a break. He sensed Gabriel needed time to process Raven's pregnancy and gather his thoughts in a place where he didn't have to worry about her reaction to them.

"Let's get out of here," she said.

He paid the bill and ushered Raven out of the restaurant and toward his car. It had been warm that day for the month of March, in the low fifties. Now that the sun had set, he pulled his wool coat tighter around him. Still, all the snow had melted, and for once he didn't mind walking the distance to the parking garage.

Raven paused. "Do you smell that?"

"No. What do you smell?"

"Like something's burning. And something else. Ozone." She held the back of her hand to her nose.

Tobias didn't smell anything, but he heard what sounded like a glass bottle rolling across concrete. He looked down to find a small blue orb. "That's strange. That looks like—"

A flash of blue light knocked him off his feet. His wings bumped against the inside of his coat as his body instinctively tried to steady itself, but the garment wasn't built for his kind and he fell to the sidewalk, Raven on top of him. Branches of white lightning exploded above them, drawing his breath from his lungs and sending hot energy coursing through his veins.

"It's... it's... Paragon." Raven rolled off him and crabwalked away from the light show above them, but she didn't get far. Her muscles were as useless as his, wracked with spasms from the Paragonian grenade. The magic attacked the nervous system, made it impossible to do anything but breathe. He heard Raven sobbing. The baby. What was this doing to the baby?

A hulking, figure stepped into view, face hidden in shadow behind the flashing lights. Helplessly immobile, Tobias watched as the man approached.

Scoria.

The Obsidian Guard loomed dark and merciless above him, the jeweled embroidery of his black-and-red uniform reflected in the dying light. The apparel didn't blend in at all with human clothing, but then Scoria wouldn't have used a Paragonian grenade if he was interested in blending in.

The guardsman drew his dagger. "Hello Tobias. I have you at last."

CHAPTER TWENTY-SIX

Boss Miller was a longtime friend to the vampires of Chicago. He'd allowed his uptown bar to be used as a safe place for monitored feeding on human guests since he'd bought the place in 1985. In exchange for a small fee, he kept the humans calm and the vampires from killing anyone. There hadn't been an incident in decades.

Sabrina handed him the envelope she'd prepared. "So then I can expect you to continue acting as a friend to my coven after my coronation?"

He tucked the envelope into his jacket. "Why spoil a good thing?" Miller's voice was as gruff as a bear's. The curtain of his beard parted to reveal a flash of white teeth.

Sabrina was still shaking his hand when a commotion at the front of the bar reached her ears. When she asked what was going on, Boss Miller shook his head, unable to hear it. She led the way toward the front of the bar where a big picture window was packed with patrons.

"What's happening?" she demanded.

A human woman turned toward her and said in a voice laced with more excitement than fear, "Some guy is mugging a couple. They're on the sidewalk. I don't think they can move. Maybe they broke something."

Sabrina moved into action, threading her way through the crowd to the front door. No one was getting mugged in front of Boss Miller's place on her watch. Not today, Satan.

Two sets of legs, one male and one female, lay sprawled on the concrete, pointed at a man who was big enough to be a Chicago Bears linebacker.

"This isn't the place for you," she said in her deepest, most serious voice. "You don't want to do that here."

The man turned and Sabrina's fangs dropped. He had the mark Tobias had shown her, two dark crescent shapes in the space between his right eye and his temple. And his hand, which was holding a sinister-looking dagger, wore a ring with a cat's-eye stone in a setting similar to Tobias's. This was a dragon!

She growled a warning. The man raised the dagger and shifted his weight toward the victims. Tobias and Raven! Why weren't they moving? Sabrina saw their faces clearly now and the rage already coursing through her veins took on a new, sharper edge.

Mine.

In a flash, she was on the attacker. Her hand caught his wrist before he could sink the knife into Tobias's chest. Clinging to him like a monkey, she tore into his throat and tried not to swallow the blood that rushed into her mouth. This was dragon blood. Pure ambrosia, but it would knock her on her ass if she had too much. She'd learned that from Tobias.

The knife nipped her shoulder, and she growled and pushed and kicked and tore. Blood sprayed across the sidewalk. A whistle like a baseball bat singing through the air engaged her vampire instincts. She flung herself off the man in time to watch the heavy bottle Boss Miller had swung connect with the dragon's temple. The glass shattered, shards raining to the pavement and mixing with the blood. It was enough. Apparently even dragons succumbed to head injuries. He toppled to the pavement.

"Mess with my girl again, fucker." Boss Miller delivered a kick to the man's ribs.

Tobias sat up and rubbed the back of his head.

"Are you okay?" she asked.

His jaw clenched. "Sabrina... Yeah. Thanks for the help. I bet you were tempted to let nature take its course."

"What are you talking about?"

"Just that it might have been more convenient for you if you'd let him stab us."

She gripped his hand and helped him to his feet, her stare digging into his. "If you believe that, you don't know me at all."

"It would help if you'd return my calls."

"Not now, Tobias. And definitely not here." She shook her head.

"Fine."

"What's wrong with her? Why isn't she moving?" Sabrina gestured toward Raven.

"Paragonian grenade. The magic has a debilitating effect on the nerves. Looks like the paralysis lingers when the device is used on humans and witches."

"Fucker." Sabrina growled at the dark man heaped at her feet.

"I gotta clean this up, Sabrina," Boss Miller said. "It's bad for business."

"I'll send two of my people to help." She texted a couple of vampires she knew would be in the area, then looked at

Tobias. "Do you need help getting Raven back to your place?"

"No, but any way you can help me get Scoria to the car before you ghost again?" The words left Tobias's mouth like he regretted every one, as if it burned his tongue to ask her for help. But Sabrina could see he had no choice. He couldn't carry both of them, and leaving the bloodied man on the sidewalk wasn't acceptable.

"His name is Scoria?" She frowned. "You know this guy?"

Tobias gave her a curt nod.

"I'll meet you at your house."

Sabrina exchanged a knowing look with Boss Miller, who'd already set the two vamps she'd called to work with mops and buckets. She reached down and grabbed Scoria by the shoulders.

Tobias began to protest. "No, Sabrina, I—"

But she was gone. She'd dematerialized before he could finish, landing in the center of Tobias's living room with the dragon in tow. Damn, he was heavy. As soon as she formed again, she flipped him facedown on the carpet and gathered his hands behind his back. Scoria was still unconscious, but he wouldn't be for long. He was twice her size, but even a dragon's wrist could snap under the right amount of pressure. She placed a knee in the center of the guardsman's spine and adjusted her grip.

An orange calico cat ran into the room and hissed at her, the hair on its back rising toward the ceiling. Sabrina hissed back.

Gabriel rushed in after it, his presence like a dark menace. Damn, Tobias's brother was intimidating as hell. His gaze floated from her to Scoria as his lips peeled back from his teeth on a growl that she wasn't sure was meant for her or the dragon.

"He tried to kill Raven and your brother."

"Raven? Where is she?" Gabriel paced toward the door, drawing his phone from his pocket. His fingers flew across the keyboard.

"Relax. She's with Tobias. They're on their way here."

A ding sounded. No doubt Raven responding to the frantic text. The tightness in Gabriel's shoulders eased somewhat.

"I need rope or wire, something to bind him," she said. "If he wakes, I'm not sure I can hold him. He's not going to stay under for long."

"He's a member of the Obsidian Guard from Paragon. The best of our warriors. I'm surprised you knocked him out at all." Gabriel ran a hand through his hair.

"I tore half his throat out. Unfortunately, it's already healed. This guy is tough."

"The toughest." Gabriel moved to her side to get a better look. The cloying scent of burnt cinnamon and old books struck her. Repulsive. The guy seriously needed a shower.

She sneezed and rubbed her nose. "Did you fall in something?"

"Hmm?"

"The smell." She turned her head to the side. "I don't mean to be rude, but you stink."

He gave her a withering look. "I'll find you something to use on him."

"What was that look for? I'm just being honest. It's not my fault you smell," she called after him.

She heard him rummaging in the kitchen drawers. Her

fangs ached. She concentrated on retracting them, but it wasn't working. She was hungry. The effort it had taken to subdue Scoria and transport him here had drained her energy, and she'd had to spit out his dragon blood. Her stomach cramped.

Gabriel returned with a fistful of zip ties. "I presume these will do."

"Perfect." Sabrina hoisted the guardsman into a heavy wooden chair that reminded her of something that belonged in a basilica. Last time she was here she'd only seen Tobias's bedroom. The man had interesting taste. Eclectic. The orange cat leaped from behind her, hissed, and swiped at the guardsman, then ran off like a holy terror.

"That thing's a menace," she said.

He chuckled. "Try telling that to Raven."

Holding the man in place with her elbow, Sabrina made short work of binding his wrists and ankles to the sturdy chair frame as her father had taught her. Too tight and it would cut off circulation. Too loose and desperate prisoners would break their own thumbs to get free. She admired her handiwork. The guy wasn't getting out of this without help.

Once he was secured, she moved to the nearest window and closed the drapes.

"What are you doing?" Gabriel asked.

"This place is a fishbowl. Anyone can see in with these open. Trust me, you don't want that. We'll have the Chicago PD at our door in a heartbeat. There's too much blood on his clothes, and I'm willing to guess once we start questioning him, there's going to be more."

Scoria's head rolled on his shoulders. They had a few minutes before things got interesting.

Sabrina addressed Gabriel again. "Seriously, what's with the smell?"

The man's eyes shifted to the side. "My scent never bothered you before?"

She shook her head. "You didn't smell before. I'm telling you, you stepped in something."

Gabriel nodded. Was he blushing? "I think this is something you need to talk to Tobias about."

"Who is this Scoria guy, and why is he in our territory?" Sabrina was growing more concerned by the minute with the way the dragons were multiplying in Chicago.

Gabriel focused on her with such intensity she had to take a step back. "Where *is* my brother?"

"I told you, he's on his way here. He had to drive Raven. I can only dematerialize with one person. It was pretty important I get this guy off the sidewalk."

His eyes widened. "He attacked you in public?"

"Not me. Them." Sabrina sighed. "He had Tobias and Raven on the ground and was ready to stab them out of existence when I took him down with the help of a friend of the coven."

"By the Mountain," Gabriel cursed, holding his head. "Humans could have been hurt. They definitely could have seen."

"That didn't seem to be a concern to this guy. We'll wipe the memories of anyone who might have seen anything. Don't worry about that." Sabrina planted her hands on her hips. "Are there more dragons coming to Chicago? What do you know about this?"

"Relax, vampire. We are not invading your territory. This is a member of the Obsidian Guard from our home realm of Paragon. He was sent to kill us over a... private matter."

She hissed. "Gabriel, that private matter was made public today. Blood was spilled in front of hungry vampires.

If anyone aside from me tasted that blood, you better believe we'll have a problem. Your blood definitely does not taste human, and shifters are not allowed in vampire territory."

An angry growl tore through the room. "Put your fangs away. You don't want to fight me, Sabrina. I'm not as nice as I let on." He was crouched, his dark eyes burning. Nothing about him looked nice. Nothing about him looked anything but deadly.

She covered her mouth with her hand. "I can't. It took energy to get him here, and I haven't fed. They won't retract until I feed."

"You need blood."

"Human blood. Dragon blood is intoxicating to my kind."

Gabriel scowled.

"Normally I can feed off energy too, but...." She shook her head. It would be far too awkward to feed on Gabriel.

Gabriel spread his hands and narrowed his eyes. "Sorry, only dragon blood here, and I'd prefer to keep it in my veins. If you'd like to go, though, I can handle this from here."

"No way. I'm not going anywhere. I need to know what's going on and if I need to get the coven involved."

A groan came from the direction of the chair. The guardsman roused, head bobbing and fingers twitching.

Gabriel growled. "He's coming to."

As the dragon blinked awake, Sabrina sagged, her stomach clenching again from hunger. This was not how the night was supposed to go. This was a disaster. Vampires had seen Scoria, and he did not look human. This, all of this, might be too much to hide and too much to forget. Not to mention the protective instinct that had flooded her when she'd seen Tobias on the ground. That was not something she could cast aside.

There was a thud from the direction of the kitchen and then the sound of the door slamming. Tobias staggered in with Raven at his side. The witch was walking but pale. Dark circles had formed under her eyes. Gabriel rushed to her and caught her in his arms.

"You're just in time," Sabrina said around her still-extended fangs. "Our friend is waking up. I'm sure you'll have questions for him and answers for me about why he is in my coven's territory."

Tobias glanced between her and Scoria, taking in his bindings. "You did this?"

"Of course I did. He tried to kill you."

"Thanks."

His roasted-almond scent met her nose and she inhaled deeply. Maybe it was because she was hungry, but he smelled exceptionally delicious. Her entire torso warmed with the delectable bouquet.

Scoria struggled against his bindings, then scanned the room, his eyes falling on Gabriel, Raven, and Tobias before narrowing into thin slits. He said something in a loud clear voice, in a language Sabrina did not know.

"What's he saying?" she asked.

Gabriel answered. "He says Her Majesty Eleanor, Empress of Paragon, demands the presence of the Treasure of Paragon in her throne room immediately."

"Fuck that," Raven spat out, shaking her head.

"What's the Treasure of Paragon?" Sabrina asked.

Tobias looked at Gabriel for a long moment and then back at Sabrina. "The Treasure of Paragon is... me. Well, us. It's what our people called my siblings and me. I told you I came from the kingdom of Paragon. We, my siblings and I, are the heirs to the throne."

TOBIAS HAD NEVER THOUGHT HE'D SEE A MEMBER OF the Obsidian Guard again, especially not here in Chicago. The elite soldiers were one part of Paragon he didn't miss. They served one purpose and one purpose only—to kill the enemies of the Paragonian crown. In his youth, Tobias had thought of them as humans might think of Navy SEALs, like honorable heroes. Now he understood that what the Guard did wasn't honorable; it was espionage. Scoria was an assassin.

"An heir... You're a prince?" Sabrina's dagger-filled gaze fell on him.

"Yes. I told you as much."

"You told me no such thing. And if you're an heir, doesn't that mean the empress is...? I thought you said your mother was dead?"

"I thought she was." Tobias balked. He hadn't meant to keep his royalty a secret per se, but had he mentioned it explicitly? "I told you I grew up in a palace."

Her mouth gaped, her fangs flashing. "You may have mentioned a shiny floor in a palace when you were a kid, but you failed to say it was *your* palace."

As much as he hated to see her angry, they'd both had their secrets. She couldn't blame him for not revealing every detail about his past in the short time they'd been together. "Can we talk about this another time?"

The tension broke when the guardsman started to laugh. He muttered an insult in Paragonian. Tobias rolled his eyes.

"What did he just say?" Sabrina asked.

Tobias sighed. "The closest expression in English..."

"Tell me."

"Pussy whipped. He called me an owned man." Tobias turned to Raven, ignoring the way Sabrina's bottom jaw dropped. "Are you capable of making a truth serum that will work on a dragon?"

He hated to ask her to do anything more. The Paragonian grenade had affected her far more than it had him. She looked exhausted.

The witch rubbed a hand over her lips. "I think so. I mean, I've never tried it before, but my instincts tell me I can."

Gabriel held her against his chest. "Are you sure you're strong enough?"

"Yes," she said. "I can do this."

"What do you need?" Tobias asked.

She tightened her black ponytail. "Candles... I have some in my things, but I need more. As many as you can find. Lemon. Salt. A bowl of water. Oh, and some fresh sage." She walked over to the guardsman and yanked one wavy dark hair from his head, holding it between her thumb and forefinger, pinky raised in disgust.

"I'll find candles. Everything else is in the kitchen," Tobias said.

"Gabriel, get my other candles from my things," Raven said. He nodded to her and disappeared up the stairs.

"Someone needs to stay here and watch this guy," Tobias said.

Sabrina wrapped her hand around her opposite fist. "I'm still standing here."

"This isn't your problem. We've imposed on you enough already."

Sabrina lowered her voice. "Let me save you a lot of time, *Your Majesty*. I'm not going to leave here until I see that witch perform her spell and I know the truth about why this guy is here. Go get the candles. I won't let him out of my sight."

Tobias looked at her—really looked at her—and it was like he was seeing her for the first time. The expression on her face was absolutely deadly. She hadn't flinched when she'd brought Scoria down. The way she'd bound him to that chair, it was like she'd been trained to do it. And of course she had, hadn't she? She was her father's daughter.

Sabrina had been telling him as much this entire time. Fully human, fully vampire. With her fangs dropped and her fist twisting in her palm, anything that was left of her human mask was gone. She looked at their prisoner like she was ready to bloody him. Sabrina was part of the Chicago vampire coven, a coven that she'd said was behind everything that happened in the city. *The vampire* mob, Tobias thought. *This is not the first time she's bound someone to a chair.*

At that moment, she was violently beautiful. And he realized that he loved both sides of her. Yes, he loved her. He loved the gentle human healer who preferred to feed on energy rather than blood, and he loved the vampire who'd saved his life tonight and would rip Scoria apart to protect anyone in this household. And as painful as it was that she had put her coven before him and their relationship, he also respected her strength and loyalty. When she looked at him, as she was looking at him now, her stare cutting through to his soul, he only wished that the feeling was mutual.

"Tobias, where's the salt?" Raven called from the kitchen.

Tobias tore himself away from staring at Sabrina and marched into the kitchen where he retrieved a round blue carton from the pantry and handed it to Raven.

"This has to work," he mumbled. "We need to know the

truth about why Brynhoff sent Scoria. The dagger he almost landed in our chests doesn't mesh with his formal invitation to the throne room."

"Why would you think Brynhoff is behind this? The guardsman only mentioned Eleanor." Raven turned on the water and started filling a glass pitcher.

He scratched the back of his head. "It doesn't sound like her. He's pulling the strings. I know it."

Raven's expression remained carefully blank. He didn't like the pity he saw veiled in her expression. She thought he was in denial. She was wrong. Raven didn't know his mother the way he did. She didn't know anything about Paragon.

She mumbled something as she poured the cold water through her spread fingers to mix with the salt, lemon, and sage already in the bowl. When the last drop broke the surface, the water sparked. She dropped in Scoria's hair and a cloud of silver poofed toward the ceiling before settling back into the bowl to form a smooth, glassy surface.

"So... how does this work? You make him drink that and he has to tell the truth?"

"Not exactly. He doesn't drink it. We soak his feet in it."

"Great. He tries to kill us and we give him a pedicure."

Raven flashed a half smile. Damn, she was pale. He wished he could tell her to go lie down, but they needed her help.

She tightened her ponytail again and shook her arms like she was loosening up. "It will make it extremely uncomfortable for him not to answer our questions. If he tries to lie, we'll know."

Tobias dug a box of candles out of the storage area above the fridge and shook them to get her attention. "How exactly will we know?"

"It'll be easier to show you." She gestured toward the living room. "Oh, Tobias, before we go in there..."

"Yeah?"

"What Sabrina said to us about leaving Chicago... I get it now. I thought it was territorial. I took it as a threat. I thought she was bullying us on behalf of her coven. That's not what it is at all. She's asking us to leave because she loves you. She risked her life tonight to save you." Raven's eyes met his.

"She helped us out of obligation. She's made it clear she doesn't want to see me anymore. I couldn't even get her to answer my texts yesterday." He rubbed the ache that had started in his chest.

Raven didn't say a word, just lifted the bowl and rounded the kitchen island to return to the living room.

Gabriel had already set up a ring of candles around Scoria. Tobias handed him the additional candles, and he made short work of a second ring.

"That's perfect," Raven said. "I need his shoes off."

Gabriel held the guardsman's struggling legs and popped off his boots. Raven slid the bowl in place and plunged his feet in. Tobias thought for sure that Scoria would kick the bowl over, but Raven settled that with a snap of her fingers. "*Fotiá.*"

The candles blazed to life, the flames stretching toward the ceiling until Tobias was legitimately concerned for his paneling. Heat blasted through the room. He darted a worried glance toward Raven, who raised a placating hand. The flames shrank to a normal, flickering burn. The guardsman stilled, his eyes wide. Raven stood and backed out of the circle.

"Goddess, I shouldn't have pissed her off," Sabrina mumbled beside him.

"He's ready now," Raven said. "Ask quickly. The spell will only last as long as the water does."

Tobias eyed the bowl. Why the rush? It would take days for that amount of water to evaporate.

Gabriel didn't hesitate. "Who sent you?"

"Eleanor, the Empress of Paragon," Scoria said immediately.

"If the empress was requesting our presence, why did you try to kill me?" Tobias asked.

The man didn't answer. He started shifting in the chair, then grimaced, desperately attempting to pull his feet from the water. But Raven's spell locked him in place, almost as if his feet were frozen into the water.

"Feel that?" Raven said to Scoria. "That's every one of your cells becoming an overfilled balloon. One by one, they will burst, causing you an increasing and intolerable level of pain until you answer us."

"Fuck you!" Scoria yelled. "I don't have to tell you anything." Then he screamed, loud and high-pitched.

"That's a lie," Raven said. "Lie to us and you'll burn from the inside. I warn you, even dragons aren't immune to this heat."

"How is he speaking English?" Gabriel asked.

"Translation spell," Raven said. "Ask again, Tobias."

"Why did you try to kill me?"

The guardsman squirmed.

"Answer him!" Raven fisted the air in front of his face. "Answer him or I will make you hurt in ways you never imagined."

Scoria growled and bared his teeth. "Because your mother wants you returned to Paragon, dead or alive!"

Tobias's entire body stiffened. No. This wasn't right. This couldn't be. "Just me or all my siblings?"

Scoria groaned before answering. "I have been ordered to return all eight of your hearts to the empress, beating or not."

The air around Tobias became hard and tight, his mind racing for the next question. All at once Sabrina leaped in front of him, hissing, her fangs bared. The rest of them covered their ears at the sound. She pointed a finger at the space between Scoria's third and fourth ribs. When she spoke to the guardsman again, it was in a voice as dark and rough as the inner mountain.

"Try it and it will be your heart in my hands after I tear it from your chest."

CHAPTER TWENTY-SEVEN

Everything stopped for Tobias the moment Sabrina lunged at Scoria. In that moment, she looked feral, all vampire and undeniably menacing. A voice inside Tobias's head shouted, *Mine.* There was no other woman like Sabrina. If his feelings for her were strong before, they paled in comparison to his feelings now.

His hand landed on her waist and he pulled her against his chest. "Easy," he said, his voice low and soft. He massaged the base of her skull until she met his gaze. Her fangs were still out, painfully extended.

"Sorry, I don't know what came over me." Her cheeks reddened. "I'm drained and hungry."

"It's understandable. Do you need to feed from me?" Her body pressed against his, no room between them.

Staring at his mouth, she edged the tip of her bubblegum-pink tongue along her bottom lip. "Maybe, just a little."

He bent his head to her and she leaned in to kiss him. Her fangs pressed against his lips, hard and sharp, interrupting the soft heat of the kiss. The energy started to flow.

He didn't fight it. He would have given her his soul if she'd asked for it. She inhaled deeply, his breath mingling with hers. After what might have been minutes or centuries for all he cared, she drew back. Her fangs receded. She stared at him with the strangest look in her eyes. What was she thinking? Did she feel what he was feeling, that there was no way they could stay apart now? Something had changed, shifted. They were bound, more deeply than the moment she'd first said she was his.

"Thank you," she said softly.

Someone coughed, and he realized Gabriel and Raven were still in the room and staring at them like they had just turned a glowing fuchsia pink.

Raven huffed. "We're running out of time. One of you needs to ask the next question."

Gabriel recognized that Tobias needed a moment and did the honors. "Why now? Why did the empress send you to kill us now?"

Scoria's eyes locked on Raven. "Because *she* is a threat to the crown! When the dark-haired witch came to Paragon in Rowan's dress, the empress could see you'd thrown the gauntlet down. Her children she could handle, especially considering she'd torn you away from your training before you could become a real threat. But a witch—a witch changed everything. It was clear to her that your next move would be to try to take back your birthright. You are a threat to her power. A threat to the throne."

Confused, Tobias demanded an explanation. "What about Brynhoff? Did he direct Eleanor to do this? He must be behind it."

Scoria laughed a low and wicked laugh. "Brynhoff? He hasn't directed anyone to do anything on his own in a very long time. He's a puppet. Your mother and her fairy witch Aborella hold all the power of the Mountain."

Tobias swallowed as cold, hard dread filled him like he was a bucket in a rainstorm. "She wasn't saving us when she sent us here; she was moving us out of the way."

Gabriel drifted closer to him. "Yes, brother. Do you see now?"

"Tobias, I'm sorry you're finding out this way," Raven said. "We tried..."

It was funny how just a few words could tear someone's entire personal construct apart. One day he was walking around thinking he'd had a wonderful childhood and was loved by his parents, parents who'd given their lives for him. And the next thing he knew, it was all a lie. He'd been thrown away like old bones.

His knees gave out and he sat down on the couch, staring at Sabrina's boots. They were Italian leather. The craftsmanship was lovely. Expensive boots for a nurse. But then she wasn't a nurse anymore, was she? And wasn't that a huge indication that his brain was done for the day that he'd prefer to think about her shoes than the life-changing events of the evening.

"The spell is wearing off. The bowl is almost empty," Raven said.

Tobias glanced at Scoria's feet. It was true. The evaporation rate defied logic, but the water was gone.

"What should we do with him?" Tobias asked.

"Kill him," Gabriel offered, looking every bit serious about the suggestion.

But Sabrina shook her head, her eyes bright with cunning. "You do that and Empress Eleanor will send a replacement to finish the job. There's no way she isn't sitting on her throne waiting for an update from this guy.

She might even have him magically tagged so she knows where he is."

"You seem to know a lot about the daily life of assassins." Gabriel's tone wasn't complimentary, but Tobias didn't have a chance to react to his brother's quip before Sabrina came to her own defense.

"Yeah, I do," she said, meeting Gabriel's stare head-on. "I was raised in a vampire kingdom. I've watched my father defend and expand that kingdom since I was old enough to walk. If you two are truly the heirs to this place called Paragon, you've got to be smart about this. You can't just kill this guy."

Raven rubbed her eyes, looking more exhausted by the minute. "Then what do you suggest?"

Sabrina glanced at Tobias before answering. "I suggest you use magic to wipe his memories, then send him back to Paragon to report to Eleanor that he couldn't find any of you. You're gone. Plant a false memory to suggest you are either all dead or have left this realm for good. Then hope she believes it."

The unflinching eye contact between Sabrina and Gabriel was making Tobias itch, but his brother's expression gradually softened. He knew that look. It was respect.

"You are one badass vampire," Tobias murmured.

She smiled and curtsied.

Gabriel paced in front of their prisoner, his hands buried in the pockets of his sport coat. "It's a good idea, but not enough. Not for Eleanor. We must take it one step further. We should plant something in his brain to make him kill Eleanor if and when he's close enough to her to do so. Turn her own weapon against her."

"Are you suggesting we murder our mother?" Tobias crossed his arms against the ridiculous notion.

"Yes, before she kills us." Gabriel raised an eyebrow.

A tingle crawled up Tobias's spine. He couldn't deny what his brother, Raven, and now Scoria had told him about his mother. But he couldn't accept it either. He wanted an explanation. He wanted to look her in the eyes and have her tell him herself why she had done it. The idea of Scoria killing her before Tobias experienced that closure, before he was totally sure that there wasn't some sort of reason, some manipulation driving her, unsettled him.

"And then what? I can get behind sending him back. Killing her means someone else needs to step up and lead Paragon. Do you want that to be Brynhoff? Or are you suggesting it will be you on the throne?"

"I am the eldest heir." Gabriel pointed a finger at his chin. "Relax, brother, no one expects anything from you."

"No, you never did. You were happy being the warrior, the backup for Marius. Who was I but the wiry and underestimated academic who could barely wield a sword? A sparring partner meant to build your confidence." Tobias ground his teeth. He was a renowned doctor in the human world. He would not go back to being his family's punching bag.

"What is it you want, Tobias? If you don't want to defend ourselves against Mother, what is your solution?"

Tobias shook his head. "Send him back with a message that we are dead. Leave her alive to rule Paragon."

"And therefore sentence Paragon to her rule. She's destroying the realm."

A growl ripped from Tobias's throat, and suddenly Sabrina was there, between them, her hand on his chest. He met her gaze, and slowly the anger drained from his body.

"He's not the enemy," she said softly.

He pointed a finger back at Gabriel. "Do as you must,

but know this: if you take back Paragon, you are on your own. I will not be by your side, and I will not be able to stop the backlash when our people learn your mate is a witch."

Gabriel's jaw clenched as he processed Tobias's statement. He did not break eye contact with him as he said, "Perform the spell, Raven. Wipe his memories and implant a false one. Then we will send Scoria back where he came from."

Raven turned to him, both hands resting on her lower belly. The circles under her eyes looked like two dark bruises. "I can't. Not now. I'm drained. You'll have to keep him until tomorrow. I need time to rest."

"Of course," Tobias said. "You've been through too much tonight already."

Gabriel grumbled his agreement.

Sabrina sighed. "You should lock him in the basement. Make sure you gag him. Once Raven's spell completely wears off, I have a feeling you'll have a howler on your hands."

"What's he doing?" Tobias asked.

Scoria had wrenched his head to the side and was biting a black jewel off the shoulder of his uniform.

"Stop him. Don't let him swallow that!" Sabrina said, lunging for the prisoner. She was too late. The dragon swallowed the stone and she swore.

"What was that?" Tobias asked.

Beside him, Gabriel cursed. Scoria began to spasm, his eyes rolling back in his head, his body contorting against his bindings. White foam bubbled over his lips. A deep crack came from his chest. Tobias cringed as a malformed and scaly protrusion broke from his torso like an alien in a horror movie and spilled onto the floor where it sizzled against the hardwood.

Tobias gagged at the smell. That was the male's dragon, or a piece of it anyway, fried from the inside out. He'd never seen anything so horrific.

Spreading her hands, Sabrina whirled on Gabriel and Tobias. "Why didn't you tell me he had a suicide pill on his uniform?"

"I didn't know."

"How can you not know? Aren't you from Paragon? Haven't you ever interrogated someone before?"

"Wait... Did he poison himself rather than be used as a weapon?" Tobias felt slow on the uptake. This was not his world. He longed to go back to the hospital where there were rules, where life and death were natural occurrences, not political weapons.

Sabrina grabbed his lower jaw and turned his head to look at her. "I'm sorry, Tobias. I know this isn't easy for you, but you need to wake up!"

❧

ON SOME LEVEL, SABRINA WAS SELF-AWARE ENOUGH TO know that she had crossed a line. She was shaking Tobias by the face. Why not go full *Looney Tunes* and smack him across the cheek? Instead, she lowered her hand and turned, unflinchingly, toward the prisoner who had died a horrific death and was oozing fluids on the carpet.

"This is reality, Tobias. This is *your* reality. I don't know much about where you come from, but war is war. And you are royalty." She laughed a little at that. "No wonder you wanted me to shed my responsibilities to my coven. That's exactly what you did, didn't you?"

"That's not fair, Sabrina. You don't know how it was."

"No. I don't. But I'm catching on quickly regarding how

it *is*. The empress, your mother, will hear of this. If not immediately, she'll figure it out when that guardsman doesn't check in. You need to prepare yourself." It was rude, in his face, but at the moment she was her father's daughter. She could almost hear Calvin's voice when she spoke.

Tobias said nothing. He glowered at Scoria's remains, his eyes vacant.

"We need to hide the body," she said, feeling annoyed. She hated dealing with this stuff, and she couldn't call the coven to do it for her. They couldn't know about Tobias or his brother, and she didn't even want to think about what would happen if her coven found out about Raven.

"It will take care of itself," Tobias said.

"What?" Sabrina glared at him. Had he lost his mind? Did he think he could leave this mess to rot on his living room floor?

A creaking sound brought her gaze back around to Scoria, whose body had gone entirely gray. Abruptly, the corpse turned to ash, collapsing into a formless pile of dust on and around the chair.

Her mouth gaped. "That's convenient."

Tobias rose and left the room, returning with a dustpan and a garbage bag. He started shoveling the ash into the Hefty. To Sabrina's horror, Raven reached into the remains with her bare hand and retrieved a cat's-eye jewel larger than her fist.

"Holy crap, what is that?" Sabrina blurted.

"His heart." Raven tossed the stone to Gabriel, who nodded and mumbled something about taking care of it.

"W-wait," Sabrina said. "That was the same stone that was in his ring."

Raven nodded. "In their human form, their ring is a magical representation of their heart. It cannot be removed without killing the dragon. When they transform, the ring is absorbed and you get that." She pointed toward the ostrich-egg-sized stone in Gabriel's hand.

"The anatomy lesson is great," Tobias said. "But can we talk about what Sabrina said? When Scoria doesn't report in, Eleanor will send another."

Gabriel growled. "We will be ready. We'll stick together. We'll find a way to notify the others."

"Others?" It would be hard enough for Sabrina to keep the three of them a secret. Sabrina couldn't handle hiding more.

"There are eight of us still living," Gabriel said. "After what Scoria said today, it is clear we are all in danger. We need to find each of our siblings and tell them what has happened."

"I have Rowan's address," Tobias said. "I've lost touch with everyone else."

"Rowan is a great place to start," Gabriel said. "If I know her, she'll have kept in touch with Alexander. If we find her and bring her here—"

"You guys know you can't stay in Chicago, right?" Sabrina interrupted.

They all turned to look at her. She straightened up and placed her hands on her hips. There was no turning back now, not after what she'd seen. They needed to know what kind of danger they were in. "Look, I like you, all of you, and Tobias is a well-respected member of the medical community. No one would ever question his being here. But this is the second magical incident in a week."

Raven frowned. She looked exhausted and Sabrina hated to put more stress on the poor woman.

Sabrina tucked her hair behind her ears. "It's not like I'm going to tell anyone about you, even though I am obligated as a member of my coven and the future master to report you immediately. I'm trying to warn you because the longer you all are here and stuff like this is going down"— she pointed at the Hefty bag full of ashes—"the greater the odds that someone from my coven is eventually going to figure out you're not human, and then shit will hit the fan. Frankly, after tonight and the blood, it might already be too late for me to cover your tracks."

Gabriel tipped his head. "And what will happen to you if Tobias leaves?"

"I just said I'm not going anywhere," Tobias said.

"I'm simply asking the question. Do you realize what will happen to you if Tobias leaves you?"

Sabrina narrowed her eyes at him and shook her head. "What are you getting at, Gabriel?"

"Earlier tonight you mentioned you couldn't tolerate the way I smelled."

"Yeah, 'cause you reek like you stepped in a pumpkin pie made of shit."

Raven looked at her and then at Tobias, whose face had gone stony. "He smells the same as always. It's you who's changed."

Sabrina didn't understand. "What are you talking about?"

In a rush, Gabriel attacked Tobias, talons thrusting from his second knuckles and wings spreading. He never got close enough to lay a hand on him. Sabrina's fangs dropped. In a flash, she'd moved between them and shoved Gabriel back with everything she had. His feet left the ground, but thanks to his wings he was able to stop himself before slamming into the wall. He laughed wickedly.

Tobias rubbed his head. "Sabrina. By the Mountain."

"What?" Her eyes darted between each of them.

It was Raven who blurted out the truth. "You're bound to him. You're mated. You're showing all the signs. Sabrina, don't you know you're in love with him?"

The words knocked her back a step, the air growing thick and close. "Of course I love him. I've loved him for years. It doesn't matter. You haven't been listening to me. None of our feelings matter."

"I love you too," Tobias said immediately.

"Don't. You'll only make it worse." There was a lump forming in her throat, and for some reason her entire body had started to tremble.

"What are you trying to say?" Tobias's brittle expression threatened to break her heart.

She rounded on him, and despite herself tears started to flow. "I'm saying that I can and will keep your secret, but I'm not powerful enough to stop the repercussions if my coven finds you and your family. Less than a month ago, I watched three werewolves have their heads sliced from their bodies moments before every vampire I know descended upon them and drained their corpses dry. I won't be able to stop it. If they catch you, they will kill you." She chewed her lip. "Once I rise to master, there are things I can do to make it easier for Tobias, but I can't keep covering stuff up like this. I keep bringing this up because my heart couldn't take watching you die. Any of you. The smart thing to do would be for you, all of you, to leave Chicago. And it's not because I want you to go. I'm trying to save your lives."

"Well, I'm not leaving you, or Chicago," Tobias said flatly. "And my brother and his future wife are welcome here for as long as they need to stay."

She nodded slowly. "Okay. But you should know I can't risk this again. Not even if you're attacked by another Obsidian Guardsman."

"Fine. We'll take care of ourselves. This is dragon business," Tobias said coolly.

Sabrina's gaze darted between Gabriel and Tobias, and all she could picture was the werewolves in Lamia's Star. She could see the three of them on their knees, being torn apart by her own coven. A powerful leader like her father might be able to stop something like that from happening, but not Sabrina. She would be new, inexperienced. What if Tristan or another vampire challenged her authority? Her stomach churned and she closed her eyes. "You don't understand the danger."

Tobias reached out and touched her face. "Thank you for helping us Sabrina. I understand that you can't protect us anymore. We'll protect ourselves."

With a final huff and a shake of her head, Sabrina twisted her exhausted shoulders and dematerialized.

CHAPTER TWENTY-EIGHT

Watching Sabrina leave was one of the hardest things Tobias had ever done. Even now, distracted and exhausted by the events of the evening, every part of him wished she had stayed. He had the strangest need to protect her, which was stupid considering that everything about tonight showed him she was more than capable of protecting herself. It didn't take a genius to conclude that Sabrina was no stranger to violence. He'd underestimated her, taken her human kindness and quirky nature at work to be the entire picture of her personality. But she was far more.

Vampire covens were prone to being territorial. Tobias understood that Sabrina wasn't lying when she said they were in danger, especially given the size of the Chicago coven. If his true identity was ever revealed, Tobias might well be in a world of hurt. He should have been more careful with her. He'd allowed his feelings for her to cloud his judgment, and he'd let her in too far, too fast. But what was done was done. Now he only hoped that after she rose to power they could find each other again.

"I'm sorry, Tobias. She'll be back. She's bound to you. Mated. Whether she believes it or not, she won't be able to stay away. She's already yours." Gabriel placed a hand on his shoulder.

"Don't put anything past Sabrina. She's the first vampire-human hybrid, and her will is as strong as her grip. If she says she can't act on her feelings, she won't."

Raven sat down on the couch and stared at the Hefty bag full of Scoria's remains. "Do you believe us now?" she asked. "About your mother?"

"Yes." He rubbed circles over his temples. "I still feel there has to be another explanation. Our mother, she was good, wasn't she, Gabriel? I remember her as good."

"I do too, brother, but she's changed." Gabriel shrugged. "We need to tell the others what's going on. They deserve to know."

Tobias lowered his hands. "I know."

"Rowan first. You said you had an address." Gabriel sat down beside him on the sofa and rubbed his palms on his thighs.

"She lives in New York. Manhattan."

"What about a phone number? Email?"

Tobias shook his head. "The last of both I had don't work anymore. I tried to contact her when you arrived here. Granted, I haven't seen her in decades. I've had three phone numbers myself since then."

Gabriel leaned back against the cushions and blew out a deep breath at the ceiling. "So, we go to New York and hope she hasn't moved."

"I might be able to do a locator spell. We have her dress at home in New Orleans. I mean, if she's moved." She leaned her head back. "And if no one kills me before I get the chance to do the spell."

"Maybe you should eat something," Tobias said, the doctor in him bubbling to the surface.

"You know what I want?" Raven closed her eyes. "Ice cream. It's been a long day. A huge bowl of mint chocolate chip would be amazing."

"I have Chunky Monkey." There was no levity in his voice. He couldn't believe he was talking about ice cream at a time like this, although he had to admit, the idea of Ben & Jerry's did give him a warm spot. Sometimes ice cream could heal what words could not.

"Chunky Monkey it is. I'll get it." Gabriel rose from the sofa.

"I better take out the remains," Tobias said. "There's an ordinance. Special tags. No dumping."

"I would offer to help, but considering what happened when we tried to park without a sticker..." Gabriel rubbed the back of his neck. He was beginning to look as fatigued as Raven.

"Don't worry about it. You don't want Mr. Gilbert on your case again. The vacuum's in the hall closet. Do you mind sucking up what remains of this guy's... remains? I'd rather not be inhaling him the next time the heat kicks on."

"Consider it done." Gabriel disappeared into the kitchen in search of ice cream.

Tobias lugged the garbage bag to the back door and pulled on his coat and shoes. As he trudged to the curb, it gave him no pleasure to have contributed to the death of a member of the Obsidian Guard. They used to be his heroes. It was like dropping his childhood on the side of the road and any innocence he had left along with it.

He'd turned to go back in the house when the biting jabs of a heated discussion met his ears. A tingle traveled his spine. It sounded like Sabrina's voice. Quietly, he moved along the street toward the sound, making himself invisible.

Around the next block, he found Sabrina talking to Tristan.

"You fucking bitch. You will regret doing this to me."

"I didn't do anything to you. Truly, if my father assigned you to the work camp in Racine rather than offing your head, he's done you a service. When I told him about what you'd done, he considered execution."

"You can't prove anything." Tristan bared his teeth.

"No? Is that werewolf hair on your shirt?" She snorted when Tristan looked down at himself. "In case you're wondering, I'm immune to that particular poison you used to coat his dagger. Don't bother trying it again."

"You will be sorry," he said through his teeth. "The coven doesn't want you. We don't need a human hybrid calling the shots. You've gotten by this far on your father's coattails. How will you survive when he's gone? No one will take you seriously, Princess. Admit it, you're in over your head."

She hissed and lowered herself into a fighting stance. "Pack all your things before you leave for Racine, Tristan. You're not welcome in Chicago ever again."

"Are you going to fight me, Sabrina?"

"No." She stood and brushed invisible lint from the sleeve of her coat. "You're not worth it."

Quickly, she poofed out of there, leaving behind nothing but the scent of honey and moonlight. Tristan's nostrils flared. His eyes shifted left, then right as he smoothed his shirt. "...gonna be sorry," was all Tobias heard before Tristan dissolved in a puff of black smoke that smelled of cigar smoke.

GABRIEL RAN THE TIPS OF HIS FINGERS ALONG THE base of Raven's neck. He loved it when she wore her hair up. There were a million things he should be thinking about. Scoria could have killed her or hurt the baby with the weapon he'd used on her and Tobias. They'd killed a member of the Obsidian Guard. If they weren't on Paragon's most-wanted list before, they sure as hell were now. The baby—he should be thinking about the baby. But as much as he tried, his attention returned to the slope of Raven's creamy skin, the stretch that ran from behind her ear to the dip of her clavicle. He lowered his lips to place a kiss there.

Raven had wasted no time tearing into the pint of Chunky Monkey Gabriel had brought her. Even after Tobias had come in from taking Scoria to the curb and excused himself to his room, Raven hardly came up for air long enough to mention her dismay at seeing Tobias heartbroken. In record time, she'd almost reached the bottom of the pint, and Gabriel thought she looked a little better, the dark circles under her eyes a bit smaller. He kissed her again as another bite found its way into her mouth.

"This is so good," she mumbled.

"So you keep telling me. I don't suppose you plan to share any of that?"

"Absolutely not. It's too yummy." She grinned at him over her shoulder and then fed him a bite. "Actually, please eat some. I can't believe I've finished most of this pint. I can't remember ever being this hungry before."

"You expelled an incredible amount of power today. Eat it. You need the calories. It's good for you and the baby." He returned to worshipping her neck. It had taken months for her to regain the weight she'd lost when she'd had cancer. He would love and want her at any size, but he was relieved to see her eating. It meant that despite their circumstances, she was healthy, happy, and strong.

"I'm just not sure it will be good for fitting into my wedding dress. Avery is going to flip her top when she finds out I'm pregnant."

Gabriel laughed into her skin. "Are you sure you want to tell her?"

"Of course I do. She doesn't need to know I'm having a dragon, but I have to tell her something. She's my sister! What would she say if we showed up one day with a child in our arms?"

"You're right. It's better to tell her. Why are you worried about fitting into a dress? I was not aware you'd had time to pick one out yet."

She shrugged and placed the empty ice-cream container on the coffee table. "I haven't, but Avery has my measurements and she's shopping for me."

"You're allowing your sister to choose your wedding dress for you?"

"Maybe. Avery cares more about it than I do."

"The oreads could make you one if you'd like, in a style that would accommodate your changing figure. Juniper and Hazel would feel honored."

She turned to face him. "Seriously? You don't think it would be too much?"

He wiped a bit of ice cream from her bottom lip. "All I ask is that you only request their help if you are committed to the outcome. You won't be able to hold them back if you do, and they would be destroyed if you did not wear their finished creation."

"Never. Nothing I could buy would be as beautiful as what they would make for me. When we get home, I'll ask them."

He gave her a shallow smile. How he wished their wedding plans weren't marred by his family's drama. He wrapped his arms around her and pulled her into his lap, tight against his chest. He pictured her in a traditional Paragonian wedding gown, peacock blue of course, a melding of the emerald stone that represented his family line and the blue of her eyes. She'd have looked lovely descending the aisle of the great hall. All of Paragon would have treated her as royalty.

Raven dropped the spoon into the mostly empty ice-cream container. "Maybe we *should* go back to New Orleans. I need to research this pregnancy, and I've put off telling my father about our engagement for far too long."

"As soon as they realize Scoria is dead, my mother and Brynhoff will send another guardsman. Tobias can't handle an attack on his own. He was never a fighter. If we go, we need to convince him to come with us."

Raven scoffed. "He won't leave as long as Sabrina is here."

"No." Gabriel shook his head. "He'll wait for her for as long as it takes."

"If her entire coven is as scary as she is, no wonder she suggested we leave. My skin wanted to peel itself off when she growled and bared her fangs. You should have seen her take Scoria down."

"Hmm." Gabriel frowned and stared at the freshly vacuumed carpet. "You and Tobias were lucky she was there this time, but based on the way she stormed off tonight, I wouldn't rely on her again."

"Do you think she'll be capable of staying away? It's clear she's bound to him."

He cleared his throat. "In Paragon, Vampires are prone to being... cold and calculating."

"Undoubtedly Sabrina is both those things. But she certainly is protective of Tobias."

"Still, I'm not sure about the nature of their relationship or if we can count on her protection long term. Until we're sure he's safe, I want to stay in Chicago. I know this is an important time for you. I am told planning a wedding is a great deal of work and should be a joyous occasion for us. Not to mention the baby."

She pressed her lips against his. "It's okay. I'm happy to be here for Tobias right now."

"You wouldn't rather be shopping with your sister?"

She laughed. "Er, no. I'd like to stay and strengthen the wards around this house. I can help keep us safe. Besides, to be honest, I know that human weddings are supposed to be über-important to girls and that people get all stressed out over wanting everything to be a certain way, but it's not really my priority. I already have exactly what I want. As long as I'm with you, I'm happy. No ceremony or piece of paper is going to change that. Sure, I'd like to have a nice day to celebrate with friends and family, but I'm in no rush."

"No?" He nuzzled her neck. "You're not interested in making an honorable man out of me?"

She drew back and took his face in her hands. "You are the most honorable man I know. But if you're referring to the human tradition of waiting for the honeymoon, I'll remind you that married or not, you've already mated me. That's for life, isn't it?"

He raised an eyebrow. "Indeed. And life is a very long

time with a dragon. Can you handle the commitment?" He swept his hand up the outside of her thigh.

Her eyes narrowed. "I think I'm up for the task. Why don't you take me upstairs and see how much I can handle?"

His wings punched out of his shirt, and he swept her off the couch. Instantly, his body responded to her proposition and his mind narrowed in on her until there was nothing else in the entire universe but her. To him, she was the most precious being alive. She squealed as he rushed her into their room and locked the door behind them. In another breath, he'd stripped off her clothing and then his, leaving it in a pile on the floor. Gently, he spread her out on the bed, his lips trailing down the inside of her thigh.

Her fingers dug into his hair. "I love you, Gabriel, with everything that I am."

He paused and looked up at her, his wings arching protectively over her naked body. She reached up and stroked her nails along the underside of those wings, sending tiny shivers down his spine. He needed to be inside her, to mark her as his and to hear her call his name. With a single flap of his wings, he hoisted himself over her and cradled her dark head in his hands. By the Mountain, her eyes were blue. Deep. Fathomless.

"I'm not sure love is a strong enough word for what I feel for you, Raven. My soul thirsts for you. Without you, I'd shrivel like an empty husk. Do you realize how thoroughly you own me?"

"My very own dragon." She thrust herself up, and he tucked his wings as she rolled him onto his back. Her red lips lowered to his ear. "Let me ride you and see if you're worth keeping."

She lowered herself onto him then, connecting with him in the most intimate way. He arched under her, his blood hot in his veins. With a swivel of her hips, she sent him to heaven. No other thoughts clouded his brain as she began to move above him except the singular desire to give her more of what she needed. To be more for her.

And he showed her as much, time and time again.

CHAPTER TWENTY-NINE

E very box was packed, every plate, every trinket
wrapped and tucked away. There was nothing left on
the walls. All the furniture was gone. Sabrina was supposed
to be staying with her father tonight. She *would* be staying
with her father. There was no other choice now. Her place
was sold, and staying with Tobias again—that was out of the
question.

A glass of wine in her hand, Sabrina sat on the carpet in
front of her sliding glass door, watching the Chicago skyline
beyond her balcony. Part of her wanted to be excited. She
was rising, taking on a powerful position that few of her
gender had taken on. Add to that her status as a vampire-
human hybrid, and Chicago needed her. She would ensure
a kind and fair vampire society. One that would coexist
peacefully with humans.

And maybe, after several years of focused attention, if
the coven was safe and she'd laid the groundwork for an
orderly rule, she could pass on her duties to someone she
trusted and return to the life she'd left behind. She'd find
time to see the sun again, even if only for fleeting moments

while the other vampires were still asleep. She'd sneak out if she had to. Bribe Paul if it was necessary.

And maybe, just maybe, she could find a way to safely see Tobias.

Draining the glass, she set it down beside her crossed ankles. Why was she procrastinating? She stared out over the city like some reject from a Hallmark movie. If she were honest with herself, she *knew* why. She'd felt it snap into place the moment she'd seen Tobias stretched out on the sidewalk. It was like all her internal organs had shifted to make room for her growing heart. It was a good thing Scoria had died the way he had, because she might have ripped him apart herself otherwise. Surely she would not have hesitated, even if it meant loss of life and limb.

Which could mean only one thing. She'd bonded with Tobias. Her vampire half had marked him as her own. What had he called it? His people called it mating. He'd asked her to be his before, and she'd told him yes, but it was only her human half speaking the word. She hadn't fully given herself over heart, mind, and soul until she'd had to protect him. Leaping on Scoria had been her vampire half's way of screaming *mine*. And now her heart might as well be wired to his for how empty she felt here without him, as if she'd left a piece of herself behind.

It was for the best.

A dark mist filtered onto her balcony and solidified into the form of her father. She motioned for him to come in and he did, unlocking the door and sliding it open with his mind.

"I thought I'd find you here," he said, flashing her a warm smile. "Having trouble letting go?"

She patted the floor and he sat down beside her, a current of cool air following him into the room. Her father always smelled of sandalwood, spices, and leather, thanks to specially made cologne he'd been wearing for almost a hundred years. It reminded her of how ancient he was— hard to believe when the person sitting next to her looked no older than thirty-five.

"It's a big change, and it came on quickly. I'm just trying to process everything."

He leaned back on his elbows and crossed his legs at the ankles. "I was already master of our coven when I met your mother." Sabrina glanced his way. His face was sober, nostalgic. "It was the early morning of 1939, and I was returning from an event at the Willowbrook ballroom. In those days we worked closely with human leaders. There were less of us then, and we didn't have to be as careful. Those were different times. Simpler times. No cell phones. No instant cameras. People didn't run to the police every time a vampire drank their blood and forgot to scrub their minds. They bought some garlic and moved on with their lives." He shrugged.

"Things have changed a lot since then."

"I met your mother in Resurrection Cemetery."

"You've told me this story. She was raising the dead."

He smiled. "I saw her talking to a grave. Your mother had red hair, just like yours, that deep, intense shade of red that reminded me of blood. Our eyes met, and it was like she could see into my soul. She knew I was a vampire. I didn't have to tell her."

"She was one of a kind." Sabrina smiled at the thought of her mother hovering over a grave. It wasn't her memory, but she could picture it clearly.

"Anyway, I was walking toward her when a woman in white raced past me toward the grave. I heard the squeal of tires behind me, her human date taking off, no doubt terrified. The ghost, whose name I would later learn was Mary, thanked your mother profusely before climbing atop her grave. Your mother waved a hand and she slipped inside again."

"The humans still tell that ghost story, you know," Sabrina said. "They call her Resurrection Mary."

"Veronica wanted to give her one more chance to dance the night away. She died tragically, you understand. She couldn't rest until your mother gave her that one final wish."

"That was nice of Mom."

"She was a good woman. Full of life. I loved her beyond measure." He leaned back and stared at the ceiling. "I still miss her."

A thought crossed Sabrina's mind and she furrowed her brow. "My mother was human. A necromancer, for sure, but a human necromancer. How did you get the coven to approve that? I thought it was forbidden."

He scoffed. "By the goddess, if I had a dime for every-thing that was forbidden in the old laws, I'd be an even richer male. Yes, she was forbidden, and it made me want her more."

She leaned forward, hugging her knees to her chest. "But what did you do? How did you keep the coven from killing her?"

"Oh, they tried. Well, one tried. His name was Seamus and he challenged me, accusing me of breaking the old law in front of the entire assembly."

"What did you do?"

"I told them that Veronica was my consort and as master I was allowed to select my personal staff. It was none of his business that I was in love with her. That I'd bonded with her. I didn't admit to that. Only to enlisting her as my human companion."

"And that worked?"

He scoffed. "No. The bastard tried to have her killed, and I took off his head."

"And that was it? No one else accused you?"

"You will find as master that if someone challenges you and you end them quickly and decisively, others are loath to follow in their footsteps. Violence is only the answer when you want them to never ask the question again."

"So you've told me." She smiled. "So, for Mom, you made your own law."

"Yes. The same as I did when you were born. Oh, the rumors. There were some who feared you wouldn't be immortal because you were born and grew up, but here you are, no longer aging."

"There are still people who want to kill me." She thought of Tristan.

"You know how to defend yourself. I've taught you everything I know."

She laughed. "I'm afraid I am not as strong or as deadly as you, Father."

He turned a serious look in her direction. "You underestimate yourself. When it matters, I know you will use all the resources available to you and you will do what is necessary. You will do what I would do."

"I just hope I can live up to your legacy, Daddy. I sometimes feel I'm not cut out for this fate."

He grunted deep in his throat. "Bullshit. Everything that has happened to you has prepared you to lead. You question yourself because you think you have to do it the same as me. Sabrina, you will do it your own way, and that will be the right way."

She wrapped her arms around his neck and squeezed. "Thank you. I needed to hear that."

"Now, are you ready to come home with me? It's almost daybreak."

"If you don't mind, I'd like to stay and watch the sunrise. It might be a while before I see another."

He nodded. "What a wondrous thing, to be able to walk in the light."

"It doesn't suck." She grinned as he strode onto the balcony and dematerialized.

She stared at the horizon until watery light bled across the floor, its warmth swallowing her balcony, then kissing her toes before it washed away the stars. The city lights succumbed one by one to the bright ball of rising gold. When the sun was fully risen, she dematerialized to the tunnels, ready to start her new life.

※

As always, Tobias embraced his work like an old friend, using his gift for healing others as a much-needed distraction. Sabrina wasn't returning his calls or texts, her apartment was empty, and when he returned to the uptown bar where she'd saved his life, the one they called Boss Miller claimed he'd never heard of her and then offered him a free beer. She was gone. Disappeared into some underground labyrinth where he couldn't follow.

"Doctor?" The nurse taking his patient's vitals nudged his elbow. "Joseph asked you a question."

Tobias snapped out of his reverie and looked down at his young patient. How long had he been lost to this churning in his brain, this feeling like he'd never be whole again if he didn't reconnect with Sabrina?

He cleared his throat. "Sorry, what was that?"

"Can I still play baseball this summer?"

He blinked rapidly. "Yes, Joseph. You'll be fine by then as long as you make sure you take your medication and follow the diet we talked about. Your dad is going to help you with those things. As long as you're not passing out anymore, you can do any of your regular activities."

With all the good humor he could muster, he answered the rest of Joseph's questions—his father's too—before excusing himself from the room.

"Are you okay, Dr. Toby?" the nurse asked. She'd followed him into the hall, looking concerned. An older woman in her fifties, she worked part-time now and was probably filling in for Sabrina until the hospital could find a permanent replacement.

"Fine. Er... thank you. Another case on my mind."

She nodded her understanding and went about her work, heading in the direction of the medication room. Thankfully, Tobias was done with his rounds. He quickly finished his documentation and headed for the door.

"Dr. Toby?" The nurse was back and she was pale. Extremely pale, like all the blood had rushed from her head.

"Yes? What's wrong?"

"Tristan says he has a message for you." She pushed the neck of her scrubs aside to reveal an ugly bite mark under her collarbone. The nurse wavered on her feet, and Tobias rushed forward to catch her in his arms. He helped her sit down behind the desk, checking her badge when he couldn't remember her name.

"Elizabeth, where did you see Tristan?"

"Outside the medication room. He said he was a friend and was looking for you."

"Is that when he bit you?"

She laughed. "Bit me? Nobody bit me. A nice man just asked me to give you a message. I gave it to you, right?" She touched her forehead. "I can't remember now. I feel a little light-headed."

The color was coming back to her cheeks. Tobias moved the phone closer to her. "I need to go look for him. Rest here for a minute. If you start to feel worse, call for help."

"Okay." She shook her graying curls. "Probably low blood sugar. I just need to eat something. I'll be fine."

Tobias gave her a light squeeze on the shoulder, then headed for the medication room. There was no one there, but a note on the door read PARKING GARAGE. SINATRA LEVEL. He tore the note from the door and crumpled it in his hand.

Furious, he grabbed his coat and took the elevator down to the main floor, wishing the security guard good night as he passed through the lobby. Across the street in the Huron Superior Parking Garage, he boarded the elevator and selected the Sinatra Level, level four. The only other person on the elevator with him got off at Tony Bennett, level two. When the doors opened again, Tristan was there waiting for him, leaning against a blue sedan.

"What do you want, Tristan?" Tobias asked. The vampire reminded him of a toad that had stretched itself into a man, his overlarge eyes giving him the look of a nocturnal animal.

Tristan smoothed back his oily dark hair. "So, you do know who I am. It seems that Sabrina didn't quite uphold the level of confidentiality she says she did."

"I don't know what you're talking about," Tobias said. "My nurse, Elizabeth, said a man named Tristan had a message for me. I followed you here." He held up the crumpled note. "Now, what can I do for you? And what does this have to do with a nurse who used to work here?"

Tobias thought he'd done a good job playing it cool and

covering for Sabrina, but Tristan didn't seem to buy it. His dark eyes became even darker slits. "Either you are weak-minded or intentionally ignorant. I know you have a relationship with Sabrina. I've watched her enter your home and not come out for days."

Tobias scowled.

"You didn't think I knew? Oh, I had humans following you, Doctor. In the coffeehouse, the museum, the zoo. They lost the trail every now and then, but somehow I could always connect the dots back to you. You must be one hell of a human."

"Go fuck yourself." Tobias turned to leave.

"I wouldn't do that. Not if you care about your patient."

Tobias turned around slowly, grinding his teeth to keep from shifting. It wouldn't do to reveal what he was to this scumbag. That would spell disaster for Sabrina. Tristan was holding up his phone, and even from a distance he knew who was featured on the screen. Katelyn.

"I've got two vamps and a human outside her house. All I have to do is say the word and she dies. Cute kid. It would be terrible if her young life should come to a tragic end, especially after the miracle you pulled off healing her."

He suppressed a growl. "What do you want with me?"

"I want to save my coven from a terrible mistake, and I need you to come with me to do so."

"And if I come, you won't hurt the girl?"

"Swear on my life."

"You're a vampire. You're already dead."

Tristan opened the car door and retrieved a length of rope. "Allow me to bind your wrists and get into the car, and I'll call off my crew." He shook his phone. The live feed of Katelyn sleeping made Tobias feel ill.

He approached the vampire. If he played his cards

right, he could save Katelyn and snap the vampire's neck in the process. A partial shift. A short reach across the seats while he was driving. Tristan wouldn't know what hit him. Tobias held out his wrists.

As soon as Tristan tightened the binding, Tobias realized he'd made a terrible mistake. His knees dipped and it felt like his blood was turning to concrete. *Enchanted*, he thought. Tristan must have the help of a witch!

"Interesting," Tristan said, a broad, froggy smile stretching his lower face.

"Tell your people to leave my former patient alone," Tobias said.

Tristan tapped the screen and raised the phone to his lips. Tobias heard ringing and then a click as someone answered.

"Kill her," Tristan said.

"You bastard!" Tobias tried to kick Tristan but could barely raise his foot off the ground.

"Nighty night, Doc." Tristan's fist collided with his face. Tobias's head slapped the concrete, and then there was darkness.

CHAPTER THIRTY

For as long as she'd been a vampire, Sabrina had never seen the tunnels look more beautiful than they did tonight. The human floral designer had sworn he'd make the underground ballroom look like spring, and he'd succeeded. The tunnels had been decorated with thousands of flowering plants. Red tulips, petunias, and an array of greenery she couldn't name lined every wall. Deep-red roses had been strung on plastic line and hung in swags across the ceiling. Lamia's Star smelled of flowers and had been transformed from gray and brick to a cherry-red floral paradise.

If the tunnels weren't enough of a departure from normalcy, the dress she was wearing certainly was. Blood-colored silk and organza wrapped high along the back of her neck and then plunged toward her waist, the bottom of a wide vee ending in the vicinity of her belly button. A full skirt with a train hid a pair of Jimmy Choos that were absolutely to die for. In white, it would have been a wedding dress fit for a queen. As it was, the color made her flesh appear alabaster and brought out the coppery tones in her hair. Along with a velvety red lip color, she'd become the queen of the undead, prepared to marry her coven.

Marriage was a good analogy. This was not a light commitment. Once a master, always a master.

She waited in the small antechamber off the side of the dais, her father by her side. A Forebear had been called in to perform the ceremony. All she knew about him was that his name was Aldrich and although he looked about fifty, he was over one thousand years old. Dressed in a kimono of red silk embroidered with a black pattern of falling leaves, he mounted the stage to the sound of a trio of violins, taking his place beside the throne, next to the gold-and-ruby tiara he would place upon her head at the end of the ceremony. The entire Lamia Coven had gathered to watch her coronation.

Her knees turned to water and she placed a hand on the wall to steady herself. Her father hooked his arm under her elbow.

"Nerves." She pressed a hand to her stomach.

"Breathe, Sabrina." He sent her a reassuring smile.

The tiara she was to be crowned with had been commissioned by her father and contained a twenty-five-carat pear-shaped ruby at the crown called the Tear of Hades. It was worth millions. Vampire legend said the stone was charged with the energy of the lord of the underworld himself.

"Your mother would have been so proud of you today." His gray eyes twinkled and he laid a gentle kiss on her cheek.

"That means a lot to me." She sent him a soft smile. "She'd be proud of you too."

That made his eyes twinkle. "It's time."

She picked up the ceremonial dagger and nodded to her father. She was ready.

"Please present the candidate for coronation," Aldrich said.

Her father guided her toward the dais. One step, then two. Her knees wobbled and she gripped her father's arm for support. And then they were face-to-face with Aldrich in front of a sea of vampires. Her coven. Her people.

"For over three hundred years, the Lamia Coven of Chicago has maintained order by rule of blood. Who presents this child of the night as master?"

"I do," her father said. He held his hand out over the jewel-encrusted chalice.

Sabrina sliced across his palm and watched his blood trickle into the vessel. "By the goddess, I accept the offering of your blood as a sign of my readiness to take your place as master of this coven."

"Do you come before the goddess of your own free will to take on responsibility for this coven for as long as you are master?" Aldrich asked her.

"I so offer my blood as a sign of this covenant." Sabrina sliced across her own palm and watched her blood mix with her father's inside the gold chalice.

Aldrich lifted his own dagger and extended his hand above the goblet between them. "Then, as a representative of the Forebears, I bestow upon you—"

"Wait!"

Aldrich stopped before the blade pierced his skin. Sabrina turned to see Tristan shoving his way to the front of the ballroom, dragging two prisoners along with him. Both were bound and wearing dark hoods. He shoved them to their knees in front of the dais.

"Tristan? What is the meaning of this?" Her father's voice was laden with menace. He wasn't happy, and Sabrina watched his fingers bend into claws near his sides.

"I think the coven needs to know that the female they are about to make master fraternizes with shifters."

Sabrina's spine stiffened. She stared at the hooded figures. One wore street clothes, the other dress pants and a tie. It could be... Goddess, please don't let it be.

Tristan pulled the hoods off the first man, and there was an intake of breath as the vampires around him got a good whiff. Even she could smell the werewolf. It was unmistakably the one who had stabbed her. But it was when Tristan pulled the second hood off that her fangs dropped and she released a chilling hiss. Tobias. He was on his knees, staring up at her. She caught herself on her father's arm.

She knew instantly that the rope binding his wrists was enchanted. Madam Chloe had warned her that Tristan had asked for enchanted bindings. Tobias would be powerless to defend himself using any of his dragon abilities as long as the rope was touching his skin.

Sabrina's trembling stopped and her bones turned to steel. Funny, it was hard to be brave for herself, but for Tobias?

"Why have you brought my coworker here?" she demanded, taking a step toward Tristan. There was no fear or embarrassment in her voice. Nor the guilt he was after. Just anger. She had to talk around her fangs as she pointed to Tobias and said, "This man is a well-known human physician. He is a healer. Return him topside at once."

Tristan scoffed. "You've been misled, Princess. This man is a dragon."

A collective gasp rose up from the coven.

Aldrich turned to her father, a scowl on his face. "Calvin, what is the meaning of this? Who is this vampire?"

"Tristan, return the doctor to his life or prepare to pay with yours," her father said. "You are not welcome here."

With a wave of his hand, two members of her father's security contingent surrounded Tristan, ready to escort him from the Star.

"Tell them." Tristan slapped the back of the werewolf's head.

"I-I saw him shift. He is a dragon." A collective inhale rose up from the crowd, and the guards looked at each other and then at her father.

Sabrina cast a warning glare at the werewolf and noticed for the first time that he was in far worse shape than the day he'd stabbed her, his face beaten and bruised, an ugly scar that might have been a burn running the length of his neck. His cheeks were sunken like he'd been starved.

"Clearly you've been torturing this wolf. He'd say anything you wanted him to say," Sabrina said.

"Such an odd story to tell, don't you think, Princess?" Tristan grinned. "Why would I risk claiming something as crazy as a dragon among us if it weren't true?"

"Dragons have been extinct for generations," Aldrich said. "What proof do you have?"

"Taste his blood." Tristan raised his chin and flashed his teeth. "I promise you won't be disappointed."

Her father turned his head in her direction and whispered in her ear in a voice so quiet it was barely more than a breath. "Do you know anything about this?"

In a soft whisper, she told him the truth. She had to. There was no other choice. If Tobias's blood was spilled that day, it would be done only after the spilling of her own.

"He is my bonded mate. And he is what Tristan says." Tears pricked her eyes, but she did not let them fall. She showed no weakness. To do so would be to hand her fate and Tobias's over to Tristan.

As she met her father's eyes, she saw no softness in his

expression. He was as still and cold as marble. She hadn't seen him look this regal since the day her mother was killed. So this was how she would die, at her father's hand. He would kill her, then Tobias. She steeled herself and nodded to him, ready for whatever punishment he doled out.

He turned to Tristan. "Very well. I will taste the blood."

Her father descended from the dais and approached Tobias. Sabrina's heart pounded against her breastbone as her father rolled up her mate's sleeve a notch. What was he doing? Toying with her? She'd told him the truth!

Sabrina met Tobias's gaze. Whatever happened, she was in this with him. She tried to silently tell him so. The worst part was, she could feel what he was feeling. It wasn't fear, although there was plenty of that coming off the werewolf. Her emotional radar was picking up nothing but love and acceptance from Tobias. He was resigned. That made her sadder than anything.

Calvin gripped Tobias's forearm, digging his thumbnail into the skin above his bound wrists. Her love's blood bubbled. Her father released him and brought the ruby-red bead to his lips, sucking it from the side of his thumb. He said nothing.

Sabrina held her breath when her father shifted to the left suddenly so that she could no longer see Tobias, nor could she make out her father's face. He must know. He must taste how Tobias was different. Sabrina dug her nails into her palms. Why wasn't he saying anything?

ON HIS KNEES ON THE COLD HARD CONCRETE THAT lined the tunnel, Tobias stared up at Sabrina's father. He was a scary son of a bitch. His dark and hardened stare was unwavering. He was *Scarface* and *Goodfellas* all rolled into one, a killer in a custom Versace tuxedo.

"Do you love my daughter?" he whispered. Tobias could barely hear the question, wouldn't have heard it if the man hadn't brought his lips close to his ear.

"Yes. She is my mate," he whispered back.

Calvin took a step back. The man's gaze burrowed into him, seeming to weigh his soul. He glanced down at the wound he'd created. It was already healed. Tobias was sure then, that he knew. Humans did not heal that quickly, and if what Sabrina had said was true, there was no mistaking dragon blood. Tobias tried not to cringe under the weight of his stare.

Calvin grabbed his arm and licked along the place the wound once was. He was sealing it closed, Tobias thought, or pretending to anyway. The vampire tugged a handkerchief from his pocket and wiped his hands as he turned back to Tristan and the wolf. Tristan was grinning, his expression smug and expectant.

"Claude and Jason, please escort Tristan and the werewolf to the dungeon. I will deal with them later." Two of the biggest vampires Tobias had ever seen came forward and seized Tristan and the wolf, dragging them toward the exit.

"What? What is this?" Tristan yelled. "You can't do this to me!" His protests faded as he was forced deeper into the bowels of the tunnels.

Sabrina's eyes snapped to Tobias's, the corner of her mouth twitching ever so subtly. *Yeah,* Tobias thought, *Daddio just made a choice, and it looks like love won this round.*

Calvin gripped the ropes binding Tobias's wrists and tore them apart, freeing him. He offered his hand to help him to his feet. With a bow, the vampire said, "My apologies for the inconvenience, Doctor. Please stay and enjoy the coronation. One of us will help you home at its conclusion."

"Thank you," Tobias said. He brushed off the knees of his pants and folded his hands in front of his hips, suddenly more aware than ever that vampires surrounded him on all sides. The room made his skin itch.

Clearly, Calvin Bishop knew what he was. Why he'd spared his life was anyone's guess and how long he'd maintain the ruse was also questionable. Leaving wasn't an option. There were tunnels everywhere he looked, but he had no idea which led to the surface and which led deeper underground. And they were all packed with vampires. He tried to calm his racing heart and trust that Sabrina's father legitimately wanted him to survive the day.

When his eyes met Sabrina's again, hers were wide and wet. Her father returned to the dais, and she kissed him on the cheek.

The older man who was dressed like a priest said, "There are always dissenters. I hope you will make an example of him, Calvin. Shall we continue?"

A smattering of laughter came from the crowd as Sabrina and her father nodded in an exaggerated fashion.

"Please, Aldrich," Calvin said.

Tobias watched as the one called Aldrich picked up the ceremonial dagger from the small altar and dragged it across his palm. Blood spilled into the chalice He raised it above his head.

"By the blood, it is done." He took a sip, then handed it to Sabrina who also drank. Calvin was the last. He drained the cup dry.

Aldrich removed the crown from the red velvet pillow beside him and reached up to place it on Sabrina's head. And that's when the waterworks started. Tobias wiped under his eyes. He was so proud of her as she turned to welcome the applause of her coven. The crown suited her. Even though he'd thought she was giving up too much to become master, he saw now that this was her destiny. She was a queen, a goddess, born to rule. Praise the Mountain, he was thankful to see this, even if it was the last time he'd ever lay eyes on her.

When everyone stopped clapping, Sabrina spoke. "Thank you for being here today. I look forward to leading this coven in the years to come, to helping continue our peaceful coexistence with humans, and to creating a safe environment where vampires can thrive."

The crowd broke into cheers. Tobias met Sabrina's eyes and gave her a small smile, which she returned but hid under the guise of thanking Aldrich. He took it all in, the flowers, the dress, the crown. He wanted to remember her like this always. She was something out of a dream.

A dream that turned into a nightmare when the screams started.

CHAPTER THIRTY-ONE

Blood sprayed across Tobias's face as bullets showered the coven. He dropped to the floor. Five enormous men with semiautomatic weapons had charged into the ballroom from one of the tunnels.

Vampires tumbled like bowling pins around him. From what Tobias knew of vampires, bullets couldn't ordinarily hurt them, but these must have been enchanted because the vampires that fell stayed down. The crowd rushed for the exits. Vampires pushed and shoved to escape, but there were too many and nowhere to go.

A team of security personnel, some of them Tobias was sure were human, had formed a wall around Sabrina and her father. They'd all drawn their guns and were firing back at the gunmen. One attacker took a bullet to the head and dropped like a rock. Another was hit in the shoulder. More bullets flew and a security guard toppled.

"Stop!" Sabrina yelled from behind the wall of bodies. "What do you want?"

The bullets stopped. Tobias watched as a man roughly the size of a semitruck and smelling strongly of wolf stepped between the fallen bodies. The wolf who had stabbed Sabrina was behind him. All wolves, Tobias could tell now. Their scent was unmistakable. The remaining team of four parted and Tristan swaggered into the great hall from the tunnel at the rear of the Star, taking his position at the front of the group. The coven broke out in murmurs and shouted accusations.

Now Tobias understood why the vampires weren't getting up. Tristan must have coated the bullets with the same solution he'd used on the dagger that stabbed Sabrina. What had Raven called it? *Keetridge Solution*. His hands balled into fists. He knew what this was. It called up his darkest memories. Scenes of Marius's head rolling across the floor of the Obsidian Palace filled his mind. This was a coup and Sabrina was the target.

The greasy-looking male gestured with his hands and the wolves cleared a large circle for him, dragging dead and dying vampires from the space. "I challenge you, Sabrina, for Lamia Coven."

"If you want to challenge me, Tristan, challenge *me*. Call off your dogs. Fight me one-on-one."

"No! He's too strong," her father yelled.

Tobias ground his teeth.

Tristan raised his hand and the wolves stepped back and lowered their guns. "Then you accept my challenge." He laughed. "Somehow I thought this would be harder."

CHAPTER THIRTY-TWO

Sabrina looked down on Tristan from her place on the dais and saw nothing but haughty rage in her fellow vampire. He'd planned this. The traitor had fraternized with their enemies to try to have her killed, and now that she was master and he had broken from the coven, he was challenging her for her role.

The crowd of security guards in front of her parted and she stepped forward, her vampire instincts raging when she saw the dead. These were her people. Immortals. Tristan could have used regular bullets. He'd coated them with Keetridge Solution to inflict maximum hurt on her and her father. He'd wanted to shake her, to wreck her human side so badly she wouldn't put up a fight.

She removed her crown and placed it on the red velvet pillow. Tristan grinned and stared at it. If he'd been a cartoon, his tongue might have extended to the floor and his eyes bulged from their sockets. *Infidel. Traitor.* He had no idea the monster he'd awakened in her.

She kicked off her shoes, then looked down at her dress. Impossible to fight in. Fisting her skirt, she tore. A female vampire cried out and a rumble of voices passed through the crowd. The expensive floor-length gown was reduced to a miniskirt.

Picking up the ceremonial dagger beside her crown, she held it up. With a raised eyebrow, she silently regarded Tristan. Would he agree to daggers?

"I accept." Tristan drew a dagger from his boot. "My personal favorite."

Sabrina nodded. Without further delay, she sprang into the circle, baring her teeth and lowering herself into a fighting stance. The growl that ripped from her lungs was something feral. A delicious drop of Tristan's fear rained down on her emotional grid.

"Tristan, if you think this is going to be easy, you don't know me," she said, making her voice as smooth and sultry as she could. *Come hither, boy. Let me slay you.*

"Bring it on, *human*."

She attacked, leaping forward and thrusting the blade underhand at Tristan's gut. He spun out of the way of her blow and stabbed at her back. So predictable. She dodged. He missed. Sabrina leaped straight up, landing behind him and kicking him squarely in the ass.

Tristan stumbled forward. That was the tang of surprise she felt in her bones. Oh yes. She could read him like a book. He regained his footing, squared low, and attacked again, his arms out like he planned to bear-hug her. She remembered this move from training with her father. Tristan planned to stab at her right side, then catch her with his free hand when she tried to dodge left.

But Sabrina had practiced this dozens of times. When he stabbed from the right, she did not react, instead catching *his* wrist in a vampire-strong grip and slicing her dagger across his cheek. She planted a foot in his chest and kicked him away from her.

She wanted to cheer. Tristan's emotions had become a jumble of fear and anger. He'd underestimated her. And she was about to hand him his ass.

Her coven closed in, their faces poking out from the tunnels again to watch the fight.

Tristan ran his fingers through the blood on his cheek. "You fucking bitch!"

He rushed her again, head-on, his arm coming high and stabbing downward, toward her face. She sidestepped a fraction of an inch. A swift flash of her blade and she'd sliced open his other cheek.

Tristan whirled, sweeping her legs. She fell hard, gracefully somersaulted backward and landed on her feet, dagger at the ready. She raised her hand and beckoned him forward with her fingers.

With something close to a roar he rushed her, stabbing fast and low. Sabrina blocked the jab, gripped his wrist, and rolled him over her back, using his own momentum to slam him into the floor. There was a pop as his wrist dislocated. Tristan's dagger went flying. He cursed.

Sabrina landed her knee in his gut with all the force she could muster. She cast her own dagger aside and held Tristan down by the throat, her nails digging in. Now there was nothing but fear on her emotional dashboard. She felt it worming in her gut. His fear.

The hall grew completely silent. She glanced up at her father who stared down his nose at Tristan, his expression cold as ice. And then her eyes found Tobias. He gave her a subtle nod.

"You lose," Sabrina said through her teeth.

Tristan opened his mouth to say something else, but she refused to give him the chance. Her fist punched through his rib cage. When her hand retracted, she was holding his heart.

Her father always said that the only time violence was the answer was when you wanted the question to never be asked again. She stood from Tristan's body and thrust the heart above her head. Slowly she turned in place, her bare feet leaving bloody footsteps in front of Tristan's body.

The coven exploded into cheers of victory. "Sabrina. Sabrina. Sabrina." They chanted her name. She cast the heart aside where it rolled to a stop on the concrete.

All at once Sabrina noticed one of the wolves who'd helped Tristan raise his gun. She growled.

"This is for the Racine pack!" He pulled the trigger.

Before Sabrina could react, a massive wall of white scales crashed between her and the wolf, and the roar that filled the tunnels was louder than the gunfire.

CHAPTER THIRTY-THREE

Tobias tore from his own skin faster than he'd ever shifted before. He was temporarily blinded by searing pain, turned inside out by his own force of will. The dragon burst through, his scaled body and barbed tail brushing Sabrina aside and taking the brunt of the shower of bullets that sprang from the wolf's gun. If he was hit, he didn't feel it.

He punched his wings out to fill the hall, turned on the wolf, and roared.

Vampires scattered, but his beast was smart enough to know exactly how to protect Sabrina. Bullets bounced harmlessly off his scales as he faced the largest wolf and made a choice. He could burn the wretch or tear him to pieces. Burning was too kind. His teeth snapped and his talons shredded the werewolf into strips of meat. Ignoring the screams and gunfire, he coiled on his next victim. He wouldn't stop until he knew his mate was safe.

Sabrina had never seen anything as beautiful as Tobias's dragon. When he'd shifted before at the museum, she hadn't had a chance to really appreciate him. She'd been blinded by pain and suffering the effects of the Keetridge Solution. But now, as her father wrapped his arms around her and drew her back into the tunnel that led to his chambers, she saw him in all his glory. He was silvery white, like freshly fallen snow, with scales that reflected blue when the light hit them the right way. Long and lean, he snaked through their attackers, his massive talons clicking on the concrete as bullets bounced off his scales. Vampires scattered around him, their screams echoing through the great hall.

When he turned, she saw his heart. Sapphire blue, the same color as his ring. It shone through his scales, surrounded by the glowing red of two fiery lungs.

"Oh my goddess," her father said once he'd succeeded in wrestling her into the shelter of the tunnel. "Where did you find him, Sabrina?"

She glanced back at her father, whose eyes were glittering like it was Christmas morning. She had not expected this reaction from him.

"Aren't you angry?" she asked. "I'm mated to a shifter!"

He laughed. "Angry?" He pointed his chin in Tobias's direction. "He will make you the most powerful master in the world. Look at him. No one will ever challenge you again."

She did look, and what she saw was *fierce*. The wolf continued his assault, unloading his weapon directly at the dragon's heart, but the bullets continued to bounce off Tobias's scales. The guns the other wolves carried were equally ineffective. Tobias ripped him in two.

Sabrina gasped as the second wolf threw down his ineffective gun and picked up Tristan's discarded dagger. He lunged forward and stabbed Tobias in the front of his shoulder, no doubt aiming for his heart. The blade sank deep between his scales, but it didn't slow the dragon down. He released a stream of fire, frying the wolf who'd stabbed him and sending a plume of heat through the tunnels.

Her father laughed behind her.

"Daddy, this is no time for mirth. Where is Aldrich? If he sees this..."

Her father snorted. "That coward dematerialized for the surface the moment the first bullet was fired."

"Good. I don't even want to think about what would happen if one of the Forebears saw this." Actually, she wished more of her coven had dematerialized when the first shots rang out. It might have saved some lives. But they'd all been caught off guard, and dematerializing took focus.

How dare Tristan bring this death into the coven? She scanned the great hall. The bodies of many vampires lay either dead or injured outside the circle where Tobias fought. She needed to help them.

Thankfully, Tobias was almost done. There was only one wolf left. The one who had stabbed her. The wolf didn't even try to run. There was nowhere to go. Vampires blocked every exit. With a pump of his wings, Tobias coiled and struck. The bite slashed the wolf in two. There was a pop and a crunch of bone. Tobias dropped the pieces of the corpse to the concrete before flattening them under his taloned foot.

And then there were none. The beast circled, scanning the crowd. Vampires gasped and flinched back into the tunnels as the dragon sniffed and chuffed in their direction. Only when the beast seemed sure that every wolf was dead did it stop and sit like a well-trained dog.

That's when Sabrina noticed Tristan's dagger still protruding from his shoulder. She pushed her father's hands off her. "He needs me." Rushing to Tobias's side, she stopped short when he whipped his head around to look at her. She held up her hands. "It's me. Let me help you."

His eyes were just as blue as when he was in his human form, although the pupils were narrow slits like a snake's. He chuffed at her and lowered his head. She ran a hand along the bony protrusions that formed his face and the two horns above his ears.

"Hold still," she said. Then she grabbed the dagger and pulled. It took several tugs to free it from his flesh and the dragon whimpered. Bright red blood spurted onto her dress. She didn't care. She pressed her hand over the wound.

"Will it heal if you change back?" she asked. Her saliva could seal a human wound. She doubted it would work on scales.

The dragon blinked, and then his flesh rippled and undulated like the churning sea. Curling in on himself, the beast was in one blink dragon, in the next man. A shimmer of white and blue coasted down Tobias's skin, and then he looked human again. Human and naked in the center of a ring of gawking vampires.

Calvin strode toward them, a dark, fur-lined cape in his hands and a smile on his face that lit up the room despite the steaming corpses that still marred it. He tossed the cape across Tobias's shoulders.

"You're hurt." Sabrina tried to reapply pressure to the wound.

Tobias bent and dry heaved toward her feet.

"Take him to my chambers," Calvin said. "I will clean this up and arrange for care for the injured." Sabrina ushered Tobias out of the room to the echo of her father's voice shouting orders to the coven.

"Your father didn't kill me," Tobias said.

He was too pale. She had to get him somewhere private and stop the bleeding.

"No one was more surprised about that than me. I think... I think he may like you."

She moved him into the guest bathroom off her father's foyer and closed the door, then pushed the cape off his shoulders. His blood had flowed through her fingers and left her hand sticky. She rinsed her fingers off in the sink, then wet a washcloth to clean the wound.

Tobias flopped against the wall and sank until his butt hit the floor. He was too pale. She watched his eyes flutter shut.

"Tobias!" Straddling his legs, she knelt, pressing a clean towel to his wound. Her dress was in tatters around her thighs. She thought about taking it off, but it was covered in blood anyway. As much as she'd love to be naked with Tobias, at the moment she couldn't get distracted.

"Hold on. I have to clean away some of this excess blood before I can seal the wound. If I do it now—" Her eyes flicked to his. "Well, you know what will happen. And I need to keep my head on straight. So many of my people are injured... dead." Her voice broke.

"I'm sorry."

She tipped her head. "You did your part to avenge their deaths." She concentrated on cleaning the wound.

"I haven't shifted that fast since I was in Paragon. I forgot what it was like." His eyes met hers again, his lids heavy.

"How did it feel?"

"Like being turned inside out by a strong wind. I'm tired Sabrina. So tired."

"Hang in there. I'm going to help you. It's pretty clean. Hold still. I'm going to seal this." She brought her mouth to his wound and gave it a slow, languid lick. His blood, his flesh, tasted like ambrosia. His scent filled her lungs and sent a throb of need straight to her core. Her fangs dropped. She forced herself to pull away before she did something stupid like feed on him. She couldn't afford to be passed out on the floor twenty minutes from now. She needed to make sure he was okay and then return to her people. They needed her. She was their master, and they had just experienced a major disaster.

"Your heart is pounding." His mouth curled into an exhausted grin. "Is that for me?"

"Always." She eyed the wound. It had stopped bleeding and was healing nicely, but she had to quell the urge to give it another lick.

His hands came to rest on her hips, the touch hot through her dress. In a single heartbeat, her position straddling his lap went from one of necessity to feeling too good, too comfortable. She resisted sagging into him.

"Sabrina... You told me it was too dangerous for us to be together. You thought there wasn't room to be both coven master and to be in love. You told me to leave the city." He gave a dark laugh and shook his head. "You thought your coven would kill me. I thought I'd never see you again."

"I know. I believed it. All of it. I was only thinking of you." She sandwiched his face between her hands. "You were a big reason I did this... became master, I mean. Not the only reason. My people... obviously. But I knew if I wasn't in charge, you'd be in danger. I guess I underestimated my father." She chuckled. "He's an enigma."

"What do you believe now? Because I can't continue like this. You are my mate. For me, there can be no other female."

"I know," she said. "I feel it." Her hand pressed over her heart as if she could stop it from leaping out of her chest and running to him. The truth was, she'd bonded with him as well.

He breathed a sigh of relief. He tugged on her hips, sliding her against him. "Say you're mine. I need to hear it."

She touched her forehead to his and tried not to weep. "I am yours, and you are mine."

"Still?"

"Still."

He grinned, his lips reaching for hers.

She put a hand up. "Hold on, cowboy. You're healed. You need to go home now. I have to help my coven. I'll come to you after sunrise and we'll talk... and things."

He raised an eyebrow. "Oh, I look forward to all the things." He helped her lift off him and rose to his feet. He was still naked. He retrieved the bloody cloak from the floor and wrapped it tighter around himself. "Take care of your coven. You're a good leader. I love that about you. I love you, Sabrina."

The warmth that flowed through her made her feel like a light bulb that had just been switched on. "I love you too."

A kiss landed on her lips and he disappeared. Invisible, she realized. The door opened and he was gone.

CHAPTER THIRTY-FOUR

Tobias dragged himself into his house, feeling numb and not from the cold. Actually, the snow had melted, and the morning was temperate by Chicago standards. He was numb because he knew that everything would change now. It had to. He'd exposed himself to the coven. Did that mean he'd be accepted as Sabrina's mate? Or did it mean that tonight, after sunset, he'd be surrounded by vampires with pitchforks?

The good news was Sabrina loved him. She'd admitted they were bound and couldn't stay apart. But the initial buzz he'd gotten from that admission had worn off as he'd made his way through the tunnels to the surface. There were practicalities. Old laws.

At least one worry was gone from his mind. He'd checked on Katelyn before returning home. Thankfully, she had not been harmed. Not that Tobias gave Tristan credit for that. No, he wasn't sure why the people working for Tristan hadn't followed through. He somehow doubted it had all been a bluff.

As he turned the corner from the mudroom into the

kitchen, a hiss from the general direction of the floor attracted his attention. Artemis arched her back and flicked her tail, guarding her domain like Cerberus at the gates of the underworld.

"Et tu, Kitte?" he said, staring her down. "Do you think you could give me a break? Just this once?"

The cat stopped hissing and crept closer, weaving between his legs. He bent down and gently picked her up, scratching her behind the ears. The kitten started to purr almost immediately. "Well, I'll be damned. I guess you're not the spawn of the devil after all."

Raven appeared in the doorway to the living room and stopped short. "By the goddess, there's a sight I never thought I'd see."

"She took pity on me."

Raven gave him a once-over. Thankfully, he'd had athletic clothes in the gym bag in his trunk and had changed out of the cloak into a pair of sweats and a fleece. "Are you doing the walk of shame?"

Tobias raised an eyebrow. "Something like that."

"Sabrina?"

He tipped his head and laughed. "I wish it was under better circumstances. Her coven-mate abducted me and took me to her coronation where I thought I would be beheaded. Instead, her father set me free, I shifted into my dragon in under a millisecond for the first time in, oh, ever, and burned a gang of her werewolf rivals to extra-crispy dead. Well, technically I bit two in half." He told her the entire story from the beginning, from Tristan's trap, to the ceremony, to the wolves and even Katelyn.

"Sweet mother of mercy!" Raven looked him over again, this time with an entirely different eye.

"I'm fine. Just exhausted."

She leaned against the kitchen island. "Well, if it's any help, I can solve one mystery for you. I warded Katelyn's place at the same time I did Sabrina's."

"Huh?"

"I didn't tell you because I knew how you felt about magic. But once you explained why Sabrina was in danger, it crossed my mind that they might target Katelyn. It wasn't difficult to find her. She was all over the papers."

"Thank you." Tobias lowered his head. "By the Mountain, Raven, thank you."

"You're welcome. That's what family is for."

Family. A warm feeling blossomed deep inside his chest and Tobias's vision blurred. He rubbed the space over his heart and blinked away the swell of emotion.

"Are you sure you're okay?"

He sighed. "It's just good to have a friend. You know, the worst part about all of this is, I'm still not sure where Sabrina and I stand. I mean, we're mated. The two of us are... good. But her coven... She's master now. I've exposed myself."

Raven took a deep breath and blew it out slowly. "I'm sorry, Tobias."

"Yeah." He stared at her for a minute, his fingers working in Artemis's fur. "So what are you doing up?"

A blush stained her cheeks as she opened up the freezer, then held up a new pint of Chunky Monkey. "Baby wants ice cream."

"It's five in the morning."

She shrugged. "What baby wants, baby gets."

He stared at her for a beat, taking in her sock-monkey-print flannel pajamas. Those were new. One definitely did not need flannel pajamas in New Orleans. "Mind if I join you? I don't think I'll be able to sleep."

She opened the drawer and grabbed two spoons. Then she reached back in the freezer and retrieved a second pint of ice cream.

"Damn, how many of those do you have in there?"

"Twelve. Don't judge me." She handed him a pint and the spoon. He set Artemis down near his feet and took the frosty container before following her into the living room and sinking into one of the two wingback chairs.

"Should I light the fire?" he asked, detesting the thought of standing up.

"*Fotiá.*" With a flick of her finger, the flue opened and the logs inside the fireplace blazed to life.

"Thanks." He pried off the lid to his ice cream and dug in.

"I think you should come to New York with us to look for Rowan."

Tobias dropped his spoon. It flipped off the edge of the carton and landed on the rug. He cursed.

"Sorry," Raven said. "Maybe this isn't a good time."

With a slanted glance in her direction, he fished the spoon off the floor, wiped it on his pants, and took another bite.

"It's just that we need you. I know you said before that you didn't believe us about your mother, but I think that's changed now, hasn't it? And if we stay together, we'll be able to protect each other should the empress send another guardsman. *When* she sends another guardsman. We all know she will. Also, if and when we find Rowan, it will be easier to convince her of the truth if we're together."

He sighed. "Don't forget you're going to need me to help with this pregnancy."

"Yes. Oh, Tobias, will you do it?"

"Hold on there, witchy poo. I'm not saying that I'm

giving up my life here to join the sibling-hunting circus with you guys, okay? And I'm certainly not leaving Sabrina. She's my mate. I couldn't leave her if I tried. Even if she pushes me away again, I'm in. I'll wait as long as it takes for her to come back around."

"Of course. Yes. You're mated. That's understandable." Raven's face fell, and she stared into her ice cream.

"What I am saying is, given what's happened, maybe I'll take a sabbatical. Go with you to New York for a few days. Be more available after that, in case something happens."

Raven reached out and squeezed his hand. "Really?"

"Seeing Sabrina tonight, I get it. I get why she rose to master even though she doesn't love everything that comes with the title. Sometimes fate calls us to be more than what we want to be. More than what we ever expected for ourselves. Like it or not, I'm an heir to Paragon. If Mother has done what it seems she's done, maybe it's time I rose too. I mean, Gabriel is the eldest. I don't want to lead. I'm just saying, well, when it comes to you and Gabriel, I'm in too."

Raven sighed, looking far too happy about the turn of events. Her smile clashed with the general exhausted funk he was in and made her hard to be around. Everything was too up in the air. He needed his mate to tell him where they stood with the coven and what would happen next. He wouldn't feel whole until she did.

"I hope Sabrina knows what she has in you. You are an admirable man, Tobias."

He sighed. "Admirable me and my ice cream are going to bed. We can talk more in the morning. I'm sure Gabriel will want to rub my nose in my backpedaling and general compliance with your plan."

"Oh, no, Tobias. It's not like that."

"Do you know your mate?" Tobias gave her a pacifying

wink before climbing the stairs to the master bedroom. Only he found that when he got there, he couldn't sleep in his bed. Sabrina had been in that bed, only days ago, naked and close and his. By the Mountain, she'd been his, if only for a night. He was afraid if he lay in it now without her, somehow he'd be jinxing himself. It was sunrise. If she was coming, she'd be there soon.

He took a hot shower and then collapsed in the armchair near the window, turning on the TV to a DVR'd episode of *The Great British Baking Show*. His eyes fell on his ring. The sapphire held his dragon magic, magic he hadn't used in centuries until recently, until Sabrina. A dragon loving a vampire wasn't logical, but as Sabrina always told him, logic was overrated. He supposed it was time to believe in magic.

He leaned his head against the back of the chair and drifted into oblivion.

CHAPTER THIRTY-FIVE

"**K**eetridge Solution." Sabrina pointed at the gritty edges of a wound on a dead vampire. "They didn't stand a chance. Without human blood, they had no defense against the necrosis."

"Some are still alive. Should we call the witch?" her father asked.

She raced to the next victim, a young female vamp with a wound in her stomach. "Hold still. I'm going to help you." Sabrina dug in her wound with a pair of forceps and tore a bullet from her flesh. The vampire cried out and bared her fangs. Sabrina handed her a bag of blood and watched her wound heal as fast as she could drink it.

She held the bullet up so her father could see it clearly.

"Silver," he said.

"It looks like the amount of solution Tristan stole from us didn't go very far. He augmented with silver and probably wood. That means we can save some of them. Go get more blood. I'll extract any bullets left in the wounded."

Her father didn't move. It suddenly dawned on her that this was the first time she'd ever ordered him to do anything.

When she turned her head to look at him, he simply smiled proudly before taking off in the direction of the blood.

It took hours to treat the remaining injured vampires. After everything, the stockpile of blood that she had created by working among humans for so long had been a lifesaver. Without it, the vampires would have still healed, but it would've taken time and left them vulnerable. This way they'd be back to normal by the time they woke up at nightfall.

As the sun rose above the tunnels, her younger patients fell asleep. While she'd felt the sunrise warm her blood from forty feet up, the sinking draw that rendered them dead until nightfall did not have the same effect on her. Her father wobbled on his feet as he handed her the next bag.

"Go to bed, Father. I'll finish."

"But..."

"Go. I'm too exhausted to carry you if you fall here."

He nodded, then slowly trudged toward his chambers. Sabrina handled the rest on her own, providing transfusions when needed and making sure each of her charges was safely in their coffin. She had to carry the last of the wounded to their beds herself.

When she was done, she took a shower in the apartment that would soon be hers and put on jeans and her softest sweater. She was so exhausted she could hardly stand up, but she refused to give in to the draw of sleep. She'd promised Tobias she'd go to him. After what he'd done for her today, she needed to see him. Needed to tell him how much he meant to her.

With every ounce of energy she had left, she dematerialized to his room. After taking a second to orient herself, she saw him sleeping in his chair, an empty pint of ice cream in his hands. She gently removed it and placed it on the end table. Should she wake him? He'd overdone things tonight. She'd watched him explode out of his own skin like the charge of a grenade. No, she'd let him sleep. He needed it.

Although she wondered if she should move him to the bed, ultimately she wasn't sure she'd be strong enough in her current state. Instead, she crawled under the covers and curled on her side. She'd be here when he woke.

Hours passed in the blink of an eye. When Sabrina woke again, it was twilight and Tobias was standing over her, staring at her with frozen, stiff limbs. The only things that were moving were his eyelids. He kept blinking, closing his eyes tightly and then opening them again.

"Tobias," she whispered.

"Are you really here?"

She smiled at him and scooted over to make room for him in bed. "I didn't want to wake you, and I didn't think I could lift you."

His biceps stretched the soft gray T-shirt he was wearing as he scrubbed his face with his hands. But instead of climbing into bed beside her, he sat back down in the chair. "I was afraid you wouldn't come."

"Why? I told you I would." She climbed from the bed and moved to kneel in front of him.

"You need to tell me where we stand with your coven. Your father didn't kill me today, but I exposed myself. What happens now? I don't think I can handle you telling me we can't be together."

She cradled his hands between her own. "No. That's not what I came to tell you." She could feel distance like a trench between them. She had done this, pushed him away one too many times. What did she expect? He was self-protecting.

309

"Thank you for what you did today," she said softly. She had to start somewhere. "You saved my people."

He swallowed. "I was proud of you. Your coven needs you. You're a good leader."

She took a deep breath and blew it out slowly. "Tobias, I will never forget what you did for us."

"Right. But you can't see me anymore because now your people want to kill me. They'll probably surround the house with torches as soon as the sun sets."

"No."

"No?"

"Before my father tasted your blood, I told him you were my mate. After you left, he explained it was the primary reason he covered for you. My coven knows what you are, and they are thankful for you. And the ones who aren't thankful fear you. I don't think they pose a threat."

He rubbed his thumb over hers. "What does that mean for us?"

"When vampires mate, they mate for life. The bond between mated pairs is so strong that if one dies, the other usually commits suicide or dies of grief. It is considered a crime among our kind to separate a mated pair."

"But mating with a dragon..."

"Is normally forbidden; however, given the circumstances, my father gave us his blessing. I'm master now. I didn't need it. But I am thankful for it."

Tobias's breath hitched, his palms rubbing nervously against his thighs. "Which means?"

"As master, I have a level of control over my coven I didn't have before. The longer I am master, the stronger that control becomes. Tristan was able to challenge me after my coronation because my father had excommunicated him from the coven. Those vampires who remain have accepted me. That means what I say goes. And frankly, after last night, it would take a very strong vampire to challenge us."

"Us. There's an us in this story?"

"My father sees our mating as a benefit to our coven. You are a protector and as my mate would never turn on us. I know it's not flattering to be thought of as a guard dog. I don't approve of that, but my father is a man from a different time. You should have seen his face when you shifted. It was like he'd discovered a new toy."

"I think I saw it when he tasted my blood." Tobias's breath quickened.

"I should have foreseen it actually. In hindsight it seems so clear. My own birth was a result of my father breaking the rules. He wasn't supposed to mate with a human, but he did. I guess the heart wants what it wants."

"What do you want, Sabrina?" His eyes twinkled.

She sat back on her heels. She was already on her knees, she might as well do what she came to do. Her eyes shifted downward to the place a shadow stretched across the floor and she steadied herself.

"I couldn't stop myself from loving you, Tobias. It's what I was born to do. And if you love me too, there's something I need to ask you."

He gave a light, breathy laugh. "If it's not clear that I love you, I've done something very, very wrong."

"I need to ask you if you'll become my consort." She bit her lip and fisted her hands.

Tobias blinked.

"It's an official role within the coven. You'd be crowned and expected to help me rule, at my side."

"I know what a consort is. We had them in Paragon. I'd be Prince Phillip to your Queen Elizabeth."

"Yes. I know it's a huge sacrifice." Sabrina rushed on

when Tobias gave her a strange, bewildered look. "It's a full-time role. You'd have to leave the hospital. Not forever, mind you. I won't be master forever. But as long as you rule by my side, it has to be your first priority. And you'd have to live with me, underground. I know that's probably scary…"

She stopped talking. Silence uncoiled between them and took an unhurried stretch. He wasn't saying anything, just staring at her.

"Tobias? Say something. If it's too much, just tell me."

TOBIAS ROLLED THE IDEA AROUND IN HIS HEAD. He couldn't escape the irony that when he'd left Paragon, the last thing he'd wanted was to rule. But here he was, considering a royal position over Sabrina's people. He hated politics. Had never thought of himself as a warrior or a protector of any kind. But maybe he'd underestimated himself. Knowing Sabrina and following her journey had made him respect the fortitude it took to step up to a challenge. She hadn't loved the idea of becoming master, but she'd felt a responsibility to her people.

"Tobias?"

He shook his head as if waking himself from a dream. There was only one answer. He would not give her up for anything. "Yes."

"Yes?" Sabrina let out a shaky breath. "You don't mind giving up your job and living underground?"

"I will always be a healer, Sabrina, but as far as leaving the hospital now, I think it's the right time. Over the centuries, I've had to change my identity every thirty years or so. I've been Dr. Winthrop for long enough. This is as good a time as any."

"Really?"

"And honestly, I was considering a break anyway so that I'd be freed up to help Gabriel and Raven if they need it—to find Rowan and help with the baby."

"You can still do that. I'll arrange it." She squeezed his hands.

"As for living underground, I was born and raised in the belly of a mountain. Your tunnels are not that different."

Another breath rushed from her lungs, her lips spreading into a smile. "So, you're saying..."

"Yes. Yes, Sabrina, I will become your consort."

Her hands landed on his face and then her mouth was on his. He collided with her. Everything he was he threw in her direction: his heart, his soul, what was left of his courage. And she caught him, fingers in his hair, limbs tangled with his. He was rough and ready, his capacity to be gentle long past. His ache for her had become pain, a hungry need demanding to be fed. Gripping the edge of her sweater, he pulled back from the kiss. She gasped for breath as he pulled it over her head.

Eager hands found the tie on his pajama pants and she eased them down, over his erection. He gripped the arms of the chair when she took him into her mouth, her tongue worshipping his hard length with long, languid strokes. The purr he rewarded her with shook his entire body. As she started to move, licking and sucking, talons emerged from his knuckles and buried themselves in the upholstered arms of the chair.

Only her eyes lifted to meet his. Goddess, she was a rare queen, a precious warrior, both steel and silk. A fang stroked along the side of his shaft. He trembled. When she pulled him in deep once again, an orgasm tore through him like a storm.

He thought his heart would burst at the seams. So much pleasure, a sharp edge after all the pain, after feeling torn in two for so long. He reached for her and pulled her into his lap.

"By the Mountain, Sabrina." He caressed her face, her neck, her waist. "Say you're mine. I need to hear it."

Hands on his face, she looked him directly in the eye. "I'm yours, Tobias, entirely and completely. For always." His body shuddered against hers, his eyes closing with the low animalistic whimper that escaped him.

"Oh," she said, as she felt him stir beneath her. "You're ready again?"

He opened his eyes and raised an eyebrow. "It's a dragon thing. I haven't shown you all my tricks."

In a heartbeat, he'd set her on her feet and stripped his T-shirt over his head, his wings punching out, shining silver in the window's light. One beat of those wings and she was on the bed. Another and her clothes were history. His fingers found her center. She arched into his hand.

"I think I'm going to like these so-called tricks," she said.

He smiled down at her, his wings arching out to fill the room.

He entered her slowly, sliding his hand under her shoulders to cradle her head. When he'd finally filled her, he paused. "I am yours, Sabrina. Forever and always."

As their souls connected, it felt like going home. That's what this was. There were no other words for what was happening in his heart. He followed her into the light, wrapped her in the shelter of his wings, and knew without a doubt that they were bound.

CHAPTER THIRTY-SIX

"And then Sabrina put a crown on my head!"

Gabriel listened to Tobias tell the story again about how he'd been crowned consort to the master of the Lamia Coven and rolled his eyes. His brother had not stopped talking about it since they'd left Chicago. He watched Raven in the rearview mirror as she attentively nodded her head. His mate had more patience than he did.

"I'm telling you, the crown was heavy. You wouldn't think by looking at it that rubies and solid gold would be that heavy, but it was. I spent the entire night wondering when I could take it off, but there were so many vampires to meet. Everyone wanted to kiss my hand. I—"

"Tobias," Gabriel interrupted. "Am I to assume you'll be putting your house up for sale?"

"The Realtor is bringing the sign on Monday. That's okay, right? Raven said it was time for you guys to move on."

Gabriel grunted his agreement, keeping one eye on the New York City traffic. "If Scoria was in communication with the empress, she will know his last breath was taken in your living room. It's best we are all moving on. Especially considering your new role and our mission to find our brethren."

"By the way, Artemis is coming with us," Raven said.

Gabriel swerved and someone honked. He straightened the wheel. "The cat? Why?"

"She can't live underground. The vampire tunnels are no place for a cat. Someone might accidentally eat her."

Tobias cleared his throat. "It's true. The tunnels don't suffer a single rat for a reason."

"Plus I'm beginning to think of her as my familiar. She inspires me." Raven smiled at him in the rearview mirror.

He grumbled his consent.

Raven turned back to Tobias. "Anyway, my sister will become homicidal if I don't return to New Orleans to plan my wedding with her."

"Aren't you afraid that's the first place our mother will look for you?" Tobias asked.

"Not really," she answered. "I think the first place will be where Scoria died. But just in case, Gabriel has someone working on buying a new place for us under a false name in the Garden District. If all goes well, I'll have protective wards on the house before we set foot in it. We'll be hidden in plain sight from anyone who means us harm."

"Smart."

"Is this the building, brother?" Gabriel asked, pulling up to the curb in front of a white brick townhouse with three large rows of windows.

Tobias gave the place a once-over. "It's been updated since the last time I was here. But I think we're in the right place."

Gabriel parked and climbed out. He hadn't been to New York in decades, and Manhattan was not an area he'd spent any length of time in. Still, he could see his sister being happy here. An older woman in a fur coat passed him on the street, her chin high, her little floppy-haired dog following behind her. Was that a diamond-studded collar around its neck?

"She reminds me of Agnes," Raven said.

Gabriel had to agree.

"Let me buzz Rowan. It will be better if she hears my voice first," Tobias said. He jogged up the stairs to the collection of mailboxes in front of the door and pressed a button.

"Looks like an apartment building," Gabriel said.

"I think it is." Raven inspected the place more closely. "I see boxes for four units.

"That's unexpected," Gabriel murmured.

"Why?" Raven turned to look at him.

Gabriel chuckled. "My sister was always a diva. The only girl among nine children. I'm surprised she's living in an apartment and not a castle somewhere in rural upstate New York."

"You and Tobias were drawn to the city." Raven frowned. "Why wouldn't Rowan be?"

Gabriel rubbed his cheek. He'd never thought about it before. "In essence, New Orleans sprouted up around me. I'm sure Tobias would say the same thing about Chicago. When we settled, our cities weren't like they are today, and after a while, a place becomes home. You change your surname. Sometimes your appearance. The bigger the city, the easier it is to be forgotten without ever really leaving."

Raven took his hand and threaded her fingers in his. "I'm sure Rowan feels the same way."

"Can I help you?" a woman's voice called through the speaker. It didn't sound like Rowan, but Gabriel hadn't heard her voice in centuries.

"I'm looking for Rowan Turner," Tobias said toward the speaker.

"How do you know Rowan?"

Tobias glanced toward Gabriel, then back at the intercom. "I'm her brother."

"Hold on a minute."

The intercom went dead. Tobias shrugged. A few minutes later the door opened and an older woman in a robin's-egg-blue pantsuit and perfectly coiffed hairdo appeared on the doorstep. "You're Rowan's brother?"

Tobias nodded. "Is she here?"

The woman pushed the door open wider, glancing at Gabriel and Raven. "Come in."

Tobias explained that Gabriel and Raven were friends of the family before following the woman inside. "I'm sorry, but who are you?"

"My name is Mrs. Fernhall. I own this building." She gestured for them to enter a well-appointed apartment.

Gabriel took a seat between Raven and Tobias on the sofa, growing more confused by the minute.

"Mrs. Fernhall, where is my sister?" Tobias rested his elbows on his knees.

Mrs. Fernhall coupled her hands and sat down in the chair on the other side of the coffee table. She cleared her throat. "I am sorry to be the one to have to tell you this, but Rowan was killed in a terrible accident three months ago."

Raven gasped. Gabriel squeezed her hand. He wished he could tell her that as an immortal, it was very unlikely that Rowan was indeed dead, but that wouldn't be prudent at the moment.

"What type of accident?" Gabriel asked.

The old woman cleared her throat. "May I be frank with you?"

"Please," Tobias said. "Rowan and I haven't been in touch in some time. I'd like to understand."

She nodded. "Rowan told me as much."

"Then you knew her?" Raven asked.

"Yes. I lived upstairs. We were neighbors, and friends." She rubbed her hands together. "Rowan was under investigation for theft, accused of stealing a large jewel from a rather famous collection. The owner said he had proof. The night after she was interviewed by the police, she leaped in front of a subway train and was killed instantly."

Gabriel forced his face to remain impassive, although inside he was laughing. Rowan had most definitely not been killed by a subway train. He glanced at Tobias, who was hiding his chuckle behind his hands, disguising it as a sob. Unfortunately, Raven's tears were real. He put an arm around her and kissed the side of her head.

"Shh, It's okay," he whispered in her ear. When she looked at him, he winked discreetly. She wiped under her eyes.

"I am sorry for your loss," Mrs. Fernhall said. "She was quite dear to me. We were neighbors for a number of years."

Tobias took a deep, Oscar-worthy breath and blew it out slowly. "Did she leave anything behind? Anything for us to remember her by?"

"After her funeral, I donated most of her clothing to the local shelter, but there was a box of personal items I saved in case you came. She spoke of you." Mrs. Fernhall shook her head. "I'll get it."

The woman left the room and returned a few moments later with a banker's box. Tobias accepted it and removed the lid. Gabriel perused the contents over his shoulder. Pictures. A diary. What appeared to be a wooden jewelry box engraved with a dragon. He replaced the cover.

"Thank you, Mrs. Fernhall," Tobias said. "I need to go now. I'm sure you understand." He rubbed his chest for effect.

"Of course." They all rose in unison and followed her to the door. "If there is anything else I can do..."

"We know where to find you," Tobias said solemnly.

Gabriel followed him down the front steps. When they were safely back inside the car, Raven slapped him on the shoulder. "What gives? Is Rowan really dead?"

The brothers broke into laughter, shaking their heads.

"No. Definitely not," Gabriel said.

Tobias rubbed his mouth. "But this does complicate things. It appears Rowan got caught hoarding some jewels and decided to go into hiding."

Gabriel nodded, turning the key in the ignition. "And a dragon in hiding is almost impossible to find."

EPILOGUE

Aldrich, vampire elder, returned to the nest of the Forebears, wringing his hands. He'd arranged for his coffin to be transported to the old country on a day flight direct from O'Hare. He'd traveled through the night hours to make it to the castle in the forests of Romania before sunrise. Now, deep within the bowels of the underground fortress concealed there, he was exhausted and wondered if he was doing the right thing.

It was risky business consulting with the other elders. Many had withdrawn from society ages ago and had feral tempers as well as appetites. But the news he carried must be shared. If he was found to have harbored this secret, his life would be worth little. He'd be thrown out into the sun.

He stood outside the door to the chambers of the eldest Forebear, the one whose voice on the matter would not be denied. A less risky venture would have been to bother one of the younger ones. Like him, they had power, but not absolute power. They would want to learn more about the situation and consult with each other on what to do. Not

Turgun. Not the ancient one. His word was law, and he was frightfully decisive.

Inside the room, Aldrich could see Turgun's lanky limbs draped motionless in his chair. His nails and hair had grown long, his body thinned. Aldrich wondered how long it had been since he'd moved. It was not uncommon for the older ones to get bored with life and allow themselves to go dormant. A servant had started a fire in the grate. At least it was warm in the room. The vampire must have some feeling left to care about the temperature.

"Master Turgun, I bring word from the New World," Aldrich said.

At first the vampire didn't move anything but his eyes. But slowly his fingers stretched. Turgun's joints cracked. His tendons popped.

"You need blood, my lord." Aldrich rang the bell near the door. A servant boy came running and offered his neck to the vampire. When Turgun barely moved, the boy crawled onto the lap of the ancient one and pressed his throat against the vampire's mouth. The strike was clean, the drinking efficient, and Aldrich watched the life drain from the boy in a merciful minute.

Turgun's cheeks plumped. His hair transformed from a thin gray mess to sleek chestnut waves. Muscle formed where before there was only bone. Renewed, Turgun stood from his throne and allowed the boy to slip from his lap onto the floor. A cloud of dust billowed from his flesh. He brushed off the sleeves of his starched white shirt. It wasn't lost on Aldrich that Turgun was dressed appropriately for the Victorian era. He'd been asleep for a very long time.

"Call someone to deal with that, will you, Aldrich?" he rasped, pointing at the boy. "And then bring me another. I'm famished."

"Of course, my lord." Aldrich tugged at the bell outside the door again. "But there is something I must speak with you about. It is of dire importance."

"Then speak. I did not awaken for idle chitchat." He crossed to the bar at the edge of the room and poured himself a draft of mead from a large barrel.

"While I was in Chicago inaugurating the new master of the Lamia Coven, the vampires there were attacked by werewolves."

Turgun finished his pint and scoffed. "Nothing unusual about that. Why wake me for such nonsense? We've been at war with the wolves for centuries."

"It is not the wolves that worry me. It is how they survived the attack. They were protected by a dragon."

Turgun set down his stein. "You are mistaken, Aldrich. Dragons are extinct. The coven likely used a witch to create an illusion."

"I saw it with my own eyes. I witnessed the man shift myself!" When the wolves had attacked, Aldrich had dematerialized into one of the tunnels and watched the entire tragedy unfold from his hiding place. He kept that part to himself. Turgun might think him cowardly, but the ancient one did not understand what it was like in the real world. Aldrich had done what he needed to keep himself safe. "Furthermore, Calvin Bishop was not able to discern the dragon's blood. He'd tasted it earlier in the night and determined the male to be human. The vampire was as surprised as I when the male prisoner shifted into the beast. The dragon was enormous, my lord, and absolutely deadly. It blew fire and it ate one of the wolves."

"A prisoner. Interesting. And you are sure this wasn't an illusion?"

"No illusion can tear a wolf in half."

"Hmm. It is no surprise Calvin failed to know the dragon. How could one discern the blood of a creature that has been extinct for millennia? Are you sure of what you saw?"

"I would not waste your time with speculation. I've brought you proof."

Turgun's eyes widened. Aldrich pulled out his phone and turned it so Turgun could see. The ancient one hissed. He hated technology, but this could not be helped. For once, Aldrich was happy to be the youngest of the Forebears and the most familiar with modern trappings. Calling up the video he'd taken from his hiding place in the tunnels, he pressed Play.

Turgun growled as the dragon appeared on screen, tearing the wolves to bits. The scaled beast's roar was frightening, even from his phone's small speaker. "It's true. A dragon... among our kind."

"As I said, my lord."

"Where is this dragon now?"

"I do not know. I had to flee for my life."

"Goddess! You were right to bring this to me." Turgun tapped the screen to play the video again. "We must wake the others."

"Which ones?" Aldrich asked.

Turgun met his gaze, sweeping a hand across his beard. "All of them."

Aldrich clutched his chest although his heart had stopped beating long ago. "All of them?"

"Where there is one dragon, there are others, Aldrich. This is a serious threat to our kind. Put out word immediately to all covens: favor to anyone who captures or kills a dragon, by order of the Forebears. Share with them what you have seen."

Aldrich bowed low. "Yes, my lord."

✤

THANK YOU FOR READING WINDY CITY DRAGON. The treasure of Paragon is in danger. It's more important than ever that Gabriel and Tobias find Rowan, only she's up to trouble of her own. Rowan is a dragon used to being in control, until she meets a human detective named Nick who changes everything. Pick up a copy of Rowan's story, MANHATTAN DRAGON wherever you usually buy books.

Turn the page to read an excerpt of Manhattan Dragon, Book 3 in the Treasure of Paragon series.

✤

SIGN UP FOR MY NEWSLETTER TO BE NOTIFIED when new books release! https://www.genevievejack.com/newsletter/

Please enjoy this excerpt from **MANHATTAN DRAGON**, book 3 in the Treasure of Paragon series.

CHAPTER ONE

S he was supposed to be dead.

Rowan felt remarkably spry for a corpse. But then she'd died multiple times since coming to America over three hundred years ago. New identities were necessary for an immortal. Every so often Rowan would shed her proverbial skin and start over with a new last name, a new address, a new life. It was easier in New York. The city that never slept rarely slowed down to notice one mysterious woman with unfinished business or the fate of one of her identities.

She wasn't a thief but Rowan came to steal.

A dragon was born with a certain set of instincts. Keen observation was one of them. A natural affinity for anything rare and valuable was another. For example, Rowan had spotted the blue teardrop-shaped diamond around Camilla Stevenson's neck from across a crowded gallery—an example of her keen observation skills. Understanding that the stone was, in fact, the six-carat Raindrop of Heaven diamond, sold at auction recently for $1.2 million? That was her talent for recognizing the rare and valuable.

She didn't need the money.

Rowan was rich. Very rich. It wasn't a need for cash that sent her sneaking up the path to the white brick mansion in the Hamptons, an enchanted lock pick weighing down her pocket. That had more to do with her history as an exiled princess of Paragon than her financial need. She'd witnessed her brother's murder at the hands of her uncle before she was cast into this world, and Rowan had no patience for corruption. What the wealthy Gerald Stevenson and his wife Camilla had done made them the exact type of elitist scum that drove Rowan to distraction. She'd steal the diamond not for its value but as revenge.

For a human, playing Robin Hood in the Hamptons would be a ticket to the slammer. The place was crawling with security and there was only one gated drive in and out of this property. Humans, though, couldn't make themselves invisible. Nor could they fly.

Besides, there was no better alibi than being dead.

The night hummed a familiar tune. Crickets chirped, insect lovers calling to each other from the grasses; the waves brushed the beach in a soft caress behind her; and a warm spring breeze off the Atlantic rustled the branches of the hawthorn trees that grew along the main drive.

"Thank you, Harriet," she murmured as she slid the enchanted lock pick into the lock of the French doors at the back of the Stevenson's home. It was a sophisticated lock. Stevenson was a real estate developer and was no dummy when it came to home security. But security systems had their limitations. For example, most weren't able to record an invisible intruder or detect a lock pick charmed with ancient Traveler magic.

The door parted like the lips of an eager lover and she slipped into the dark interior. No alarm. No dog. That was fortunate. A few lights were on but she knew no one was home. Gerald and Camilla were hosting one of the biggest political fundraising events in the city that evening. How could they effectively rezone and gentrify every part of Manhattan if they didn't consistently line the pockets of their political allies?

Fucking assholes.

The gem practically sang to her from the master bedroom on the second floor. It was time to save the jewel from the Stevenson's filthy hands. She trailed down the hall, allowing her invisibility to fade to conserve energy. Invisibility and flight took their toll; she'd need that energy for the journey home.

The hardwood creaked beneath her footsteps. Rowan paused outside the bedroom. A delicious scent she'd never smelled before met her nose, sandalwood and dark spice. She breathed deeply and felt her eyes roll back in her head at the intoxicating fragrance. What the hell was that?

A fine shiver traveled through her body straight to her core. Whatever it was, she wanted to roll in it. She made a mental note to find out where Gerald Stevenson bought his cologne. It couldn't be Camilla's. It was too masculine. Too heady. It took effort to pull herself together but she managed to slip into the master bedroom and refocus on the task at hand. The Raindrop of Heaven wasn't going to steal itself.

The room was a white-walled wonder with decor that belonged in the museum of modern art. At its center, a bed the size of a barge was flanked by twisted wire sculptures Rowan's keen assessment marked as worth more than most people's yearly salary. No doubt they were paid for in cash. People like the Stevenson's loved to use art as a way to launder their wealth and evade the taxman. All the more reason they were overdue for some bad luck.

And she planned to deliver it.

Once she oriented herself, she found the door Harriet had described in her vision and had to smile at the traveler's accuracy. The best decision she'd ever made was to save her dear friend from tuberculosis in 1904 with the gift of her tooth. She'd never regretted using dragon magic to bind herself to the powerful traveler, whose psychic gifts and practical magic rivaled any witch's. Harriet's friendship had proved priceless over the years and her magical abilities had come in useful on more than one occasion.

The Stevenson's giant walk-in closet was built of cedar and had a convenient keypad on the jewelry drawer that served as a safe. Rowan held the lock pick against the keypad and watched the keys glow purple, one at a time. The magic revealed which numbers to push and in what order, and she enthusiastically followed its suggestions. The drawer popped open with a hiss.

The Raindrop of Heaven winked up at her from a bed of blue velvet. She caressed the cool facets of the diamond before plucking it from its bed. Along with two matching earrings, she shoved the lot in the zippered pouch around her waist, pure satisfaction curling the corners of her lips.

Take that, you corrupt piece of shit.

Rowan's nostrils flared. The delicious smell from the hall was back, even stronger than before. Cloves and sandalwood. Her inner dragon stirred and licked its lips. She whirled to find a man standing in the bedroom behind her, staring at her through the open door to the walk-in closet. A bear of a man, big, rough, and all male. He scratched the stubble on his jaw, amaretto colored like his hair, and scanned her with eyes the gray of stormy seas. His arms crossed over the chest of his sport coat, and his head cocked to the side.

She cursed under her breath. She'd been so distracted by the smell, she'd forgotten to make herself invisible again. Too late now. He'd seen her. The real her.

Thankfully, he was alone. She could handle one man. It wouldn't be pretty, but she could handle it. Their eyes met.

In a voice edged in grit, he asked, "Who the fuck are you?"

⁂

DETECTIVE NICK GRANDSTAFF STARED AT THE WOMAN in the Stevenson's closet and tried to decide if she was real or a lovely hallucination. He was leaning toward hallucination. After all, he'd been awake for going on twenty-four hours now and she was too perfect to be real. Only a figment of his imagination could strike all his personal erotic notes. Long, dark waves that cascaded down her back. Silky. Shiny. Touchable. He imagined his fingers buried in that hair. He'd startled her and when she turned toward him, her amber eyes overwhelmed him as if he'd stared into the sun. And oh God, her curves. Curves for days. Curves that made his palms itch to touch her.

"I'm a friend of Camilla's," Fantasy Woman said, moving toward him. She folded her hands innocently in front of her hips. "She said I could borrow a pair of shoes."

He snorted. After years working as a homicide detective, Nick was a human lie detector. He could hear the lie in her voice as clear as if the words came out of her mouth colored red. Whoever this woman was, she was up to no good.

"I wasn't aware Camilla had any friends," he said.

Fantasy Woman laughed through her nose as if she

couldn't help herself. He thought he might die from the thrill the sound sent through his body.

"What's your name?" she asked.

"Nick." He frowned. She was supposed to be giving *him* information, not the other way around.

She inhaled deeply. Those amber eyes narrowed on him. Bedroom eyes. Soul-stealing eyes. Goddamn, she was sexy. He felt her presence warm his bones like a tropical breeze.

"What are you?" she asked.

"Detective," he mumbled. What the hell was with the oversharing? He mentally shook himself.

"*Detective* Nick." Her gaze flicked down to the gun holstered under his shoulder. "If you know what kind of people Camilla and Gerald are, why are you here?" Again, she inhaled, leaning toward him. Did he stink? It had been a long night. He resisted the urge to sniff himself.

"Look, sweetheart, I'm on duty here. Security. You need to tell me your full name. Nobody cleared you to be here. I'm going to have to call this in and get a verbal confirmation from Camilla."

One of her hands reached out to dance her blood-red nails across the tops of Camilla's shoes. God damn, he could imagine how those nails would feel on his skin. Gently trailing down his chest. Digging into his back. He shifted, wishing he had something to hold in front of his pants. He needed a cold shower and to get his brain out of fantasyland.

Ignoring his request for a name, she hooked her long, elegant fingers into a pair of black Louboutins. The overhead light glinted off her ring as she removed the shoes from the shelf. That thing was a monster. Anyone who could afford a ruby of that size didn't need to be borrowing anyone else's shoes. Close now, she looked at him through her lashes and waved the shoes as if they were all the explanation he should need to let her go. He blocked the door with his body.

"Easy enough to clear this up," he said. "I'll give Camilla a shout." He raised his phone to his ear.

In the blink of an eye, her hand wrapped around his wrist and squeezed. He paused, his finger hovering over the call button. Her touch sent a delicious rush through him that made his cock twitch. He lowered the phone.

"Did you know the Stevenson's actions are shutting down a community center that serves at-risk kids?" She glared at him. "How can you defend people like that?"

"Huh?" All he could see was her lips. All that existed was her perfume, a smoky citrus and cinnamon scent that drove him wild. His breath hitched.

"Camilla and Gerald bought the land out from under them. They're shutting it down. Over a hundred needy kids use that facility. It's a lifeline for some of them. You know how guys like Stevenson work. He'll probably turn it into a Baby Gap."

Nick swallowed. He'd been an at-risk kid himself at one time and spent many afternoons inside his local community center. While he wasn't aware of the specific scenario, he'd be the last one to approve of such a thing. Still, it didn't matter. Although he sympathized, she didn't belong here and it hadn't escaped his notice that she still hadn't told him her damn name.

"I don't know anything about that." He planted his hand on the doorframe, boxing her in. "Tell me who you are now and I'll clear this mess up with Camilla." He suspected she wasn't there for shoes, but he wished she was, wished there was a reason he could let her go and maybe get her number while he was at it.

He blinked and she was gone, ducked under his arm. She strolled through the bedroom toward the doors to the balcony. Damn, she moved fast. And as he looked back into the closet, he could see why. A jewelry drawer was open and whatever had been inside was gone, three empty impressions in the blue velvet.

He whirled and drew his gun, leveling it on the woman. "Stop!"

"Are you going to shoot me, Detective? For borrowing shoes?" Her red lips spread into a smile.

"Drop the shoes and put your hands up," he said firmly. "Don't make this harder than it needs to be."

She set the shoes down on the bed and opened the doors to the balcony. The ocean breeze coasted in around her, delivering another dose of her scent to his nostrils. He loosened his grip on his gun. He wasn't worried. She was unarmed, and there was nowhere for her to go.

"You can't get out that way, ma'am," he said, his voice thick. "You're too high up to jump without injuring yourself. Step back into the room and let's talk about this. Tell me who you are."

She backed onto the balcony and flashed him a wicked grin. "I'm a ghost."

Nick almost discharged his weapon. In the blink of an eye, his fantasy woman completely disappeared.

❧

PICK UP YOUR COPY OF MANHATTAN DRAGON wherever you buy books to continue the story.

ACKNOWLEDGMENTS

When I started writing Windy City Dragon, I was living through a Chicago area winter. The tension from the snow and the cold was with me every day and I started to view Tobias and Sabrina as two tightly coiled springs that longed to release toward each other. Both of them are headstrong and deeply burdened by their pasts. I love how Tobias and Sabrina grow toward each other in this novel and want to thank those who helped me bring their story to life.

Author TM Cromer, thank you for being a friend and a sounding board. This book is better for your input. Author Sara Whitney, thank you for your keen eye and clear wit and for challenging me when you knew I could do better. Your help is much appreciated.

Also, thank you to editor Anne Victory for helping me buff this manuscript to high shine. Your careful attention is a godsend.

And finally, thank you to the readers, bloggers, and reviewers who have made this series a success. I appreciate you and I hope you love this one as much as I do.

ABOUT THE AUTHOR

USA Today bestselling author Geneviève Jack writes wild, witty, and wicked-hot paranormal romance and fantasy. Coffee and wine are her biofuel, the love lives of witches, shifters, and vampires her favorite topic of conversation. She harbors a passion for old cemeteries and ghost tours, thanks to her years at a high school rumored to be haunted. Her perfect day involves the beach, her laptop, and one crazy dog. Learn more at GenevieveJack.com.

Do you know Jack? Join my VIP list for exclusive perks available nowhere else.

Know Jack ➤ News

https://www.genevievejack.com/newsletter/

f facebook.com/AuthorGenevieveJack

🐦 twitter.com/genevieve_jack

📷 instagram.com/authorgenevievejack

BB bookbub.com/authors/genevieve-jack

GENEVIEVE JACK

Knight Games Series

The Ghost and The Graveyard, Book 1

Kick the Candle, Book 2

Queen of the Hill, Book 3

Mother May I, Book 4

Logan, Book 5

Fireborn Wolves Series

(Knight World Novels)

Vice, Book 1

Virtue, Book 2

Vengeance, Book 3

The Treasure of Paragon

The Dragon of New Orleans, Book 1

Windy City Dragon, Book 2,

Manhattan Dragon, Book 3

The Dragon of Sedona, Book 4 (coming Soon)

CPSIA information can be obtained
at www.ICGtesting.com
Printed in the USA
BVHW072024160919
558564BV00004B/789/P

9 781940 675503